I0772969

BONITA Y. MCCOY

Billionaire Sheriff on the Move

By Bonita Y. McCoy

Sign up for Forget Me Not Romances newsletter and receive a special gift compiled from Forget Me Not Authors!

Join our FB pages to keep up on our most current news!

Forget Me Not Romances Readers and Authors
Take Me Away Books
Winged Publications
Soaring Beyond

ISBN-13: 978-1-962168-84-7

Dedicated to my siblings Glenn, Janice, and Renae

Who taught me the importance of family roots.

Let your roots grow down into him, and let your lives be built on him.

Then your faith will grow strong in the truth you were taught,

and you will overflow with thankfulness.

Colossians 2:7

Chapter One

When would that woman ever learn? Wade had received complaints about her from Charlie Giles from day one of his new job.

He tossed his purchase into the passenger seat of his SUV and snapped his seatbelt into place. Checking his reflection in the rearview mirror, he chuckled. "Let the games begin." He flipped on the siren and moved the flashing blue light dome to the roof. The magnet dropped to the metal with a thud. He'd reached seventy before he had her in his sights.

The red Ford truck slowed but didn't stop as he neared. There weren't any other vehicles nearby, so who did she think the siren was for? Aggravated, he pulled behind her and matched her speed. Rolling down his window, he stuck out his arm and waved her over to the side of the road.

At the next turn bay, she pulled in and parked, barely leaving enough room for him to ease in behind her. He grabbed the ticket book from the dash and pushed the computer on the console out of the way. Picking up the mic on his police radio, he alerted dispatch of his stop. "I've got a red Ford truck license plate H-O-M-E-4-U. Run a 10-27."

"Really, Sheriff? You and I both know who it is, and you'll never in a hundred years give her a ticket." Penny Martin, the afternoon dispatcher, clucked her tongue.

"What makes you say that?" The receiver on the radio squawked as he released the button.

"Well, for one, she's your realtor, so if you want first shot at the new houses on the market, you're going to have to play nice."

"I don't think my need of a home should impede my ability to perform my sworn duty." Wade released his seatbelt and waited for Penny to do as he'd asked.

"Fine. I've punched it in. It's the same as last week when you pulled her over. License current, up-to-date insurance, Bernadette Pauline Stewart, age thirty-one. Wait, I didn't notice this last time."

Wade furrowed his brow. "What?"

"Her birthday is this month. In fact, it's this weekend."

"Great, let's get her a card or better yet a cake that says, 'Slow Down.' And if Charlie Giles calls in, tell him it's been handled." Groaning, he signed off. Wade had to admit it was hard not to like Bernadette Stewart. She was spunky, full of fun, and always rooted for the underdog which endeared her to everyone in Orange Blossom, Texas, including himself.

He remembered the first time he'd laid eyes on the daring red head— the summer between his junior and senior year of high school when he'd worked at Pop's ranch, Silver Spur. She'd been there helping with the program for the foster kids. Her parents had sponsored several of them from the Careway Children's Home. Pops had provided riding lessons as part of their summer activities.

Wade tucked the ticket book into his utility belt as he approached the truck. Leaning his right forearm on the roof, he hung his sunglasses on the top button of his uniform shirt and peered into the cab. Bernadette sat with her hand resting on the steering wheel, a half-smile on her full pink lips.

"Well, well, well, if it isn't Sheriff Wade Everette Thibodeaux, as I live and breathe." She slid her shades to the top of her head, drawing his attention to the cute brown freckles scattered across her cheekbones. A waft of sweet citrus floated under his way.

Man alive, she looked good today. Wade shifted his shoulders to block the afternoon sun from her eyes. "Bernadette, we need to stop meeting like this. People are starting to talk."

She shrugged, the sparkle in her eyes warming his heart. "You could just ignore me when I'm in a hurry. It'd save us both a lot of time."

"I find it very hard to ignore a pretty redhead in a pickup going twenty miles over the speed limit." Wade settled his forearms on the ledge of the window facing her, as if he planned to hang around for a while. He'd spoken his mind too easily, so, he moved the conversation back to business. "Now, where do you need to be in such a hurry?"

"A client." She glanced at the digital clock on her dash display and straightened in her seat. "I really do have to go. No kidding."

He pulled the ticket book from his utility belt, flipping it open. "Okay, this will only take a minute."

"Oh, please, Wade. If I get another ticket, they're going to raise my insurance. If you'd check my record, you'd see I've never had an accident. I'm super careful." Then she grinned. "Just fast."

"Um, I see." He rubbed his chin. The stubble prickled against his hand. "Which property are you showing this client?"

"Don't worry. I'm saving all the best ranches for you. Trust me, it's unusual to have a client where money isn't an issue."

Wade hated that money was so central to his identity. But Edward Harris was his Pops, and the man had a head for business and cattle. The Harris name carried a lot of weight throughout Texas. Wade had heard people in the county refer to him as the billionaire sheriff since he'd taken office six months ago. It'd been easier when he worked in D.C. with the FBI. Here, everyone knew about his family connections.

"Yeah, I guess I should consider it a blessing, not having to worry about money as much as others." He glanced at the ticket book and closed it. "I hear your birthday is coming up."

"That's right. Saturday." She twisted in her seat and shielded her eyes against the sun to face him.

"I thought we were meeting Saturday for a few showings. Do you need to reschedule?" Wade pushed off the truck and stood to his full six-foot-four stature.

"No, I don't. Mom is planning a little get-together for me that evening. In fact, if you'd like to come, Nikki and Dan will be there. Mom invited all the Blossom Bible Babes and their spouses."

"Is this so I won't give you a ticket?" Wade squinted, skeptical. "'Cause, I've already decided to let you off with a warning. Consider it an early birthday gift."

"Thank you." She beamed. "But no, I asked for selfish reasons. I don't want to be the third wheel. It seems I'm one of the few single Bible Babes left. This way if you come, I won't be the odd woman out."

"So, I'd be there with you? Like a date?" A rush of adrenaline flooded through him. He'd wanted to ask her out ever since he discovered she was part of his sister-in-law's Bible study group, but the timing never seemed right. *Thank you, Lord. Help me not to mess this up.*

"Yeah, you'd be my date." Her green eyes flashed with a hint of mischief. "Surely, you won't leave a damsel stranded, dear sir." She flung her arm across her forehead. "Not the handsome sheriff of Reseda County."

Placing his hand over his heart, he played along. "It'd be my honor, Miss Bernadette, to be your date for your shindig." He bowed slightly with full dramatic effect. "I vow to stay by your side all evening." His heartbeat revved up a notch, at the thought of spending more time with her, not simply as a realtor and a client.

"A true southern gentleman. And they say chivalry is dead." Giggling, she touched the key in the ignition. "I really have to go. See ya Saturday."

Wade nodded and backed away from the vehicle, finding it hard to quash the smile threatening to appear on his lips. He wanted to be cool about this, professional. Then it dawned on him he needed more information. "Wait." He jogged back toward her. "What time does it start? Should I pick you up, or do you want to meet there?"

"It starts around seven, and we can meet there." She lowered her sunglasses from the top of her head, hiding her bright green eyes from his view. "I'll see you in the morning. We can firm everything up then. You're in for a real treat. Mom's been cooking all week." Her truck roared to life, and with a quick wave, she pulled onto the road.

Real smooth there, Thibodeaux. He shook his head. At times, it was difficult to think straight around that woman.

Then her words popped into his mind. *The handsome sheriff of Reseda County.* His heart flip-flopped like a fish out of water as he watched her truck disappear around the bend. A date with Bernadette Stewart. Maybe moving back home hadn't been such a bad idea after all. Not only to reconnect with his family, but maybe God had other plans for him, too. Plans he'd never dared to dream.

~

"So, did you give Bernadette a ticket?" Penny called to Wade as he passed the dispatcher desk on his way to the break room for coffee.

He poked his head into the space that was lit by computer screens and dancing flashes of light. "No."

"I knew it." She crossed her arms and pinned him with a triumphant stare. "Donnie owes me ten bucks." Lifting one brow, she asked, "When are you going to ask that woman out? You've been chasing her one way or another for over six months."

"Well, it just so happens I have a date with her this Saturday."

"Her birthday." Penny clapped her hands together and giggled with glee. "Hallelujah. It's about dog-gone time. Maybe now we can get some real work done." She smirked, but her eyes sparkled. "Instead of wasting time looking up facts we already know."

"All right, no need to get all worked up. It's only a date for her birthday bash. She didn't want to be a third wheel at her own party. Nothing to alert the news about." He waved off her enthusiasm with a flick of his hand.

"You might say it's no big deal, but the goofy grin on your face tells a whole different story, big guy."

He rolled his eyes and continued toward the break room for his afternoon caffeine infusion. Back at his desk, he found a sticky note with a message from Harry Branson waiting for him. The message read: *Found three more items missing. A sleeping bag, a heavy, long-handled flashlight, and an eight-pack of floss. Thought you'd want to know. Harry.*

"Hilda," he called to his secretary through the open door.

"Yes, Sheriff?" Hilda Matthews appeared in the doorway with paper and pen in hand. "What can I do for you?" The older woman stood tall with her head up, shoulders back, ready for his instructions.

"This message, when did Harry leave it?"

"About half an hour ago. Right before you got back from patrol." Hilda held onto the doorknob. "Anything else?"

"Did Harry say what color the sleeping bag was?"

"Yes, pink. But he wasn't sure. He'd ordered several a few seasons back, but they didn't sell. So, he stuck them on the bottom shelf on aisle nine and forgot about them. It took him a bit to figure out they were missing. And when he did a quick count of some other items, he found one of the flashlights missing as well."

"Okay, thanks. I'll add it to the report he filed this morning."

"Open or closed?" Hilda motioned towards the door.

"Closed. Will you send in Donnie?"

"Sure, Boss." The door shut with a thud.

Wade pulled out his electronic notepad and pulled up the shoplifting report he'd started at Harry's Hardware. He added the pink sleeping bag, flashlight, and floss to the list of stolen items.

Harry had been heartbroken to think anyone would steal from him. "All they had to do was ask. I'd have given them whatever they needed," he said.

As softhearted as Harry Branson was, the man would've done just that.

A rap sounded on the hard wood. "Come on in."

Deputy Adams strolled into the office, standing tall in his black cowboy boots. The first time Donnie had worn them, Wade had noted they weren't part of the regulation uniform for the department, but he'd decided to ignore the infraction. It wasn't a hill he wanted to die on with Donnie.

"Hilda said you wanted to see me?"

"Yeah, did you get any additional information from the Camerons this morning during your interview? About the break-in."

The deputy slid into one of the two seats in front of Wade's desk. "The wife did remember seeing someone in a white van parked by the utility poles near their property several days in a row the week prior to the break-in. She didn't get the plates, and she couldn't remember the model of the van. 'They all look the same to me,' she stated." He leaned back in the chair, making himself comfortable. "When I asked her if she got a look at the driver, she said he was a male with black hair."

"Does she have any idea how many males in southern Texas have black hair?" Wade shook his head. "Not a lot of help. Did you check it out with the utility company to see if they had anyone working in the area?"

"Sure did, Boss." Donnie tapped his fingers on the arm of the chair. "They hadn't had anyone in that area since fall when they replaced the wooden poles with the steel ones."

The third break-in in two months. Not what he'd call a crime wave, but here in Reseda County and the small town of Orange Blossom, it was close. Short of the summer, Peyton and Donnie had spray painted graffiti all over town, hitting shops, schools, and several churches. The graffiti was one thing. Their choice of words … well.

Wade chuckled as he remembered the deputy as a teen. "Hey, do you remember the summer Sheriff McCain caught you painting graffiti on the water tower?"

Donnie grinned and rubbed his chin. "Yeah, sure do. I spent the entire summer doing community service, but it let me see the inner workings of the sheriff's department. Once, McCain got a call while I was in the patrol car with him. I knew the instant the lights flashed, and the siren wailed I wanted to be in law enforcement."

"Glad to know something good came from it." How things had changed. Donnie, a deputy sheriff,

McCain retired, and Wade, well, he'd come home to put down roots. He hadn't planned on running for sheriff, but here he was, in charge. And he'd beaten out Donnie Adams to get the position.

"So, how do you want us to proceed?" Donnie asked.

"Tell everyone on both shifts to keep their eyes peeled for any suspicious vehicles parked where they shouldn't be, particularly a white van, and let's try to be aware of any residents who are traveling. Seems the perps like houses that are empty and isolated. So, let's keep a patrol circling out in the county for the next week. Maybe we'll get lucky."

Donnie rose and walked to the door. Hesitating, he turned. "Speaking of lucky, I hear I owe Penny ten bucks." He chuckled. "You sure have a soft spot for that one."

Wade leaned back in his chair. "Yeah, I sure do." He laced his fingers together and rested them on his midsection, satisfaction coursing through him.

Donnie sobered, hooking his thumbs on his utility belt. "Be careful she doesn't use you to get a sale and then dump you."

"What makes you think she'd do something like that?"

"I've known Bernadette a long time. Long enough to know she's broken a few hearts in her day. And she's been single for a while. So, don't take it personal when I say, I doubt she's looking for anything permanent."

"I'll keep that in mind." Wade nodded, forcing his lips shut. She'd tell him about her past in her own good time. Well, if they survived their first date. It had been a while, quite a while since he'd gone out with anyone.

Besides, what did Donnie know about Bernadette's dreams for her life. Dreams change. His own life was a prime example. His plan had been to work for the FBI doing what he loved, law enforcement, until he retired. But the long hours and the lack of relationships outside of the bureau took its toll. He needed more. Maybe Bernadette's desires for her life had changed too.

Chapter Two

Bernadette slid onto the stool and propped her elbow on the counter, waiting for her best friend, Nikki Thibodeaux to reach a stopping point in her work. As she waited, she studied the newly painted beige walls of the Cowboy Community Church. For decades the walls, carpet, and chairs had been blue, but now, due in part to Nikki, the church office and waiting area had been updated. Score one for the nesting mother-to-be.

"So, are you and Dan coming to the party tomorrow night?" Bernadette twisted, so she could see Nikki's face.

"Give me one more minute." Nikki held up her index finger. "Okay, all done. The sermon notes have gone through their third edit. That should satisfy Pastor Connor." Rolling her chair back, she placed her hand on the edge of her desk and pushed herself to a standing position. "Now, what did you ask?"

"Are you and Dan coming to the party?"

"We sure are." Nikki winced, setting one hand on her back and the other on her tummy, as she moved toward Bernadette. "Wade mentioned last night at supper he'd be there as well." A twinkle sparked in Nikki's eyes.

Bernadette suppressed a laugh as she watched her friend's prenatal progress. Nikki was seven months pregnant with twins and waddled when she walked, reminding her of an overfed duck.

"Yes, he's going to be my date." The heat of a blush whooshed up her neck, making her pull at her collar. She willed her heartbeat back to normal. *Breathe.* The very idea of a date terrified her. And one with Nikki's brother-in-law, Wade Thibodeaux, made her question her sanity. "I needed someone, so I wouldn't be a third wheel at my own birthday party."

"Keep telling yourself that." Nikki smirked and rested against the counter. She pushed the empty stool back under the counter out of the way. "You know you look for him every month when the Bible Babes meet at my house."

Before Bernadette could answer, Purdy Thomas strolled out of the copier room. "I thought I heard your voice, Bernadette. How is your mother?" She laid the stacks of papers she carried on the counter and went to her desk.

"She's well. Up to her eyeballs in cake batter and appetizers. Couldn't be happier." Bernadette grinned at Purdy, the sixty-something church secretary she'd known most of her life. "Are you and Sarah still planning to come?"

"Wouldn't miss it. Sarah's excited. She gets her braces off this afternoon and can't wait to show everyone at the party what she calls her new teeth." Purdy heaved a wistful sigh. "Ah, to be sixteen again."

Bernadette scowled. "I wouldn't be sixteen again for all the money in the world. High school was tough. Although I tried, I never did quite fit in. The social structure had no pigeonhole for me."

"I know what you mean. Let's see, there were the nerds and the geniuses, who ruined every grading curve in the school." Nikki shook her head, resting her hands on her protruding middle.

"Don't forget the jocks, and also the kids in the band and the ones in choir." Bernadette counted on her fingers.

"Yeah, we called them the music jocks." Nikki grinned.

"Then there was me—" Bernadette shrugged. "I floated from one clique to another trying to find a place. I did make a lot of friends, but I never found my thing. Guess if they'd had a 'future realtors' group, I might have clicked." She giggled.

"In my day, the classes were too small to segregate like that. Oh sure, we had a few jocks, and there was always a smart kid or two, but we did everything together," Purdy said.

"Maybe you should've joined the car racing club. I hear you like to burn rubber when you're behind the wheel," Nikki smirked.

"Um, sounds like you've been talking to the local sheriff."

"A girl likes to cut loose every once in a while, right, Bernadette?" Purdy nudged her elbow propped on the wooden surface.

"I'll admit I do enjoy going a little faster than the average Joe Motorist, but I'm always careful. Never had an accident, and I've been driving since the ripe old age of fourteen. Of course, my first vehicle was an old stick shift. I ran up and down the gravel drive at my parents' place out in the county before I ever got my license."

"That's how I learned, too." Purdy chuckled. "An old stick shift and a couple of dirt roads where the only traffic consisted of a few tractors."

"Tractors." Bernadette gasped and glanced at her watch. "I gotta go. I was supposed to meet with Mr. Percy at the office ten minutes ago, and I think he might be selling the perfect ranch for Wade." She hopped off the stool.

"Then you'd better go. He's counting on you to find him just the right house," Nikki said. "Not that Dan and I want him to move out, but he seems bent on having his own place. I thought part of the reason for his career change was to be closer to family." She glanced down at her bulging midsection covered in a maternity shirt of blue and pink polka dots. "Living with your family would make you closer to them, wouldn't it?"

"Well, I'm sure Wade just wants to give you and Dan time alone with your new family. To get adjusted without someone always watching. Besides, my hope is to find him not a house but a home." Bernadette pushed her shoulders back, lifted her chin, and saluted. "Because that's the William Key's Realtor's promise."

The two women laughed as she scooped up her purse, raised the partition in the counter, and scooted through. Waving over her shoulder, she hustled through the door and out to her truck. If everything went well, she should have the contract signed to represent the owner, and she'd be able to show the ranch to Wade tomorrow on their tour.

Tomorrow. A whole day with Wade and then their date. Her first in five long years. Bernadette shook her head. She had no idea what had possessed her when she'd seen him yesterday morning. The invitation to be her date had floated off her lips like a cloud on a wisp of air. Before she'd even realized what she'd said, he'd smiled that heart-stopping, mischievous grin of his, and there it was. A date.

Admittedly, she'd had a crush on Wade Everette Thibodeaux since the summer before her junior year in high school. Just a tiny one. After all, he had saved her life.

The memory flashed in her mind as if it were yesterday instead of fifteen years ago. A gentle smile formed on her lips as she slid behind the steering wheel of her truck, letting the memory play out.

She'd been helping at the Silver Spur ranch during the Cowboy Camp for the foster kids as part of their summer activities when her horse got away from her. The gelding, Sampson, reared and snorted. Bernadette lost her grip on the reins. She'd never forget the terror raging through her as the horse charged toward the woods in a full gallop. She held on to the horn of the saddle for dear life, dodging low-hanging limbs and squeezing her legs tight against the leather to keep her seat, certain she would die.

Then Wade showed up out of nowhere. He maneuvered his horse so he could reach the dragging reins. Sliding to one side of his saddle, he leaned forward grabbing for the leather strap just below the horse's head, all the while avoiding the pounding hooves. It happened so fast. With a gentle voice, he spoke soft words to the spooked gelding. "Whoa. Whoa. Easy boy. It's going to be all right." The horse slowed, and Wade led Bernadette and the worn-out horse back to the barn.

He'd helped her off the gelding and kept her close all afternoon. Bernadette never forgot the look of relief on Wade's face once she was safe. Before the end of the day, he'd made sure she'd climbed back on a horse so she wouldn't shy away from them.

Perhaps, that's why she'd invited him to be her date. He'd kept her safe once. She could trust he'd keep her safe now. That's what she needed, someone safe. But one thought of Wade's broad shoulders, those smoky green eyes, and his chiseled jawline made a very different word pop into her mind. And it had nothing to do with being safe.

~

Bernadette watched out the window as Mr. Percy pulled out of the parking lot of William Key's Realtors with a copy of the signed contract for representation tucked in his briefcase. Turning, she threw her hands above her head still clutching her copy of the document and let out a whoop-whoop.

Marilyn Kemp poked her head out of her office, one of four offices with the reception area in the middle. "What's up, Bernie?"

"I just signed a new client, and I have the perfect buyer for him." She shimmied her shoulders and shuffled her feet in a happy dance. "I love it when a plan comes together."

"That's wonderful. A big fat commission makes a great birthday gift." Marilyn smiled and leaned her shoulder against the doorjamb. "Speaking of gifts, what can I get you? I've wracked my brain trying to come up with something you'd like that you don't already have."

"I know. Thirty-two is such an awkward age." Bernadette giggled and walked toward her colleague. "Throw in the fact I'm single, own my own house, and don't have kids, I'm nearly impossible to buy for."

"I guess I could buy something for that dog of yours." Marilyn shook her head. "What's his name? Freddie?"

Bernadette strolled past her and dropped into one of the chairs opposite Marilyn's desk. "Frodo. He's named after the hobbit in *The Lord of the Rings*."

Marilyn skirted her desk and plopped into her own seat. "Why on earth did you name him after a hobbit?"

"Well, hobbits live in holes, and my dog loves to dig them. Plus, they both have hairy feet." Bernie laughed and hugged the sheet of paper to her chest, threads of satisfaction coursing through her.

"Bernie, you're one of the best people I know—kind, thoughtful, and full of fun. You need someone special in your life who can celebrate birthdays and conquests like today with you."

"I have you and my other friends. Plus, my mom and dad. My life is full."

Marilyn tsked. "You're hopeless. I have no idea why some man hasn't swept you off your feet. You're single because you want to be."

"No, I'm single because I don't want to settle. I want the one God has for me, but I haven't found him yet." Bernadette's heart fluttered at the memory of her near miss.

"Or he hasn't found you." Marilyn straightened. "You should come with me to one of those speed-dating groups over in College Station. There are some cute professors."

"Not on your life. That's so not me. Besides, for your information, I have a date." Bernadette met Marilyn's skeptical gaze.

"Dogs don't count as dates, girlfriend."

"Ha-ha. No, I mean a real date. I asked Wade Thibodeaux to be my escort to the party tomorrow night." She still couldn't believe she'd asked him.

Her colleague's eyes grew as round as doughnuts, and she smacked the desk pad in front of her with a thud. "No, not one of the Thibodeaux brothers. They're loaded."

"That's not why I asked him. We have … history." Bernadette dangled the bait in front of her friend.

"History?" Marilyn leaned in closer, placing her forearms on the desk.

"Yeah, he stops me for speeding about once a week, so I decided it was time for our relationship to move beyond speeding tickets to something more substantial like double parking." Bernadette grinned.

Marilyn sat silent for a moment then clasped her hands together in front of her. "So, you like him. That's good. The new sheriff is handsome, brave, and a godly man. Maybe, he's the one you've been waiting for all this time."

Bernadette sobered as the idea fluttered into her mind and landed like a butterfly on the memories she held of him. She squirmed in her chair at this new line of thought. Glancing at Marilyn, Bernadette forced a smile.

Marilyn raised her eyebrows. "He's possibly your soulmate."

Bernadette rolled her eyes. "I don't believe in soulmates. I believe in God's direction. Besides, I've known Wade for years. Why would God wait this long to bring us together if he's the one?"

"I don't know." Marilyn sat back in her chair. "But I do know God works in weird ways."

"You mean mysterious."

"Whatever. The point is—"

"The point is, unless Wade has very hairy feet and can dig a superb hole within five minutes, he'll never replace Frodo, who at this point in my life has my undivided affections."

The squeak of the front door caught Bernadette's attention right before the motion sensor chimed a sweet melody of "Deep in the Heart of Texas." The voices sounded familiar, but she took the opportunity to dodge the rest of the conversation with Marilyn. Hopping up, she peeked into the lobby to see if it was a client. But it was only Burt Williams, the owner and resident broker of the firm, and Terry Jenkins, the other realtor, coming back from inspecting two foreclosure properties they were hoping to represent for one of the local banks.

"Hey, there's the birthday girl," Burt blurted out.

"Not until tomorrow. Please, let me have every minute of my youth."

"I'm with you. We're all going to age. No one needs to stand behind us and push. Right?" Terry nodded and headed into Burt's office.

"Is Marilyn here?" Burt asked, stopping outside his door.

"Right here. What do you need?" Marilyn called from behind Bernadette without leaving her chair.

"You and Bernie join us in my office. I want to go over this week's stats. See how we're doing compared to this time last year. With the economy, we really need to step up our game."

"Sure, be right there." Marilyn stood and grabbed a file folder from her desk.

Bernadette hurried to her office to grab her numbers. The month had been much slower than last June. She didn't need to meet with Burt to know that. The housing market had slowed to the speed of backwards, which was disheartening since summer tended to be their busiest season.

Entering Burt's office, she found Marilyn sitting in the chair closest to the wall on the right. She took the seat next to her. Burt leaned back in his rolling chair behind the desk with his fingers steepled in front of him. Terry had pulled in a chair from the receptionist area—a blue plastic thing Bernadette avoided sitting in whenever possible. She settled into the well-padded client chair, shifting to get comfortable. If she'd read Burt's body language correctly, he was worried. Which meant they were going to be here for a while.

After a thirty-minute discussion about the economy and a five-minute pep talk from Burt, Bernadette decided to change the subject. She'd been waiting for the right time to tell her boss what had happened. "I do have something I wanted to address before we go home tonight." She fiddled with her pen. "Earlier this week, I discovered one of my digital lockboxes had been hacked. I notified the owners who are no longer living in the house, but I'm not sure what needs to be done."

"That is concerning. Did they damage the box? Because if so, we'll have to report it to the state association."

"No, that's the strange part. I found the lockbox on the counter in the kitchen. It still works. How they got my shackle code is beyond me. Someone hacked into it but left it where I could find it instead of chucking it into some bushes along the roadway."

"That is strange. In my experience, thieves aren't overly concerned about the damage they do to the houses or the lockboxes. I mean, they steal stereo systems right out of the walls."

Bernadette stood. "I know. There wasn't any damage to the house, and if I hadn't known better, I'd have thought I'd forgotten to put the lockbox back on the door after changing the code or something."

Marilyn frowned. "I had a similar incident maybe two weeks ago. The house was in perfect order except for a few food wrappers from Burger King and a magazine."

"Was the house vacant?" Bernadette asked.

"Yes, the owners have already moved, and I've been having open houses there on Sundays. So, after church, I always head right over to get everything set for the viewers. One Sunday, I found the wrappers and a copy of a magazine in one of the bedrooms, as if someone had been staying there. Nothing else was disturbed."

"Which properties? Where were they located?" Terry asked.

"Mine was in the county. The Lester property." Bernadette glanced over at Marilyn.

"Mine, too. The Cordova residence."

"Okay, first thing Monday, I want both of you to go file a report with the Sheriff's Department since both houses were in the county. See if they can figure out how they're hacking into our digital boxes. We can't afford to have vagrants using our homes as hotels. What if we walk in on one of them, and they become violent?" Burt's face flooded with concern.

Bernadette waved off the suggestion. "I don't think it's anyone dangerous. Maybe someone just wanted to get out of the heat during the day."

"More like stay out of sight." Terry's eyebrows drew together as a frown settled on the corners of his thin lips. "You ladies need to be careful going in and out of those houses alone. The next time you find one of the lockboxes gone. Call for help, and don't go in."

"Terry, you're overreacting." Marilyn scoffed. "One hacked lockbox doesn't mean disaster is waiting for us around the next corner."

"Two hacked lockboxes, and Terry's right." Burt nailed them both with a stern, fatherly glare. "Don't take any chances. Your safety comes first."

Chapter Three

Wade held onto the grab handle as Bernadette took a sharp curve. They agreed it was silly to take separate vehicles, and since she was the one showing the properties, he let her drive. Big mistake.

The wheels of the red pickup spewed gravel from the driveway in all directions. As they cleared the stand of trees, a two-story house came into view. She slowed a bit, pulling into the circular drive and stopping at the front porch.

"Here we are." Bernadette rested her arms on the steering wheel and studied the structure.

Glancing out the window, Wade noticed a small round window at the top which suggested a third floor, probably an attic.

"Come on. I think you'll love this one." She grabbed her electronic pad and headed for the front door.

Wade released his grip on the handle and flexed his hand to get the blood flowing again. His white knuckles testified to the speed at which his realtor liked to drive. He hopped from the truck slamming the door behind him. "You know we have all afternoon, right? You don't have to drive like you've been shot from a cannon."

"I love to drive fast. It makes me feel alive." Bernadette grinned at him then turned her attention to the pad in her hand. She punched in the four-digit lockbox code. A light on the top of the lockbox blinked red, and she pushed a button at the bottom of the gray box.

"Well, you should be feeling pretty spry after that trip then."

Bernadette cocked an eyebrow. "What, you don't like my driving?" She tossed him a teasing grin as she removed the drawer and pulled out the key. Inserting it into the doorknob, she unlocked the door.

"Let's say I find it questionable." Wade moved in front of her, cutting her off, to open the door for her. He intended to be every inch the gentleman both this afternoon and this evening.

"I have a feeling the next time you stop me, I'll be getting a ticket." Stepping into the foyer, she laid the key on a small table that sat under a mirror near the door.

"Let's just say it might be for your own safety and the safety of your passengers if I do." He lifted his lips into a half-smile. A waft of her citrus perfume tickled his nose as he passed by her. Without thinking, he inhaled.

"I'm sorry. I know it's a bit stuffy in here, but the family moved out in April, and with the heat, it's not unusual for houses to be a bit musty." She wrinkled her nose.

"It's not that." *Why did he say anything*? He should've just rolled with her assumption. Now, she looked at him with a glint of curiosity in her eye.

Clearing his throat, he changed the subject before she asked for an explanation. "So, how many bedrooms does this place have?"

"It has four upstairs, and the master suite is downstairs. That should be a bonus. This house could work for you while you're single, and then if you ever started a family, you'd have the space to grow." A deep blush sprouted on her cheeks as she met his gaze. "You know, sometime in the future. Later, when you marry. *If* you marry." Bernadette pressed her lips together.

Wade smiled. The light pink hue accentuated her freckles sprinkled across her nose, making her auburn hair more pronounced. His fingers ached to stroke the blush away, but instead, he stuffed his hands in his pockets.

She cleared her throat and turned her gaze towards the staircase. "Why don't we go up and see the bathrooms. I believe there are two. One Jack-and-Jill style and the other accessible from the hallway." She led him to the second floor and walked him through each room, showing him the closets and pointing out special features like the tray ceilings or the wood flooring.

He moved into the third bedroom, leaving her bustling around in the other two, closing blinds and turning out lights. Wade was relieved to find this bedroom had carpeting. He preferred it over hardwood floors but carpeting according to Bernadette had gone out of fashion. Examining the layout of the room, he spotted a food wrapper and a crumpled-up bag from one of the local burger joints lying in the far-left corner. He walked over and picked them up.

"What'cha got?" Bernadette asked as she entered

the room.

"Wrappers." He held them up to show her. "Is this common? All the houses have lockboxes on them, right?" Wade asked, even though he knew the answer.

"No, it's not normal. In fact, Marilyn and I are planning to come to the sheriff's office Monday to file a report. We've both had our digital lockboxes hacked in the last few weeks. My incident happened at the Lester property." She pointed toward the paper in his hand. "I found food wrappers there as well, but the lockbox wasn't on the doorknob like this time."

"Makes it less suspicious if the neighbors know the property is up for sale. They'd expect to see a lockbox on the door."

"Easier too. The hacker only needs to have the code for the key drawer. He wouldn't need the shackle code as well. Cuts his work in half."

Wade scowled, shifting into sheriff mode. "I don't like the idea of you ladies entering houses where the safety has been compromised."

"You sound like Burt. He's worried we might walk in on someone who might turn violent."

"That's a legitimate concern." Wade scanned the floor for any other clues as to who may have been in the room while Bernadette opened the white blinds to let in more light. A ray of sunshine pierced through the slats as the late afternoon sun passed below the trees, washing the floor in light. Something sparkled on the carpet. "What's this?" Leaning over, he picked up a gem and placed it in the palm of his hand.

Bernadette touched his forearm, forcing his hand to lower. "A bedazzle rhinestone."

"A what?" Wade asked.

"It's a gem you use to dress up your purses or jackets or whatever you want to jazz up. It's called bedazzling." Bernadette grinned. "It's all the rage with the teenage girls. Ask Sarah Thomas, Purdy's granddaughter, about it. She'll tell you all you want to know. I think she's dressed up most of her wardrobe and half the clothes in her friends' closets as well."

"So, she's an expert." Wade laughed. "On bedazzling."

Bernadette's eyes lit with mischief. "She could probably tell you which company makes this particular rhinestone, and who in town uses them." The sunlight played on the floor under her feet giving her an ethereal air. "If we catch our culprit, you may need to call Sarah as an expert witness." Her soft pink lips curled into a smile.

Wade took her hand in his as he pocketed the gem. "And you'd be an expert on fast driving." His heart revved up a notch or two. "I guess I could use you as an expert witness the next time I have to defend issuing a speeding ticket." He ran his thumb across her knuckles.

She pulled her hand from his, but she didn't step away. Clasping her hands behind her back, she stood inches from him with her chin lifted. Her perfume surrounded him, demanding his surrender.

"In that case, you shouldn't give me a speeding ticket. It might bias my opinion about the whole experience." Her eyes crinkled at the corners as an impish gleam sparkled from them.

The warmth he found in her green eyes had him fighting the urge to kiss the woman. She not only knew how to rev a car engine. For a split second, he considered capturing her lips with his. He gravitated toward her, and she closed her eyes. But then, he stopped. One day and soon, but not today. Not before their very first date. Instead, he touched her cheek. Her eyes fluttered open.

A heavy thud sounded above their heads, making them both jump.

Bernadette stiffened. She opened her mouth to speak, but Wade covered it with his hand. He shook his head and let go. Placing his finger over his lips, he motioned for her to remain quiet. He cocked his head, listening. Footsteps skittered across the ceiling further down the hallway. Pointing up, he moved close to Bernadette's ear and whispered, "Is there an attic?"

She nodded, hugging her middle.

"Where's the entrance?"

"In the closet of the first bedroom, I think."

Her breath left his cheek warm. "Stay here." Wade speared her with a look, trying to nail her feet in place. He didn't need her following him. If it were someone dangerous, he needed her safe and out of the way.

She hugged her arms around her middle and nodded her agreement.

The footsteps sounded closer as he reached the closed door as if the intruder were on this level. He could've sworn they'd left the door open after viewing this room. Turning the knob, he found it locked.

Jiggling it, he banged on the door. "Sheriff's Department. Open up."

The sound of steps echoed from the other side. Then a swoosh and a loud clang rang out.

Bernadette appeared by his side. "What was that?" Her eyes huge, filled with fear.

Wade backed up as far as the hallway would allow

and lowered his shoulder.

"What are you doing?" she wailed.

Without explaining, Wade rammed the door, cracking the doorframe as the lock gave way. Spotting the open window, he sprinted toward it. He scanned the area below him. A window screen dangled on the edge of the porch roof. Then he saw someone dressed in a black hoody drop from the porch roof to the ground. He watched as the person fled into the woods lining the driveway. Turning toward Bernadette, he grinned.

"Who was it?" Confusion clouded her face. "Why are you grinning?"

"Because I might not have gotten a good look at the culprit's face, but I did get a glimpse of their shoes. They were hard to miss." He pulled the rhinestone from his jean pocket and held it between his finger and thumb. "They were covered in these little darlings."

~

One quick look in the kitchen told him Nikki wasn't in there. Wade slung the two shirts he carried over his shoulder, letting them dangle from the hangers, and groaned. He'd dug through his closet, trying on every shirt he owned, and he still couldn't decide what to wear to Bernadette's party. Nikki would know.

Moving to the living room, he found his sister-in-law sitting on the sofa with her feet propped up on the matching ottoman with a book in her lap. Her head rested on the back of the cushion, and her chest rose and fell with her shallow breathing.

Wade hated to interrupt her moment of quiet, but he needed her help. He wanted to make a good impression on Bernadette. Clearing his throat, he waited. No movement. This called for a more direct approach. Placing the shirts in the chair adjacent to the sofa, he sat on the ottoman next to her feet. Her swollen toes looked like tiny stuffed sausages about to burst out of their casings. An idea crept into his mind. What good was it to have a sister-in-law if you didn't get a chance to have a little fun? Giving into temptation, he touched the swollen digits, running his finger lightly over them.

She moved her foot, groaning but didn't open her eyes.

He suppressed a chuckle and ran his finger over the little piggies once more. This time she stirred. Her eyes fluttered open.

"Wade, I must've fallen asleep. What time is it?" She straightened, pulling her feet off the ottoman.

A smile pulled at his lips. The urge to confess what he had done pricked at his conscience, but he decided not to. "Right around five-thirty."

"That late?" She nodded toward his wet hair. "I see you've showered, ready for the big date." She wiped the sleep from her eyes.

"Yes, and I need your opinion." He rose and held out the hangers with the shirts dangling from them. Sticking the blue checkered, button-down under his chin, he asked, "This one? Or—" Then he switched to the green polo. "This one?"

Nikki cringed and rubbed her side.

"Are you all right?" He sank into the armchair, concern rising in him. What kind of man wakes a pregnant woman for clothing advice? A desperate one.

Nikki shrugged. "I'm okay. It's just Braxton Hicks contractions." She inhaled and let her breath out slowly. "The doctor said it's normal. Just my body getting ready."

"I shouldn't have awakened you. Sorry. I guess I'm nervous about this date tonight."

"Why are you nervous? You've been in relationships before, haven't you? And they all started with a first date." Nikki squirmed in her seat and stretched her shoulders.

"Actually, my policy in the past has been to keep things light. My job in the FBI kept me running around the country from one detail to another. I never knew where I'd be assigned as a field agent. So, to be fair to the other person, I didn't have too many deep, long-term relationships." Wade shrugged. "But you're right. I've had plenty of first dates."

"So, why are you so nervous about this one?"

Wade laid the hangers on the arm of the chair and sat. Leaning his forearms on his knees, he clasped his hands together. "It's because it's Bernadette. We're friends, and I don't want to mess that up. We have fun together even when I'm issuing her a speeding ticket." The corners of his lips lifted as he remembered their last encounter on the side of the road. He'd kick himself if he wound up losing her friendship. Ever since that summer when he'd saved her from the runaway gelding, Sampson, he'd wanted to ask her out but didn't dare. The spunky redhead with the quick wit was way out of his league, still was.

"Then my advice to you is, don't mess it up." A smile spread across her face. "Bernadette is a lovely woman, who like all of us has made some mistakes. But she loves the Lord and has a zest for life that is hard to resist."

Wade heard the back door close. "Yeah, she is hard to resist."

Dan appeared a few seconds later. "Who's hard to resist?" He strolled toward his wife and planted a kiss on her cheek.

"Bernadette," Nikki answered.

"That's right, her party is tonight." Dan checked his wristwatch and looked at Nikki. "I'm surprised you're not ready. Are we still going?"

Nikki's brows knit together. "What do you mean? I *am* ready." She glanced down at her freshly pressed hot pink shirt and white maternity shorts then back up at her husband. Her bottom lip quivered, and tears moistened the rims of her eyes.

Dan cringed. "Oh Nikki, I'm sorry, honey. You look great."

Nikki waved a dismissive hand at Dan. Turning her attention to Wade, she said, "Show me the shirts again."

Wade, not sure what to do, sprang from his seat in obedience to her request. "That's right. You never did give me your opinion." He waved the checkered blue shirt under his chin. "What do you think? Blue or green?"

She shot Dan a look and sniff before answering Wade. "I like the blue one. It brings out the warmth of your complexion." Struggling to the edge of the sofa, she pushed to a standing position. Dan stuck out his hand to help her, but she swatted it away. "You, on the other hand, should wear black. Because of your sunny disposition." With great effort, she waddled toward the doorway. "I'll be in the kitchen," she called over her shoulder. "Eating for three."

Dan collapsed onto the sofa. "I never know what to say these days. It's the hormones. They make women crazy, and men run for the hills."

Wade shook his head. "Bro, I feel for you."

"Yeah, right. You're doing your best to get out of Dodge." Dan grinned. "Did Bernadette show you anything you might be interested in today?"

"Not really. But she says she's got a new listing she wants to show me next weekend. It wasn't ready yet. They had a few repairs she wanted them to do to get it into move-in condition. She thinks it's the perfect one, though." Wade shrugged. "But then she is an optimist."

Wade considered telling his brother about the intruder but decided against it. He didn't want to alarm folks without good cause. Besides, Bernadette and Marilyn were due to come into the office Monday to make a formal report which would give him more information about the digital hacker. No sense alarming anyone at this point.

Chapter Four

"Why didn't you tell me you were bringing a date?" Darlene Stewart whispered as she sidled up to her daughter who stood in front of the punch bowl. "And Wade Thibodeaux of all people."

Bernadette ladled the pink ginger ale and ice cream mixture into her glass cup. "Mom, don't start. He's just a friend." Scanning the room, she spotted her date on the other side of the screen porch in a deep conversation with Asa Stewart, her father, Dan Thibodeaux, and Wilson, the Stewart's handyman. "Speaking of friends, I thought you said you'd only invited a few of my closest friends. I expected the Blossom Bible Babes, their spouses, and maybe my co-workers." She cut her eyes at her mother. "I saw Leon from the Sack and Save filling his plate full of sandwiches. Now, tell me how he qualifies as a close friend."

Darlene inspected the plate full of food she held in her hands. "Well, you two were in Mrs. Epson's second-grade class together." She shrugged. "It just slipped out I was giving you a birthday party, and—" She tilted her head and met Bernadette's gaze. "Before I knew it, the list had expanded."

"It didn't expand. It exploded. The house is full of

people I hardly ever see. It's as if you invited the whole town." Bernadette sipped her punch and tried to remember the name of the woman in the sleeveless shirt and orange shorts standing next to Nikki.

"I'm sorry, baby girl. You know I can't turn anyone away. Hospitality comes easy to me. That's why our bed and breakfast does so well. Most guests say we make them feel like family. It's my talent."

Bernadette took pity on her mother who loved people and loved to entertain. "I know. It's okay." She wrapped her arm around her mom's shoulders and hugged her. "It's a great party, and I love the decorations. Who strung the lights on the front and back porches? They're beautiful."

"Your dad and Wilson. They worked all day yesterday and today to have the place ready for tonight. Purdy and Sarah helped by picking up the cake from the bakery, leaving me time to make the sandwiches and the dips for the strawberries." Darlene lowered her voice. "I even convinced Marilyn to help. She managed the food list for the Bible Babes."

"Well, it turned out terrific. Thank you. You always do throw the best shindigs in town."

"Now you're just laying it on a bit thick." But her mother blushed under her praise.

"I'd better go rescue Wade. Dad looks like he's telling one of his old rodeo stories again."

"Yeah, he's got one hand on his hat and the other one in the air, twirling his wrist. You'd better go save the poor boy, or he'll hear about all thirty wins before your father's done."

Bernadette headed across the white wooden planks of the porch floor to the group of men who stood hanging on Asa's every word. She nestled into a spot beside Wade. "You can't believe a thing this man tells you," she joked.

"Well, it's fair to say, most of what I'm telling them is true." Asa cackled and slapped his thigh. Laughter skittered around the small circle.

Wade smiled at her. "These have been some good tales. I never knew your dad had been on the rodeo circuit. That's amazing."

"What's amazing, son, is that I didn't break my neck." Asa's eyes widened. "I can attest to the fact there were several times nothing, but the Lord's hand saved me from killing my fool self." Then his eyes landed on his wife talking with Marilyn, and a peace lit his face. "Then the Good Lord saw fit to bring Darlene into my life, and I knew the time had come to hang up my rodeo spurs."

"Now, why did you do that?" Dan asked. "It sounds like you were living your dream."

"It's hard to have a family and be out on the circuit. Too much time away, and it wasn't fair of me to ask Darlene to take on the responsibility of a ranch on her own." He glanced at Bernadette. "Then when our little bit of Heaven showed up, I had no doubts I'd made the right decision. My daughter is worth a thousand rodeo wins."

"Awe, Dad." She waved away his compliment.

Wade bumped her shoulder. "Yeah, she is pretty great."

Her dad chuckled. "Come here and give your old pa a hug."

She moved across the small circle and wrapped her arms around his pudgy middle. "You're not old."

"You're right. You're the one aging today." He threw back his head and roared.

Bernadette wiggled out of his arms. "Then I say, 'let them eat cake.'"

"All right, then." Her father turned to face the crowd on the porch. "Everybody, it's time to cut the cake."

Following her husband's lead, her mother herded the guests in the direction of the dining room.

Bernadette rolled her eyes and looked for the nearest floorboard to crawl under. All this fanfare was great when she was ten, but at thirty-two, it came off as a bit ridiculous. But then she glanced at her mom who glowed with joy and decided she'd play along for the sake of her parents. She followed her mother into the dining room. A large sheet cake decorated with pink roses sat on the table, waiting to be cut. The candles in the middle caught her attention. They took up most of the space on the cake.

Stopping, she studied the number. Where had the time gone? Only yesterday, there'd been a cake like this one that touted the promise of adulthood when she'd reached eighteen. That had been fourteen years ago. Her eyes widened and sweat formed on the palms of her hands. She was no longer a spring chicken. Another year or two and she'd be considered an old biddy by some people. Grabbing the chair in front of her, she steadied herself.

"You all right?" Nikki whispered in her ear from behind her as others jostled their way into the room to watch.

"I'm fine. This just brings back memories. I've celebrated a ton of birthdays in this house."

Nikki squeezed her shoulders. "That's what a happy home does. It gives you great memories."

"Yes." Bernadette patted her friend's hand. "And your home is going to be one big happy playground."

Sarah Thomas sidled up to her. "Look." She spread her lips apart in a wide smile, exposing all her front teeth.

Bernadette squealed. "You got your braces off. How wonderful."

"You look stunning," Nikki offered. The two women pulled the teen into a group hug.

When Bernadette released Sarah, her mother pressed through the crowd to the table holding matches. After several attempts, all the candles flickered to life. "Okay, Dan, since you sing in the choir, would you get us started?"

"Sure thing, Mrs. Stewart." He lifted his hands like an orchestra conductor. With a wave, he began. "Happy Birthday to you …" The voices blended, off-key, cracked, and full of love.

Bernadette drank in the sight of her friends, close and otherwise, singing to her. As the group finished the song, she pressed her lips together to keep from crying. The affection poured out overwhelmed her.

"Don't forget to make a wish," Leon called from the hallway.

Bernadette closed her eyes, but she didn't make a wish. Instead, she said a silent prayer of blessing for all who were there. Then she asked the Lord once again for the one thing her heart desired. *Lord, you know I've tried to do things my own way. And we both know how that turned out. I want what you want. I don't want to settle for anything less.*

Then she blew out the candles and opened her eyes. There across the table with his smoky green eyes focused on her stood Wade Everette Thibodeaux, her plus one.

Marilyn's words popped into her mind. Yes, she believed God worked in ways different from her thinking, but she wasn't sure if this was one of those times. She'd been wrong before, and Wade, well, he was a friend she didn't want to lose.

Wade's brows pulled together. He mouthed, "You, okay?" from across the table.

She nodded right before her mom leaned in for a hug. "Happy Birthday, baby girl. I hope this is your best year yet."

~

Wade's antiquated pickup rolled over the speed bumps near the stop sign at the entrance to Bernadette's street. The first time she'd seen the dented Chevy, she'd called it old. He'd called it vintage. Apparently, it had been his grandfather's. The movement bounced her to one side of the bench seat.

When she'd invited him to the festivities, her plan was to meet him at her parents' ranch, The Belles and Beaus, for the party. But that morning while they were touring houses, he'd insisted on picking her up, since it was a date and all.

Bernadette had wracked her brain at the time to come up with a good reason for them to drive separately, to avoid any awkwardness that might occur when the time came to say goodnight. She'd been in similar situations once or twice before when she'd gone out with a friend. She'd thought one thing. He'd thought another. Which was why she didn't want to go through that scenario with Wade. She respected him too much to embarrass him.

But no excuse had presented itself. So, at six-thirty, Wade had pulled into her driveway smelling of an earthy musk and looking too handsome for his own good in a blue checkered button-down and a pair of well-worn jeans that hugged his hips. That's when the mantra began looping in her head. The 'we're just friends' one, she repeated all evening because she kept forgetting.

Like when he charmed her mother by complimenting her chicken salad and her heart had fluttered, or when Wade laughed at her dad's dumb jokes and little tingles of joy coursed through her. Or when he appeared at the precise moment, she needed him, and her knees went weak. He'd been the perfect date, but now came the dreaded goodnight … kiss? Hug? Handshake?

She ran her damp palms along her jeans and glanced at Wade. He sat eyes front, both hands on the steering wheel. If she didn't know any better, she'd think the county sheriff was nervous too.

As they neared her house, Wade asked, "So, did you enjoy the party?"

"Yes, I did." She nodded with too much vigor. "But there were more people there than I had expected. Mom had made it sound like it would be a more intimate gathering. You know, close friends."

Wade chuckled. "Unless you're close to half the population of Orange Blossom, I think your mom got carried away."

"Boy, did she. Big time." Bernadette groaned and let out a series of nervous, hyphenated chuckles. "But she loves to entertain, and after all the hard work she put into this evening, it's hard to stay mad at her."

"Oh no, I think it's great. Your parents must really love you. Not everyone gets that as a kid, much less as a grown-up."

Bernadette pressed her lips together. Wade and his brothers had already lost both of their parents and their grandfather. "I'm sorry. I guess I sound like a brat, complaining about something so trivial. It's just that I hate to be singled out. I'm much more a group person." She cast a glance at Wade in the glow of the passing streetlights.

"I remember that about you from the summer activities at Silver Spur. You always liked being a part of something bigger. Helping the kids from the Careway Children's Home seemed to give you a real thrill." He cut his eyes in her direction, and a lopsided grin spread across his lips.

The mantra kicked into gear. *Just friends*. "I did enjoy working with the kids." She sighed. "It gave me such a sense of accomplishment to see one of them learn how to shoot an arrow or sit on a horse. There's nothing like it."

"I'm surprised you aren't a teacher as much as you loved it." Wade pulled into her driveway and parked, rolling down his window with the hand crank. He turned off the headlights and cut the engine.

Bernadette turned toward him. The streetlight behind him cast a shadowy outline of his broad shoulders. She forced herself to concentrate on the conversation. "Part of the reason I didn't pursue a teaching career is because I don't think I could stay in one room every day with the same people over and over. The monotony would drive me crazy. But I love being a realtor. I get that same sense of joy of helping others I got helping the kids from Careway, but with more freedom." Butterflies fluttered in her stomach as the scent of his musky cologne lingered on the warm June breeze. "Plus, I love putting people in the perfect home. There's just something about knowing the place fits the person."

"I like that." Wade ran his arm along the back of the bench seat and squeezed her shoulder. Surprised, she stiffened. "I didn't mean to—"

"No, it's all right. I'm just nervous," Bernadette winced, wishing she could snatch back the words.

Wade dropped his hand and rested back against the seat.

"I'd better go." Bernadette picked up her purse and shifted to open the truck door, sure she had ruined the moment with her rude response, causing the very awkwardness she'd wanted to avoid.

"Let me." Wade jumped from the truck and jogged around to the passenger side door. With a quick jerk, Wade swung the door open. It squeaked on its hinges. And then, he stepped forward and offered her his hand.

A prickle of delight zinged through her. Laughing, she said, "Persistent, aren't you?" She slid her hand into his, letting him help her out of the truck. "Thanks." She squeezed his hand, and he met her gaze. A mischievous gleam danced in his eyes, and he shut the door without releasing her hand.

Falling into step with her, he said, "If I'm honest, I'd admit to being a little nervous myself." He shrugged. "It's just that we're such good friends in a way. I mean, we don't hang out often, but I see you at

Dan and Nikki's when you come for the women's Bible study, and you see me when I stop you for speeding, so we see each other about once a week." His eyes crinkled at the corners.

She giggled, thinking how much she liked their verbal sparring. "Well, you could remedy that by not pulling me over."

"But then when would we have the chance to visit? You know, have quality time alone." A low rumble worked its way up from his chest. The laugh came out full and masculine. She liked the sound of it.

They stood outside her front steps, facing one another, him still holding her hand. The porch light flooded the small area with a yellow hue, drawing the beetles and moths to it. Frodo barked from the other side of the door as if aliens were invading, and he needed to alert the entire neighborhood.

"I tell you what. How about instead of me stopping you this week for speeding to get our alone time, you join me at The Flying Pig Barbeque for dinner Friday night. I've been wanting to try it out and—"

"Sure," she blurted out, before she had the chance to think about it. "Why not." *We're just friends* popped into her mind, and she shook her head to dispel the words.

"That's great." He beamed, then seemed to hesitate. Catching her other hand, he gazed into her eyes. The warmth that greeted her sent prickles dancing across her skin.

Looking away, she worked to corral her emotions. She licked her lips wondering if he'd try to kiss her. It might not be so bad to give the guy a goodnight kiss. She rose on tiptoe. As she did, he bent down.

A thud sounded. "Ow." Wade pulled back.

A sharp pain radiated from a spot on her head. She'd whacked the poor man. It figured, that's what she got for forgetting the mantra. "Oh, sorry." Stepping back, she met his gaze. "Are you all right?"

With a wince, Wade covered his nose. "I'm okay. How about you?" His eyes watered, and a trickle of blood appeared beneath his finger. He wiped it away.

"I'm fine. Hardheaded. It takes more than that to hurt me. But you. Your nose." She dug in her purse for a tissue. Reaching up, she dabbed at the injured area.

Peering down at her, he covered her hand with his and moved it but didn't let go. "I'm fine. Just fine." Leaning down, he brushed her cheek with his warm lips. "I'll see you tomorrow at church."

She touched the spot where he had kissed her. "Tomorrow at church."

He walked toward his truck. "I'll wait until you're inside, then I'll leave."

She wanted to argue with him, protest that she didn't need a guardian. But then she decided against it. Let him wait for her. Let him be her protector. It was her birthday after all. What harm could come from a little spoiling by a handsome man with smoky green eyes?

Once inside, she peeked out one of the windows by the front door. Wade stood by the truck, watching her. He dipped his chin when she waved and then climbed into the cab of his old Chevy truck. Leaning her back against the door, she closed her eyes. What was she doing? She'd known Wade forever. So why was her heart doing flips like a college cheerleader at a football game?

Chapter Five

Early Sunday morning, the call came from dispatch. There had been another break-in. Wade had gone into the office, even though Sunday was his official day off. He needed to hear the facts for himself from the officers before they left. Their notes would be useful but catching them while the memories were still fresh would be even better.

Apparently, two of his deputies had interrupted the burglars. His idea of patrolling the more remote houses whose owners were on vacation had paid off. Officer Regan Perez had noticed a white van parked in the vicinity of Old Pines Road. Calling into dispatch for backup, she approached the house and found the front door ajar. Entering, Regan heard a racket in the back bedroom of the one-story ranch house. By the time she reached the room, the perps had gone out the window, running for the side of the house. Backup arrived two minutes too late.

After debriefing the deputies, Wade hustled home, showered, and rushed to church, but he'd missed the announcements and the singing. Slipping into the pew next to Nikki and Dan, he scanned the sanctuary and spotted Bernadette without any trouble. The soft blue dress she wore made her easy to find. His heart hammered against his chest, and the palms of his hands became damp. Wiping them on his pants, he accidentally elbowed Dan.

Dan frowned but slid closer to Nikki, giving Wade more room but pushed Nikki closer to Rod Carson, their ranch manager, and his wife, Dolly, who sat in the middle of the row.

Wade tried to relax and focus on Pastor Connor's reading from the Bible. A second later, he felt a sharp jab in his arm. He cut his eyes in Dan's direction, but Dan sat concentrating on the front of the sanctuary. Another jab sent pain tripping through his shoulder. Looking past Dan and Nikki, Wade discovered Rod grinning at him with a smile that spread from one ear to the other. Then he nodded and winked. *What was he missing?*

Harry, who sat in the pew behind him, reached forward and patted his shoulder. "Did you have a good time last night? You and Bernie sure make a cute couple."

Wade tensed and tried to direct his attention to the podium where Pastor Connor stood reading the scripture for the day.

"Jesus replied, 'Foxes have dens and birds have nests, but the Son of Man has no place to lay his head,'" Pastor Connor's voice rippled out over the small congregation.

Out of the corner of his eye, Wade noticed Rod's wife nudging him with her elbow. The older man squirmed in his seat and turned to face forward. Running his arm along the back of the pew, he draped his hand over her shoulder. She nestled against him and shifted her Bible where he could see it. Wade grinned at the pair. He'd known Rod and Dolly Carson his whole life. If ever two people were made for each other, it was them.

Wade stole a glance in Bernadette's direction. She sat up front in the second row with her mother and father as she did most Sundays. Bernadette must've felt his eyes on her because she glanced over her shoulder and met his gaze. She closed her eyes and shook her head before returning her focus to the stage. Not sure what was going on, Wade concentrated on the sermon.

"We rarely think of our Lord Jesus as someone who was homeless. But when His ministry started, He left his home with Mary and ventured out in obedience to God, His Father. Homeless, like so many today in our cities. He had nowhere to lay his head. Nowhere to call home."

Home. A concept Wade had been wrestling with since he'd left for college at eighteen. His four years at Texas A&M didn't yield him any ties to the college town, nor did his time in Washington D.C. give him an attachment to that city either. Sure, he'd had apartments and townhouses, but never a home.

Dan leaned close, breaking into Wade's thoughts, and whispered, "So, you and Bernadette? I approve." He bumped Wade's elbow with his own and chuckled.

Wade resisted the urge to roll his eyes. So, that's what Bernadette's look was about. If he got nudged, congratulated, and peppered with encouragement during the sermon, what had she endured before the service started? Maybe it had been a blessing he'd run late in getting to church.

"Not everyone is called to leave home and family,

but we are all called to count the cost of following Jesus. The cost of obedience to God and His Word. Though in our scripture reading today, the religious leader wanted to go with Jesus, but Jesus warned him of the cost. There is the contrasting story of the miracle of the demon-possessed man whom Jesus delivered. The man begged to go with him, but Jesus said no and sent him back home to his own people to tell of the miraculous change in his life."

Yes, there had been a miraculous change in Wade's life. A bullet in the chest, leaving him keenly aware of his own mortality. The bullet had changed his perspective of what was important. Without thinking, he touched the spot on the right side of his chest, then ran his finger along the scar on his left cheek. Marks of his life before his profession of faith.

"Our home as believers is in Christ Jesus. As Jesus said in John 14:23, 'all who love me will do what I say. My Father will love them. And we will come and make our home with each of them. We are in Christ, and Christ and the Father, are in us and make their home with us.'"

Not long after his conversion, the invitation came to attend Dan and Nikki's wedding which stirred a longing in him to be near his family. He'd been able to come for the big day to reconnect with his brothers, but the trip had only worked to increase his desire to be back in Reseda County.

Pastor Connor closed his Bible. "Whether we are sent to the mission field in a faraway land or sent to the mission field among our own people, our home is in Christ, and as long as He is with us, we are never spiritually homeless." He paused, his gaze moving across the congregation. "If you know of anyone who is spiritually homeless, bring them out of the cold. Tell them about Jesus." Bowing his head, he prayed.

Wade leaned his forearms on his knees and clutched his hands together. *Lord, You are my home. Please put me where You want me to be.* He lifted his eyes and glanced at Bernadette. *And I hand over the situation with Bernie. I want Your will, Father. Your will, not mine.*

With those words, his throat tightened. What if God had a different idea? Could he let go of his feelings for Bernadette, the feelings which had grown so quietly in his heart, he'd nearly tripped over them when he realized how much he cared for her? Hopefully, he wouldn't have to find out. Maybe, God's infinite plan was at the center of all this.

~

Sitting behind his desk in the sheriff's office, Wade examined the notes he'd taken Sunday morning from Deputy Perez. She'd spotted the white van Saturday evening around twilight, assuming it belonged to someone living in the house. When she made a second pass two hours later and discovered the vehicle had backed into the drive, she decided to pull up the vacation home checklist, a service Reseda County offered to its citizens. When the address popped up on the list, Perez pulled the squad car to the side of the road and approached on foot.

Frustrated, Wade picked up his own notes about the lockbox hacking and what he and Bernadette had found at the Hudson property. He didn't believe the burglaries and hacking were connected, but it was strange these two events were happening in the same area at the same time. Wade couldn't imagine that the bedazzled shoes he'd seen on the culprit running from the house belonged to a hardened criminal. A kid, yes. But someone who went around stealing televisions and computers along with the good silver didn't seem probable.

"Sorry to interrupt." Hilda stood in the doorway. "Bernadette Stewart and Marilyn Kemp are here. They want to file reports on some hacked lockboxes."

"Send them in. And if you could hold my calls."

"No problem, Boss."

A few minutes later, the two women sat across from him. He was glad Bernadette had taken Burt's advice and had come to file the report. Marilyn's presence was a bonus. Maybe with her statement, a pattern would emerge that would help him find the hacker.

Marilyn Kemp, a bottle blond around forty, pushed her sunglasses to the crown of her head and blinked to adjust her eyes to the fluorescent lighting. "Well, Sheriff, I don't have to tell you how unnerving it is to know someone's been nosing around a place that I'm responsible for." Marilyn crossed her legs and let her satchel drop to the floor beside the chair. "It gives me the creeps." She shuddered.

"I'm sure it does. That's why I wanted the two of you to come in and let me hear what you have to say. The more my department knows, the more likely we'll be able to catch the perps."

Marilyn shifted in her seat. "I heard from Purdy that the Nortons were robbed while they were on vacation. The thieves took all the big electronics and Mrs. Norton's diamond necklace—the one her mother gave her for her wedding day over fifty years ago. It was a family heirloom." Marilyn's lips curled into a snarl. "Dirty, rotten scoundrels."

"I'd forgotten about that," Bernadette said. "Do you think the burglaries and the hacked lockboxes are related?"

"I don't think so, but at this point, I'm looking at all the angles." Turning his attention to Marilyn, he asked, "Can you tell me what happened concerning the lockboxes?" Wade needed to get the conversation back on track. It would do no good for rumors to start flying around Orange Blossom about the burglaries. He'd do his best to keep the information quiet for the time being. People in a panic would only make his job harder.

Marilyn inhaled and squinted, letting her breath out slowly through her pursed bright red lips. "About three weeks ago on a Sunday, I drove out to the Cordova property in the county near the Sine River." She met his gaze. "That's what makes the property special, the location."

Bernadette interrupted, a mischievous glint shimmering in her green eyes. "Location, location, location."

Marilyn shot a disapproving glance in Bernie's direction. "Anyhoo, when I arrived at a little past one, I noticed the key drawer dangling from the lockbox. I removed it to see if the key was still inside, and it was. So, I thought I had accidentally left the lockbox open."

"With it being digital, don't you receive a notification if you leave a lockbox open or if someone else opens it?" Wade asked.

"Not if the right code is entered, but the company

who sells the boxes does keep a log of their use."

"Yeah, if the right code is entered, they post the activity to the user log." Bernadette confirmed.

Marilyn frowned, before turning her attention to Wade. "Next, I entered the home and headed upstairs. You know, to do a once-over before people started showing up for the open house. Everything looked fine until I got to the last bedroom near the back of the house. In there, I found about a week's worth of food wrappers. Apparently, the hacker likes Burger King Whoppers because the floor was littered with brown paper. The whole room smelled of cheese and onions."

"Good. Wrappers from Burger King." Wade jotted down the information on the official form. "Anything else?"

"Yes, a magazine. I found it tossed to one side of the room, and it had some pages torn out."

"What kind of magazine?" Wade glanced up from writing.

"One of those teen idol types. Let's see. Maybe *Tiger Beat*?" Marilyn snapped her fingers. "No, *Teen Rage*. That was it. I checked the date of publication, and it was four months old."

"So, four months old, that'd be March. And the pages missing? Did you have any idea what might be on them?"

Marilyn smirked. "Of course, I knew. I was a teenage girl once. It had to be pictures of that month's featured heartthrob. I can't remember who it was, but any teenage girl worth her salt would be able to tell you who the popular teen idols are these days."

Wade wrote *Teen Rage* magazine on his paper, then under it he wrote *teen girl* with a question mark beside it. Bedazzled shoes, heartthrob magazines, and a love of Burger King Whoppers with cheese and onions. A picture of the hacker began to form in his mind. Nothing quite as dangerous as he'd thought the other day at the Hudson property.

"Is there anything else you noticed that might help?" Wade had learned to be patient when interviewing a witness. Sometimes silence worked to his benefit. It allowed the witness's brain time to recall the small details of the event. Ones they deemed unimportant.

"I don't think so." Marilyn tilted her head to one side. Her lips puckered.

"What about the packet of floss?" Bernadette asked.

"Floss?" Marilyn's brows drew together as her lips dropped into a frown.

"The one you said you found in the bathroom," Bernadette added.

"Oh yeah, I completely forgot about that. I guess I'd figured it had been left by the owners and I hadn't noticed it before. Easy enough to overlook. But Bernie's right. The Sunday prior to coming across all that mess, I'd found a packet of floss on the bathroom counter sitting next to the sink, as pretty as you please."

"Floss. Got it." Wade slid further back in his leather chair. "You've been very helpful, Marilyn. I appreciate your time. This should give me a good sketch of our hacker."

"I always like to be helpful where I can, Sheriff." Marilyn leaned forward and placed her elbow on top of her crossed knees, planting her chin on her fist. A smile snaked across her lips. "Now, I have a few questions for the two of you. Just between us, how serious is this relationship? Everyone's dying to know. I mean, you two make the cutest couple, and I've always heard opposites attract."

"Who's everyone?" Bernadette shrieked, twisting in her seat to face her.

"Well, your mother did invite half the population of Orange Blossom to your birthday party, Bernie. You can't blame them for talking about how adorable you guys were together."

"Good glory. Have you taken leave of your senses?" Bernadette straightened her shoulders and sat to her full height. The blush marking her cheeks displayed the depth of her embarrassment.

Wade had heard enough. He wasn't going to sit still and let the witness become the interrogator. Nor was he going to let Bernadette be put on the spot. "Miss Kemp," he said with an edge of authority in his voice. "I have all I need. Hilda will see you out." Wade stood and moved to the door. Stepping out, he signaled Hilda to join them.

"I get it. You want a minute alone. No problem. But people are going to want to know if they need to start planning a wedding." Marilyn stood, picking up her satchel from the floor by the chair. "I'll catch up with you later, Bernie."

Wade held the door open for Marilyn. As she passed by him, he remembered something he wanted to ask. "One more question. Do you recall the color of the room where you found the wrappers?"

"That's an odd question." Marilyn paused to consider it. "Pink, I believe. A girl's room for sure."

Wade nodded. "Thank you. That's very helpful."

Marilyn followed Hilda to the front of the squad room.

Wade turned and closed the door, his gaze meeting Bernadette's. "She's right, you know. Your mother did invite half the population of the town."

"Well, if you include Harry Branson and Leonard, then it'd be more than half." She giggled.

Wade adored the fact she could make light of the situation and allowed her good humor to rub off on him. "Aren't you angry with Marilyn?"

"Not really. She's just honest enough to say what others are thinking." Bernadette plopped back in the chair. "I want to apologize for getting you into this predicament. I had no idea that many people were going to be there. Mom had told me, and I quote, 'a quiet gathering of close intimate friends. At the most, ten.'" Bernadette shook her head. "If I'd known what we were walking into, I'd never have asked you to come as my date."

Wade rubbed his hand across his jawline. "It doesn't matter. I'd rather have you ask, and all those people be there, than you not ask at all. Now, we can get to know each other a little better—" His nerves pulsed at the thought of their Friday night date. "On a much deeper level than speeding tickets." Not sure where to take the conversation, he brought it back to the reason for her being there. "Now it's your turn. Can you tell me what happened the first time you found the lockbox hacked at the Lester property?"

"Let me see. I entered the residence and found the lockbox on the kitchen counter. When I went upstairs—"

"That house also had an upper level."

"Yes, it did." Bernadette's eyes widened. "That's something all three houses have in common."

Wade nodded. "Sure is. Didn't you tell me Saturday you had found food wrappers like Marilyn did?"

"Yes, and they were also from Burger King. Although there were a few plastic bags with the word *thank you* on them as well. The generic kind."

"The kind that might be used at a gas station?" Wade asked.

"Yeah, that's right. I believe the Stop and Go has that type of bags."

"Can you remember anything else?" Wade sat in silence. The sweet citrus scent of Bernadette's perfume floated around him. The way she tapped her finger against her lips while she considered his question drew his attention to her heart-shaped mouth. The urge to be closer to her made him shift in his chair.

"No, not really. At this point, I think I've told you everything that's relevant."

Wade chuckled. "You'd be surprised by what you can learn from what most people consider irrelevant." Wade straightened in his seat and pushed the forms he worked on toward Bernadette. She moved forward to examine them. "If we take everything you told me, what Marilyn told me, and what I saw, can you guess what would be the most significant piece of information?"

Bernadette studied his notes on the forms. "Is it that the culprit appears to be a teenage girl?"

Wade shook his head. "I'll give you two more tries."

She narrowed her eyes. "Challenge accepted." She

picked up the papers and ran her finger down the pages one at a time, occasionally stopping to study a particular item. She glanced up after several moments. "Is it that all the houses have two stories?"

"Nope." He leaned back, crossed his arms, and hummed the theme song from *Jeopardy*.

She scowled at him before she scanned the sheets one more time. "The bedazzled shoes?"

Leaning toward her, he folded his hands on his desk. "There are actually two significant facts we know now because you and Marilyn gave your statements. One is that the culprit has a connection to Burger King. Nobody loves Whoppers that much. She must be getting the food free. Which means, she must know someone who works at one of the locations. We have three Burger King locations throughout the county. So, that gives us a place to start looking. We can see if anyone knows a teen with bedazzled shoes." His chest swelled at the expression of awe radiating from Bernadette's face.

"Wow, you really are good at this sheriff thing." Bernadette beamed. "What was the second piece of significant information?"

"The date on the magazine. It appears whoever is hacking the lockboxes is doing it to have somewhere to stay. That's what all the mess tells us. Someone desperate for money wouldn't waste any on something like a magazine. So, I'm thinking the kid took it with her when she left home. She must've run away sometime after March since that's the publication date. It may be a long shot, but it gives my team a place to start with the missing-persons reports."

"So, do you think between the Burger King lead

and the magazine date you'll be able to figure out who our hacker is?"

"I do. All because you came in and filed a report." He reached across the desk and took her hand in his. "Well, and the fact you're dating the sheriff."

Her eyes widened to the size of tennis balls, and her shoulders tensed.

Why had he said that? She looked like a deer caught in the headlights of an eighteen-wheeler going ninety. "Easy, Bernadette. No one thinks we're serious. They know we've only been out the one time."

"That's not true. According to Marilyn, half the town wants to know when we're getting married." Bernadette popped up and paced beside his desk. She took three steps, pivoted, and returned to the spot by her chair, then repeated the action. "I don't know if I can do this. Why did Marilyn have to talk about weddings?"

Wade figured the poor woman was going to break out in hives the way she twitched and wiggled and paced. "What's really wrong?" He stood and caught her by her shoulders, stopping her in midstride. "Talk to me, Bernie. This isn't like you. What's the problem with weddings?"

Bernadette met his gaze. "It's not you. It's me."

"That's not an answer." Wade stifled the groan rising in him. The old *it's not you but me* jab. She might as well have hit him in the gut with both fists. It couldn't have hurt any worse.

"I ... I ... I need to go. I can't handle this right now." Bernadette pulled from his grasp and grabbed her purse from the chair. "I'll call you."

"What about Friday night? Are we still on?" Wade reined in his thundering heart, not wanting to scare her any more than he had.

"I don't think it will work," Bernadette said.

"Will you at least think about it?"

"Yeah, I'll think about it. I'll let you know either way." Bernadette turned the doorknob and swung the wooden door open. "I'm sorry, Wade. I have a history of making a mess of relationships."

"For the record, I like messy. Messy usually means it's interesting and worth the trouble."

She glanced over her shoulder at him. "Not this kind of mess."

Chapter Six

Bernadette's heart pounded as she entered the reception area of the Cowboy Community Church of Orange Blossom. She hated the idea of missing Bible study tonight, but she didn't see any way around it. She'd been avoiding Wade and half the population of the small town since Monday and going to the Bible Babes meeting tonight at Nikki's wasn't in her plans. She wasn't ready to face him.

The reception area of the church held a certain warmth for Bernadette and calmed her nerves. The recent makeover gave the well-used area a more upbeat vibe. A wreath of spring flowers hung on the wall above a line of chairs, with a 'welcome, neighbor' sign tucked in it. The mishmash of bright colors brought a dash of whimsy to the room.

Bernadette inhaled the scent she equated with peace and friendship—two things she desperately needed. Strolling to the L-shaped counter, she spotted Purdy at her desk.

Looking up, Purdy smiled. "Hello there, stranger. I haven't seen you since Sunday's service. Where've you been hiding yourself?" She rose and walked the short distance to the counter.

"Here and there," Bernadette answered the sixty-something grandmother. Looking around, she asked, "Where's Sarah? Doesn't she work here during the summer?"

"She does, but I have her over in the sanctuary vacuuming. Mrs. Dodson, our usual cleaning lady, had surgery on her rotator cuff last week, so, she'll be out of commission for the next month. I thought Sarah would be perfect to fill in for her." Purdy chuckled. "Plus, it'll give her a new respect for all her mother does around their house."

Bernadette tossed her satchel onto the counter near the partition which separated the waiting area from the workspace and rested her chin on her hand. "Being a teenager can be hard."

"Hey, I thought I heard you." Nikki entered from the copier room off to the left of the workspace. "Did you ask her?" She directed her question to Purdy.

"No, I haven't." A gleam played in Purdy's soft eyes.

"Ask me what?" Bernadette straightened and scowled. "If this is about Wade, don't."

"Come on, Bernadette. We need the inside scoop. You know Wade isn't going to tell me anything juicy." Nikki grinned and rested her hand on top of her protruding belly.

"There isn't anything juicy to tell. You of all people should know that." Placing her fists on her hips, the heat of anger washed over her. "I swear if one more person asks me about Wade, I'm going to go postal." She blinked, fighting to keep the tears at bay. "That seems to be all anyone can talk about. Harry stopped me to ask if we were an item the other day at the café."

She pointed toward the door with her thumb. "Then Leon mentioned what a sweet couple we made while bagging my groceries. Even Pastor Connor made a crack about the church getting booked up quickly, so we'd better put our names on the calendar." She threw her hands into the air, then crossed them over her chest. Tears of frustration trickled down her cheeks.

Purdy clucked her tongue and moved to the partition, lifting it. "Come here, sweetie." She opened her arms wide.

Swiping at the tears, Bernadette moved straight into Purdy's arms.

"Oh, Bernie, I'm sorry. I didn't mean to upset you." Nikki crossed the floor and wrapped her arms around her two friends. The three stood in a group hug.

Bernadette let the tears flow, releasing all the pent-up anxiety she'd carried since Monday when she'd called off her second date with Wade. The day when the memories had flooded over her and made her doubt her ability to have a committed relationship. The day the fear had set in, taking hold of her timid heart. After a few moments, Bernadette straightened and stepped back, wiping her eyes with her knuckles. "I'm sorry. It's just that it's been a tough week. Wade and I seem to be the hot topic."

Nikki reached under the counter and produced a box of tissues. Pulling two, she stuffed them in Bernadette's hand. "It's all right." Nikki shook her head. "I'm usually the one in tears these days."

Bernadette chuckled and dabbed her eyes.

Purdy pulled the second stool out for Bernadette and offered the other stool to Nikki. "I'm a little confused." Purdy frowned. "Why is it a problem that people are curious about the relationship?"

"I broke off my second date with Wade."

"I see." Nikki nodded. "That explains a lot. He's been so moody, and every time Dan or I bring up the subject of the party or house hunting, he shuts down the conversation." Nikki patted Bernadette's knee. "What happened? Why did you call it off?"

Bernadette rested her hands in her lap, twisting the tissue with her fingers. "Marilyn."

Both women groaned. "What did she do?" Purdy demanded. "She didn't try any of her old tricks, did she? Chasing after him, or sweet-talking him?"

"No, nothing like that. She just mentioned marriage and weddings. And you know my history with that." She rolled her eyes and sighed a deep, heavy breath. "I just don't trust myself."

"Oh, honey, you're going to have to put that behind you. We've all made our share of mistakes." Purdy slid her arm around Bernadette's shoulders. "Don't let your past ruin your chance for a beautiful future."

"It's not that simple." Bernadette met Nikki's gaze. "You know that." Bernadette had confided in Nikki the whole ugly truth, but she hadn't told anyone else except her mother, one of the godliest women she knew. "Look, I stopped by to let you know I won't be at tonight's study. I don't want to make Wade uncomfortable."

"Well, you're in luck. Wade's not even going to be there. He said something this morning before he left the ranch about a stakeout and a pair of bedazzled shoes. I don't know exactly what that means, but he hasn't made much sense the last few days." Nikki smiled. "So, please come."

"No, I don't want to run the risk of seeing him until I'm ready."

"What about helping him to find a house? You're going to have to face him sometime. Wouldn't it be better in a more relaxed atmosphere when business isn't part of the equation?"

"Maybe, but not yet." She stood, grabbing her satchel from the counter. "Speaking of business, I have a client I'm meeting. I'd better shove off." She tossed the tissue into the trash can before lifting the partition.

"Well, let us know if there's anything we can do to help," Purdy said.

"Yes, or if you just need a listening ear." Nikki stood, supporting her back with her hand. "You know we're here for you."

Bernadette stopped at the glass door. "I know. And thanks for letting me get it out of my system. I feel much better." Pulling her keys from her satchel, she unlocked her truck with the fob. Sliding into the driver's seat, she found her cell phone and hit her mother's number on her favorites list.

"Hey, Bernie, how's my girl?"

"Not so good. Do you think you could meet for a late lunch? I need some advice." Bernie willed herself not to cry. It would upset her mother too much. And then they'd have the whole conversation over the phone, which wasn't what she wanted.

"Sure, honey. How about one at Joan's Place?"

Bernadette tapped her knife on the white cloth napkin and checked the time on her cell phone. Her mother had said one but later texted she'd be late. Not a big surprise. Her mother often ran late if she was in the middle of one of her creative projects. Where her dad was a savvy businessman, her mother overflowed with all the creative juices in the family.

That's what made their venture into owning a bed and breakfast a perfect fit for the two. The Belles and Beaus had opened a year before Bernadette entered the world. They'd started out by advertising the ranch as a tourist destination then added horses and trail riding as part of their packages on the forty-plus acres. Eventually, they hosted a group of kids each year from the Careway Children's Home, and by the time Bernadette was fourteen, her parents had applied to become foster parents. Their hearts were focused on those who needed a temporary haven while the world sorted out what needed to be done with them.

"Sorry." Her mother slid into the chair across from Bernadette, dropping her purse in one of the empty seats.

"It's all right, Mom."

"No, it's not. I got swept away with choosing the paint for the fourth bedroom and lost all track of time. Your dad agrees it needs an update." She bent closer. "I wanted to strike while the iron is hot, so to speak." She nodded and leaned back into the seat. "Besides, the yellow wallpaper screams eighties. So, we're thinking smoky gray with splashes of yellow to keep the theme." After taking a breath, she asked, "What do you think?"

Bernadette grinned. Her mother, the whirlwind. "I think whatever you decide will be lovely. You have impeccable taste."

"Well, that's a high compliment coming from a seasoned realtor."

After ordering, her mother unrolled her silverware and spread the napkin over her lap. "Now, what did you want to talk about?" Her mother studied her, making Bernadette shift in her seat. "I can tell by the wrinkles on your forehead, it's not good." Pushing a strand of her light auburn hair behind her ear, she leaned closer to Bernadette and lowered her voice. "Is this about Wade?"

She nodded, biting her lip, not knowing where to start.

"Are you two still seeing each other?"

She shook her head.

"What happened? Are you okay, honey?" Her mother groaned and answered her own question. "Of course, you're not okay, or we wouldn't be here, having this conversation." Reaching out, she grasped Bernadette's hand in hers. "Oh, baby girl, what can I do?"

"Pray, Mom." Bernadette patted her mom's hand and then pulled her hand away. "You know how things have gone in the past with men. Wade and I are friends, and I don't want to ruin it."

"So, why would going out ruin your friendship? It's because you're friends it's a good idea."

"You know my history. None of my relationships have ended well. Train wrecks, the whole lot."

"How can you say that? You haven't dated that much." Her mom rested her crossed arms on the table. "You make it sound as if you've had a trail of romances."

"I left a man at the altar brokenhearted. It took Peter months to get over the humiliation and hurt, and in the end, the poor guy had to move away to get a fresh start."

Her mom waved the words away. "You're being

overdramatic."

Bernadette released a low groan. "I left the man in shambles."

Acting as if she hadn't heard her, Darlene continued, "Besides, it's better that you called it off before the I dos. If you didn't love him, both of you would've been miserable."

"You're right. I just don't want to make the same mistake again. And I keep asking myself, if Wade's the one God has for me, why did it take this long for us to come together?"

The waitress appeared at their table, carrying their lunch orders of chicken salad on crescent rolls with bowls of fresh fruit on the side. Bernadette offered a weak smile to the waitress.

"Can I bring you two anything else?" She smiled, making eye contact with each woman in turn.

"No, this is fine. Thank you." Her mother picked up her fork and turned her attention back to Bernadette. The waitress hurried away to greet a new customer. Once she was out of earshot, Mom said, "Only God knows why his timing works the way it does. But keep in mind, there are two hearts involved here."

"So, what are you saying?" Bernadette took a bite of her sandwich. The chicken salad made with creamy mayo and grapes melted on her tongue. She licked the corner of her mouth to get every last crumb from the crescent roll before using her napkin.

"I'm saying. Maybe Wade wasn't ready when he came to work on his pops' ranch. Maybe, he needed the college experience and the time with the FBI to work out some heart issues."

"I suppose. But what if he's still not ready? I'm

thirty-two. I'm not getting any younger." She pressed her lips together not wanting to voice the real fear rambling around in her mind, but it spilled out anyway. "What if *I'm* not ready?"

"Now I see. We've hit upon the real problem. You're afraid you can't commit."

Bernadette fiddled with her fork in the fruit bowl, poking the pineapple and twirling it against the bottom of the little glass container. She shrugged, avoiding eye contact.

"Bernie, the only way to find out if you're ready is to try. But I can guarantee you'll never find out by hiding." Her mother arched one eyebrow. "You know I'm right."

"Yeah, maybe." She didn't want to concede that her mother's take on the situation might be correct. She wanted to hold onto her fear like a shield to keep her heart safe.

"So how did you leave things with Wade? Is it completely over, or can you salvage what you started?" Taking another sip of water, she studied her daughter.

Squirming, Bernadette put down the fork with the pineapple still stuck to the prongs. "I told him I'd let him know by tomorrow night. We were supposed to go to The Flying Pig for dinner on Friday."

"Then go. See what happens." After a few bites, she studied her daughter. "What brought on this fight-or-flight response? Did something happen?"

"Marilyn might have mentioned weddings in reference to me and Wade. Plus, after the party, everyone kept asking me about us, as if we were an item." Bernadette held her hands palms up. "It took me by surprise, then all the guilt I'd carried about Peter came rushing back."

"Making you doubt yourself." Her mother nodded. "And maybe God a little." She held her thumb and pointer finger an inch apart.

"Yeah, a little bit." How she rated such a wise, godly mother, she didn't know, but she thanked God for her two parents and the happy home she'd grown up in almost daily. The fact they had shared their love of family with kids who needed a safe haven only made her love them more.

"Well, just remember God doesn't give us a spirit of fear." She met her gaze.

"I know," Bernadette interrupted. "But of power, and of love, and of a sound mind."

"Right. So, don't let what happened in the past keep you from finding out if this is a path the Lord is opening for you."

Bernadette reached out and squeezed her mother's hand. "What would I do without my own personal prayer warrior?"

"I don't know about you, but your father's life would still be in danger. Those outrageous rodeo stories he tells. It's a wonder he lived to meet me." They both laughed. Then as quickly, her mother's face sobered. "You know one day the Belles and Beaus will be yours to run. I just hope whoever you do settle down with will appreciate what we've built."

A spark of mischief stirred in Bernadette. "Well, I'm sure they will because you've probably included it in your laundry list of must-haves that you've given to the Lord." A smile rose to her eyes causing them to crinkle at the corners. "Must be handsome, must love my daughter, must be a godly man, must love horses.

I'm sure the list goes something like that."

A sly gleam entered Mom's eyes. "Maybe."

"I just hope loving me rates higher than loving the horses." Bernadette cocked her head to one side, placed her chin in her hand, and studied her mother.

"It does." She paused. "Most of the time."

Chapter Seven

The handheld radio in Wade's truck crackled with static before Ken Berg's voice boomed across the air waves. "Sheriff, we've had a sighting of the white van on Maple Lane off Highway 87. I sent Donnie to check it out."

Picking up the device, Wade pushed the button on the side before he spoke. "Sounds good. Let me know what he finds."

"Will do. Have you had any luck on your own fishing expedition?" A snort of derision floated from the speaker.

Wade scowled. "No, not yet." Crinkling the empty brown wrapper from his burger, he tossed it to the floorboard of his beat-up old truck. He'd been there since lunch, and the pile of trash had grown with the passing hours. "But it's early. They don't close until midnight. Is Regan still at the other Burger King?"

"Yes, she checked in about an hour ago. She hasn't seen the teen either. Oh, and Charlie Giles called to complain about a red Ford truck speeding past his property." Ken chuckled. "I hadn't heard from him in a while about Bernadette."

"I guess Bernadette's been busy." Wade signed off

and chucked the radio into the passenger side of the bench seat. Wade had driven his vintage truck to the stakeout. He needed to blend in with the other cars in the parking lot. As smart as the lockbox hacker was, she'd keep an eye out for the police or sheriff.

Vintage. The word made him smile. That's how he'd described his pop's truck to Bernadette. She'd called a spade a spade and considered the truck old and broken down. He straightened behind the steering wheel. Bernadette's image drew his thoughts to their current predicament, making his heart a bit heavy.

He'd never seen a woman freak out like she had at the mention of weddings. And she'd put his idea about going out Friday night to The Flying Pig on ice. She'd promised to let him know either way, but he figured she would cancel. The fear he'd seen in her eyes left little doubt. He glanced at his phone. Nikki had told him Bernadette decided not to attend the Blossom Bible Babes meeting, which meant she'd be home. Picking up his phone from the dash, he considered calling her but decided against it. She needed time, and he didn't want to pressure her.

Lord, you know how I feel about Bernadette. But if you have other plans, then that's what I want. He swallowed the lump sticking in his throat. He'd come a long way from the man who thought he had it all together and didn't need God anymore. A bullet in the chest will do that to you. Instead, he dialed Regan's number. "Hey, you got anything?"

"No, Boss. I've seen tons of teens in and out all day, but no one wearing a dark hoodie and blinged-out shoes."

They'd chosen two locations based on the intel

they'd gathered from other local realtors. It appeared the lockbox hacker kept within a ten-mile area. And the two Burger Kings fell within those lines. So far, hanging around the fast-food joints for the past two days hadn't brought the success he'd hoped for.

"Well, keep me posted, and I'll do the same." Wade tapped the screen, ending the call.

Sliding his phone back onto the dashboard, he noticed a tall, lean young man in a Burger King tee-shirt and black pants emerge from the building. The kid ambled across the pavement toward the two metal dumpsters in the back of the parking lot.

Something was wrong with this picture. Then, it dawned on Wade the kid wasn't carrying any trash bags. Instead, he had two takeout bags and a drink. He kept his eyes on the youth.

Of course, the kid could be headed to his car for his break to listen to music or make a call, but something had Wade's gut tingling.

The young man scanned the parking lot as he walked, then quickened his steps.

When he passed the truck, Wade caught a good look at his face. Thank goodness for daylight savings time. In late June, even at eight o'clock, he could make out his features. The boy couldn't be more than sixteen. Straightening in his seat, Wade hugged the steering wheel, watching the progression of the young man.

The teen stopped beside the trash bin and looked around. A minute later, a figure dressed in a dark hoodie stepped out from the wooded area abutting the dumpsters.

The two exchanged words, but Wade couldn't make out what they were saying. The young man handed over one of the bags.

His friend dug out a burger and pushed back the hoodie exposing her young face. Her honey blond hair hung long and limp, elongating her jawline making her look tired. She pulled back the corner of the wrapper and stuffed the sandwich into her mouth. Holding the bag, she used her other hand to fish out several fries and shoved them into her mouth.

She must be starving. Assessing the situation, Wade decided the best way to approach the hacker would be in the truck. She'd be distracted with her friend and the food and be less likely to be spooked by a moving car in the parking lot than she would someone approaching on foot.

Cranking the engine, he shifted the truck into drive and circled the building to the back by the bins. Pulling into the parking spot closest to the dumpsters, he slid out and glanced to his right to see if the hacker was still there.

The two teens stood behind the dumpsters talking. They didn't even look his way as he strolled by.

Passing along the front of the metal bins, he moved as if he were headed for the entrance, but once out of their line of sight, Wade eased along the side of the first blue metal box until he heard what they were saying.

"You need to be careful, Leanne. If they find you, they'll hurt you."

"I'm being careful."

"Well, you said someone almost caught you last week in one of the houses. You can't keep breaking into vacant homes. You're gonna get caught. That's how you got into this mess in the first place, girl. Being somewhere you shouldn't."

"Look, I don't need a lecture. It's not my fault they spotted me. Besides, you sound like Nadine when you talk like that. And look what doing the right thing got her."

"Nadine was a good woman, and she treated us right."

Wade stole a glance around the corner of the dumpster. The young man held the drink and one of the bags while Leanne dug out fries from the other one. "Nadine was a sucker, just like all of them. They all want something from the system. None of them care about us." She stuffed the fries into her mouth, then mumbled over them, "Don't forget that."

The young man pulled his phone from his pocket. "I'd better get back. My break is almost over, and they'll start looking for me."

As he turned to leave, Leanne grabbed his arm. "Thanks, Jay. Sorry for crabbing on you. I'm just hungry."

He nodded and took a step, then stopped. "I'm serious about being careful. If those guys find you, they won't leave you around to be a witness."

Wade ducked back before Jay saw him. He counted to ten, then moved from the cover of the dumpster toward the spot where the two had been standing. The girl had her back to him.

He inched his way toward her. Two steps out of his reach, he knocked a plastic cup on the ground with his foot and sent it rolling across the pavement.

Leanne's head jerked in his direction.

Before he had time to think, she dropped the bag and dashed into the woods flinging limbs and twigs as she ran.

Wade set off after her. "Stop, Leanne. Stop. Sheriff's department." He might as well have been talking to the wind. Her bedazzled feet sped away as if she had wings instead of rhinestones on those shoes.

Frustrated at losing the girl, Wade backtracked to the Burger King parking lot. If he couldn't catch her, he'd corral the next best thing, her friend, Jay.

Pushing open the door, he scanned the dine-in area. Everything looked normal. Nothing triggered his warning bells. Jay stood in the back by the long grill slapping frozen burger patties onto the hot surface. Wade didn't want to cause a scene. Stepping to the side, he tried to catch the manager's attention. The guy did his best to ignore Wade by filling the drinks for the next two orders and then shaking the salt on the fries.

Wade planted his feet and crossed his arms over his chest, doing his best imitation of an immoveable mountain. He'd worked in law enforcement with the FBI for six years, and he'd learned to outwait some of the toughest offenders on the books. The green button-down-clad manager didn't stand a chance.

"Can I help you?" The odor of grease and cologne drifted in Wade's direction as the man approached.

Wade kept his voice low. "Yes, I need to speak to one of your employees. I believe he goes by the name of Jay."

"Can I ask what this is about?" He glanced over his shoulder at the teen who was busy flipping burgers.

"I'm Sheriff Thibodeaux, and I just—"

"Whoa." The man held up his hands in surrender and took a step back. "We don't want any trouble here. Whatever Jay has gotten himself into, it doesn't have anything to do with this restaurant." The man sniffed.

"We want to help our community where we can, but I figured hiring that foster kid was a big mistake. I can't afford to have this location associated with any bad press, like drugs or theft."

Wade glanced at the guy's name tag. "Look, Doug." He scowled. "Jay's not in any trouble. I just need to ask him a few simple questions about a young girl he knows. I believe they met in the foster system, and it's her I'm looking for, not him."

"Well, in that case." He sniffed again and turned his back to Wade, "Hey Jay, there's a cop here to see you."

Every head in the place turned in his direction including Jay's. Wade's eyes met Jay's two seconds before the kid bolted for the back door.

Groaning, Wade rushed to the glass door, hitting the metal bar hard and swung it wide. He sprinted to the back corner of the building and scanned the area. Jay stood wrestling with his keys to open the car door.

Wade jogged over to the vehicle, an old Pontiac Firebird, metallic green with a black hood. He slowed and held his palms out as he neared the frightened teen. "Jay, it's okay. You're not in any trouble."

Whipping around, Jay pressed his back against his car, and with a rolled fist, hit the metal. "Look, I don't know anything."

"You know that's not true." Wade stopped a few feet from him. He didn't want the teen to feel trapped, but he didn't want him to run either. "I think you know a lot about the girl you were with by the dumpsters. You've been supplying her meals from here. We found the wrappers at some of the vacant houses—" Wade chose his words carefully, "where she's been staying."

He didn't want to call it breaking and entering.

The teen's face hardened. "Since you know all about it, what do you need me for?"

"I heard you tell your friend to be careful. Is she in some kind of danger? I can help her, but I need to find her first." Wade hadn't liked the sound of the conversation he'd overheard. If someone was after her, Wade needed to protect her.

The teen jutted out his chin but didn't answer.

"Tell me Leanne's last name."

More silence.

"Look, you can either tell me what I need to know here, or I can take you into the sheriff's department, and we can work it out there. If you tell me here, your boss is less likely to have a meltdown and fire you." Wade hated to be so brutal, but from what he'd seen, he didn't think he was far off the mark.

"Fine. Leanne's last name is Hopkins." The teen kept his eyes on the tree line behind the dumpsters not far from his car.

Wade shifted a little to his left, filling up the space, hoping the kid wouldn't make a break for it. "How do you know her?"

"I thought you had everything figured out." He met Wade's gaze.

"I know you stayed with Nadine for a while." He bluffed. "She was good to both of you. Why did she send you guys away?"

A sadness washed over the youth. The vim and vigor that had been fueling him evaporated before Wade's eyes. "She got sick and couldn't take care of us anymore. We found out months later she died." Jay stared at his feet, shaking his head. "They didn't even have the decency to tell us, so we could go to the funeral."

"I'm sorry about that, kid." Wade hung his head and stuffed his hands in his jean pockets. "If Leanne is in trouble, let me help her. Let's keep her safe."

Jay crossed his arms and inhaled. "She saw something she shouldn't have. A robbery. Now she thinks they're looking for her because she knows what one of them looks like. But the truth is, she barely got a glimpse of the guy."

"How many were there?"

He shrugged. "I think she said three. They drove a white utility van."

The sound of the back door closing alerted Wade to the presence of the manager. He turned to find the man standing on the cement block outside the back door. "Are you coming back in, or do I need to find a new fry cook?"

Meeting Wade's gaze, Jay straightened. "Sorry, I gotta go. I need this job. I'm hoping I can save enough for college before I turn eighteen and age out of the system. Who knows what'll happen to me then." The teen jogged back toward the manager who waited.

Wade followed.

The manager opened the door and let the teen pass, but before the man could enter, Wade stepped in front of him. Leaning close, he said, "I hope I don't hear that Jay's been fired for assisting my investigation. Because if I do, I'll come back and arrest you for obstruction of justice, and I'll throw penal code 148 at you so fast it'll knock the breath right out of you." Wade pulled to his full six-foot-four inches and tipped his chin. "Have a good evening, you hear?"

Back in his truck, he radioed dispatch and left word for Regan that the perp had been spotted and to call it a night. Wade didn't figure Leanne would risk going out again. He drummed his fingers on the steering wheel. If only he could locate her. Picking up his phone, he called Bernadette.

"Hello?" She sounded hesitant.

"Hey, Bernie. Listen—" Wade started but didn't get far.

"Look, Wade. I still haven't decided about the Flying Pig. If you could give me until tomorrow night like we agreed, I'd appreciate it."

Wade bit his tongue to keep from telling her he hadn't *agreed* to anything, but he didn't have time to argue or try to persuade her, so he focused on his original intent. "I'm not calling about that."

"Oh." The surprise was evident in her tone. "Then why did you call?"

"Is there any way you could text me the addresses of any vacant houses on the realtor listing site that are located between Oakside Estates and Lovers Lane? It's a ten-mile radius, and I think our lockbox hacker is somewhere in there."

"That could be a lot of addresses."

"I only need the ones where the house is vacant. Surely, there can't be that many," Wade pressed. He needed those addresses if he and his deputies were going to search for Leanne Hopkins. "It could mean the hacker's safety. Apparently, she saw something she shouldn't have and could be in danger." Wade played on the fact that Bernadette couldn't resist an underdog in need.

After a moment's silence, she relented. "Sure, I'll

check the MLS listing."

Wade pumped his fist in the air, grateful the appeal had hit home.

"But it may take a while. It's not just William Keys Realtor's listings, but it also includes all the realtors in the state."

"That's all right. I've got nowhere to be." Wade rested against the seat. The silence between them hummed.

"It'll probably be tomorrow or Friday. Is that okay?"

"Yeah, that works." Another beat of silence. "Listen, I'd better go. I'm on duty."

"Of course."

His voice grew raspy even to his own ears. "I'll keep my eye out for your text."

"Sure, and Wade, I'm sorry. I didn't mean to make this such a big deal."

"It's okay. I can wait until you've made up your mind." He wanted to tell her he'd wait for as long as it took, but that would just freak her out worse than she already was.

Her reply came as a soft whisper. "Thanks, Wade. You're the best."

A click, and the screen faded to black. But the questions whirling in his mind shone with a new brilliance. Why had Marilyn's comment about a wedding sent Bernadette running? And why had she said yes to the date in the first place, if she had no intention of going?

Chapter Eight

Sitting on her couch with her dog, Frodo, snuggled against her side, Bernadette tried to read the magazine in her hands, but it was no use. No matter how hard she tried to focus on the article, the words kept running together. She'd attempted the same paragraph three times. The topic of house renovations couldn't push the conflicting thoughts she wrestled with from her mind. She needed to call Wade. It was Thursday night after all. But what should she say?

After her lunch with her mom, she'd resolved to accept his invitation to dinner. But now, as the evening neared, her old fears clamored in her heart and paralyzed her. All the what-ifs marched through her thoughts. What if this wasn't God's plan? What if she ruined their friendship? What if she couldn't commit? She groaned, pitching the magazine onto the coffee table.

After all, she'd left one groom at the altar and a string of half promises to one or two others. Maybe she did have a commitment issue.

Frodo stirred. Lifting his head, he nuzzled her hand. She stroked the white furball, who weighed close to eighty pounds.

"Well, I don't have a commitment problem with you, do I?" She baby talked to the two-year-old mutt who had come from Snowball and Blue's first litter. "Wade's a good friend. I actually enjoy our conversations even when he stops me for speeding. And of course, I enjoyed our time together when we were out house hunting." She rested her cheek on Frodo's head. What if they dated and things went wrong? She'd never forgive herself for putting their friendship on the line. She kissed the dog's head.

Bernadette picked up the cell phone from the coffee table and stared at it. The empty screen made her hesitate. "Call? Don't call?"

Frodo whined and rolled onto his back. He pushed against her hands with his paw, begging for tummy rubs.

Biting her bottom lip, she tossed the phone to the other end of the couch. "How do you feel about something sweet?" She asked Frodo, who was a big fan of vanilla wafers. Hopping up, she scurried to the kitchen and flung open the pantry door.

Frodo followed on her heels and skidded to a stop. He stood with his tongue lolled to one side.

She groped around in the back of the pantry until her hand fell upon the right-sized box. Pulling it from the corner, she read the label. Wild Rice. Pushing the box aside, she rifled through the back of the second shelf again, certain she had vanilla wafers. They were one of her comfort foods. Hot chocolate and vanilla wafers had fixed many of her childhood problems. Leaning further into the pantry, her hand landed on the right box.

Opening the lid, she took out a handful and gave

one to Frodo who sat drooling. A few drops had splashed onto the white tile floor. He gently took the offered treat and scampered off to the living room to devour it.

She decided a mug of hot chocolate would be a necessary addition.

The buzz of her phone on the couch caught her attention. She dashed from the kitchen and grabbed it, thinking it might be Nikki or one of the other Bible Babes checking on her since she'd missed the meeting the night before. A number flashed on the screen. Her heart skipped a beat. Wade. She recognized his number. She'd dialed it hundreds of times in the name of business.

Ignoring it, she silenced the buzzing by sending it to voice message, then tossed the phone back onto the couch. She still hadn't made up her mind.

Wade had been sweet, charming, and oh so thankful when she'd texted him the list of vacant houses earlier that afternoon. He'd pulled out all the stops when he'd replied and even used a few emojis. A smile tugged at her lips.

When she returned to the kitchen, she checked the clock on the stove. Almost nine. She had to make the call soon. She'd give herself until ten o'clock, and then ready or not, she'd give him an answer.

Placing a mug of water into the microwave, she pushed the one-minute button and waited. A ding sounded, and she removed the steaming hot liquid. The chocolate created a puff above the mug as she dumped the powder into the water.

Settling back on the couch, she sipped her hot chocolate and reached for the television remote on the coffee table. Clicking on the screen, she chose a rerun of one of her favorite sitcoms. The vanilla wafers, hot chocolate, and the old television show summoned a wave of nostalgia. The only thing missing was her mom with her sage advice.

But she'd already received that, hadn't she? She simply didn't want to heed it. *God didn't give you a spirit of fear.* The words rang in her ears. *So, don't be afraid, baby girl.* She shook her head to dislodge them and focused on the scene playing out before her.

Her phone buzzed three more times, each one from Wade. She silenced her phone telling herself she'd call at ten and not a minute sooner. Hurting Wade wouldn't be easy.

Halfway through the hot chocolate and the sitcom, Frodo sprang from his spot and scampered to the door, barking. Bernadette figured it was one of her neighbors out walking their dog, so she ignored Frodo.

The doorbell rang. Pausing the show, she hurried to the entryway, wondering who it could be. "Coming. Give me a minute." Turning to Frodo, she praised him. "Good boy, but it's okay, now." Frodo stopped barking but sat next to her, eyes on the door.

Bernadette peeked out one of the windows that flanked the front door. There standing on her porch was the very subject of her inner debate. He looked good too, in his faded jeans with his cowboy hat pushed back on his dark brown curls. Her heart fluttered as she straightened the curtain.

Opening the front door a few inches, she said, "What are you doing here?"

"I tried calling, but when I didn't get an answer—" He scowled. "My imagination went into overdrive, and

I had to come check on you. What with all these break-ins and the lockbox hacker on the loose—" He crossed his arms over his broad chest and widened his stance, anchoring his square-toed boots to the porch floorboards. "So, I came to see for myself if you were all right."

Heat rose to her cheeks. She should've answered. It had been childish of her to make him worry. "I'm s-sorry," she stammered. "I saw your calls but let them go to voicemail." She glanced down at the white-worn boards. "I wasn't sure what to say."

"I see. You've decided then." He stuffed his hands in his front pockets.

She heard the hurt in his voice. "No, that's the problem. I haven't decided."

A low growl sounded from behind her. Glancing over her shoulder at the dog, she made a quick decision. "You'd better come inside. Frodo won't settle down until he's sure you're not a threat."

Wade stepped across the threshold but stopped a few feet inside the door.

Smart man. She jogged over to the coffee table where the box of vanilla wafers sat and pulled out two. "Here, give him these." Handing them to Wade, she stood beside him and called Frodo to them. "Come, boy. It's okay."

Stooping, Wade held out the wafer for Frodo to sniff.

The dog moved toward him. He sniffed Wade's hand and hesitated only a moment before taking the wafer from his palm.

Grinning, Wade stood. "It's good to know you have such a wonderful protector."

"You're right. Now that you've fed him his favorite snack, you can enter my home anytime and steal me blind. Just leave the box of cookies somewhere he can reach them."

Wade laughed, and the warmth of the sound had a disquieting effect on her heart. Tall, very tall, handsome, and even more important, a man who loved God. Why in the world would she say no to a simple date with this man? "How do you feel about hot chocolate?"

"I love hot chocolate." Wade ran his hand over Frodo's fur, and the dog fell in step with him as he followed Bernadette into the kitchen.

As she poured the water, Wade leaned against the counter. She could feel his eyes on her.

"So, can I ask what the problem seems to be with going out tomorrow night? And why weddings scare the daylights out of you?"

She turned to face him, surprised at his directness.

He gave her a mischievous half grin. "Most women love weddings. You certainly are an anomaly. Of course, I already knew that."

The sweetness in his words sent shivers skittering along her arms. She brushed a strand of wayward hair back behind her ear. "I've been called a lot of things over the years, but you are the first to call me an anomaly." The microwave dinged. She pulled the mug out and added the powder. "Perhaps we ought to get comfortable. This might take a while."

"Okay, but I only have until tomorrow evening, and then I have a date with someone I want to get to know better." His dark green eyes sparkled.

Playing along, Bernadette said, "I hear she's an

excellent realtor."

"You got that right." He took the mug from her and followed her into the living room.

"Make yourself comfortable."

Wade chose the recliner adjacent to the couch and tossed his cowboy hat onto the coffee table. He missed knocking over the box of wafers by an inch or two.

She sat in her usual spot with her feet tucked under her. Frodo jumped onto the couch beside her. "So, weddings." She pressed her lips together, working to gather her thoughts. How did she explain Peter? "To clarify, I'm not afraid of all weddings."

"That's good to know. I'd hate to think of you freaking out if you attended one." He chuckled before taking a sip of the hot liquid.

"In fact, I have attended a few over the years without incident. Even Nikki and Dan's, if you recall."

"But?" Wade asked.

"But there was this guy and this girl. And they were planning their wedding."

"So, it was serious between *this* guy and *this* girl." Wade placed his mug on the coffee table and rested his forearms on his knees.

"Yes, it was serious. But then the girl had doubts. Maybe you could even call them fears. She wasn't sure if this was the guy for her. You know, the One." She stroked Frodo's fur and searched for the best way to explain what had happened. "The girl was so in love with the idea of being in love, she didn't pay attention to the red flags that kept popping up."

"I can understand that. Often, we see what we want to see."

"Yeah, and the bad part was this girl had friends

who warned her, but she wouldn't listen. Then when they started planning the wedding, it became real. I … she started noticing little inconsistencies. He wanted to move. She wanted to live near family. She wanted children. He wasn't sure. But the clincher was his attitude toward God. She loved going to church and hanging out with her church friends. He went occasionally to please her, but he often belittled the sermon over Sunday dinner." She stopped petting Frodo, who jumped down and wandered to the foyer to lie on the cool tile.

"Wow, that is a big issue. It's hard to be unequally yoked in a marriage. One's loyalties are always torn."

Bernadette nodded and hugged her middle. "So, standing in front of the mirror in the bridal room of the church, I made my decision, and I left. Hopped right into my dad's pickup, wearing my Rebecca Ingram designer bridal gown, and headed to my parents' ranch. To hide."

Wade moved from the recliner to the couch. Sliding his arm around her shoulders, he pulled her into his chest. "Bernadette, you didn't go hide. You made the only decision you could under the circumstances. If you'd married that guy—"

"Peter." She mumbled into his tee-shirt.

He lifted her chin with the crook of his finger, forcing her to meet his gaze. "Peter was not the man for you. You did the right thing."

She scooted to the edge of the seat and faced him. "Don't you understand? I ruined his life. He was so embarrassed and so miserable that four months later, he moved. I literally ran the guy out of town." She groaned and sank back onto the couch.

Wade grinned. "Bernie, you didn't ruin the guy's life. In fact, you probably saved him more heartache. If the marriage wasn't right for you, then it wouldn't have been right for him either. You'd both been at odds with one another until the marriage fell apart. By then, there could've been kids involved."

"I hadn't thought of that. About what could've happened. Kids. Good gracious glory, that would've been a mess." She turned to face him. His arm still rested across the back of the couch, so she leaned her head against his shoulder.

He stroked her cheek. "You didn't ruin anything. In any relationship, God is dealing with two hearts and two lives. You weren't God's plan for him, and he wasn't God's plan for you."

"That's the second time I've heard that recently." Bernadette sighed. "You make it sound so simple."

"It is. As long as both people are seeking what God has for them, it can be easy."

"What about the other three before Peter? With each one, I thought he was it." She gazed into his intense green eyes. "I don't want to make the same mistake—" Her voice faltered. "Again. I'm afraid if we date, it'll cost me your friendship."

Wade dropped his hand and stood, moving to the recliner. "Okay, then, let's take it slow. Let's make sure we're on the right track each step of the way."

Surprised by his reaction, a thread of hope wrapped around her heart. Could this work? Perhaps, if they took it slow and prayed over each step.

"What do you say?" He asked. "Friday night. A date. No thoughts of weddings or obligations. Just a fun date with no strings. We'll take everything nice and slow."

Bernadette had the feeling that even *slow* with Wade would be dangerous for her heart. "Going out as friends?"

"Right. Pray about it and call me in the morning and let me know." Wade stood and grabbed his cowboy hat from the coffee table. Sliding it onto his head, he strolled to the door.

She followed. Standing there in the entryway, she wasn't sure how to say goodnight. Should they hug or maybe exchange a gentle kiss?

"Guess I'll talk to you tomorrow." He smiled at her but didn't try to kiss her, not even on the cheek.

A spark of disappointment ignited in her. Closing the door behind him, she propped her back against the wood and let the thought of kissing Wade linger. She imagined his kiss would be addictive and delicious, like vanilla wafers or hot chocolate. Her heart raced at the possibility, but he was right. She needed to pray about it and make sure. One step at a time. Just one date.

Chapter Nine

"Settle down. Don't make me cuff you again." Deputy Regan Perez threatened the young teen who refused to take a seat. Pushing on the girl's shoulders, she pressed her into the chair in front of her desk.

"I want a lawyer," The girl yelled and jerked her shoulder out of the deputy's hand.

The deputy dropped a large black backpack to the floor beside the chair before making her way around the desk to her computer.

"I have rights." She smacked her fist against the wooden surface. A grimace spread across her face, and she rubbed her hand, hugging it close to her body.

Wade smothered a smile and pushed to a standing position in the doorway of his office where he'd been watching the commotion. "You're absolutely correct."

The girl looked over her shoulder and met his gaze, her big blue eyes filled with panic. "Who are you? The sheriff?"

"Right again." Wade sauntered over to where the girl sat across from Regan. Propping on the edge of the desk facing her, he asked, "How old are you?" He threw out a lower number than he thought, so she might volunteer the information. "Eleven? Twelve?"

She lifted her chin. "Some cop you are. You're not even close. I'm fourteen, and I can take care of myself." Plopping back against the chair, she crossed her arms and averted her eyes.

Regan smirked as she tapped on the keyboard, filling out the information on the processing form. She'd have to fill out another form for Child Services and give them a call when they were done with the girl. The process was tedious but necessary.

Regan flashed him a thumbs-up when she'd finished typing. He shook his head, needing her to be more sympathetic and less combative—maybe play the good cop. They had to persuade the teen to talk about what she had witnessed and why she was in danger. "Say, Regan, do we have any of those cupcakes left from Roberta's party yesterday?"

Regan tossed him a quizzical look. "Yeah, Boss. Why?"

He tilted his head toward the teenager. "I thought Leanne here might be hungry." He focused on the girl. "Are you hungry? Would you like a cupcake or maybe something from the vending machine?"

"What? You think you can get me to tell you my life story for a cupcake?" She sneered. "Whatever."

"Why don't you bring her a cupcake and a soda into my office."

Regan shrugged and pushed back her chair, heading to the break room.

"Come on, Leanne. Let's go to my office and talk. We may be able to help each other. I understand there are some people looking for you."

"I think I'll stay right here." She raked her eyes

over him. "I don't trust you. You're a man. From what I've seen, I can't trust any of them."

"Not even a sheriff?" Wade arched an eyebrow.

"Especially a sheriff. Cops have never helped me; they've only made my life worse. Separating me from my mom. Then my sister, Mia. And now—" She fanned her hand around in the air as if she were Vanna White. "I'm stuck here away from my friends."

"So, there are more of you breaking into vacant houses," Wade pressed.

She rolled her eyes and shifted her shoulders away from him.

Regan returned carrying a cupcake with blue icing and a can of Dr. Pepper. "Here you go." She placed the napkin with the cupcake on it in front of Leanne. The can of Dr. Pepper sat beside the napkin.

The girl shook her head. "Pa-the-tic."

Regan scowled. Her lips grew pencil thin. "Why, you br—"

"Deputy Perez." The sharpness in his voice got her attention. Wade stepped in. He'd better do something, or Regan would strangle the little twerp.

"I think you'd better come with me, Leanne. We have a lot to talk over."

"Fine. But you're wasting your time. I ain't got nothing to say." She stood, grabbed her backpack, and followed him, her rhinestone-spangled shoes slapping against the tile floor.

He waited in the doorway for her to enter and take a seat. Out of the corner of his eye, he caught Regan pitching the cupcake and drink into the trash can. Tilting his head, he motioned to Regan. She joined him. "See what you can find out about the sister, Mia

Hopkins. I'd like to know where she's been placed and how long they've been apart."

Regan nodded and returned to her desk.

Leaving the door open, he took his seat, not sure how to approach this interview. Sure, he'd drilled hardened criminals, spies, and even a few terrorists in his day. But how to handle a blond haired, blue-eyed, jaded adolescence was a little out of his wheelhouse. They didn't teach that at Quantico.

Honesty. The word floated into his thoughts. Yes, he needed to meet her cynicism with a dose of good old-fashioned honesty. "Okay, I'm going to be straight with you. I overheard you talking with Jay the other night at Burger King. I know that you witnessed something that has you scared."

She glared at him over the top of the backpack she held in her lap.

"I also know there have been a string of burglaries in the county. And I'm going to venture a guess that you saw something to do with those burglaries, or you know something about them." Wade placed his forearms on his desk and fiddled with a pad of sticky notes. "I can't help but think since you've been staying in empty houses up for sale in the county, and the robbers have been hitting houses in the county while their owners were away, maybe your paths crossed somewhere along the line."

Her brows popped up, and she lifted her shoulder. "Think what you want."

Okay, so much for honesty. What did he expect—she'd blab nonstop once he'd been straight with her? He groaned. Her body language told him this would be a long and arduous process. Catching sight of the backpack, Wade recalled the shoplifting report Harry Branson had made. "So, what's in your backpack?"

"None of your business." She pulled the backpack closer and tightened her hold on it.

"Sorry, Leanne, but I'm going to have to look inside your bag." He stood and walked around the desk with his hand extended.

She jumped out of the chair knocking it to the floor and backed up against the wall near the door.

"There's nowhere to go. I just want to look. I'm not going to take anything as long as it belongs to you." Wade inched toward her. He didn't want her to make a dash for the door.

Leanne chewed her bottom lip. "It's all mine. You don't have to look."

"I wish I could take your word for it, but I've had a few complaints about items going missing. You wouldn't know anything about that would you?" Wade stopped in front of the small, framed figure whose chin lifted in defense. "Just let me look."

Groaning, she thrust the backpack into his stomach.

He clutched it to his chest before it could drop. It weighed more than he expected. Placing the backpack on the desk, he unzipped it, inspecting each item. Sure enough, he found a long-handled flashlight like the one Harry said was missing from his hardware store. He held it up. "Where did you get this?"

"A friend." She crossed her arms with a huff.

Digging into one of the side pockets, he pulled out an unopened toothbrush and a package containing several individual packets of dental floss. Half of the packets were missing, but the quantity on the package read eight.

Wade met Leanne's gaze, her blue eyes questioning, vulnerable and then in an instant, they turned hard. "You know shoplifting is a crime. I could put you in jail for this."

A red flush rose on her cheeks. "What? I only took what I needed."

"You needed floss?" Wade fought to keep a straight face.

Furious, she stepped over the chair on the floor and snatched the floss out of his hand. "Dental hygiene is very important. You shouldn't make fun." Moving to the bag, she began stuffing the items back into their pockets. "Miss Nadine said you can face anything if you can keep smiling. So, she made sure we took good care of our teeth." Zipping the main compartment, she snatched the bag off the wooden surface, hugging it to her body. "I bet when I'm ninety, I'll still have all *my* teeth, but you'll probably be gumming your food like old man Summers down at the mission."

So, she'd been to the mission house. He took that as a good sign. Wade bent over and picked up the chair, righting it. "Have a seat, and let's start again."

She flopped into the chair but kept a tight hold on her backpack. "Are you going to arrest me?" Her voice wobbled.

"Not at the moment." Wade let out a long sigh, studying the young teen in front of him. "First, I'm going to call Mr. Branson who owns the hardware store and see if he wants to press charges, then I'll contact the gas station owner where you've frequented and do the same. I'm hoping I can get them to let you work off what you owe."

"Do you think they'll let me?" She chewed her

bottom lip again. Moisture gathered on the rims of her lashes as she blinked back the tears.

A wave of sympathy washed over him. "Well, I know Mr. Branson doesn't want a half-used package of floss, so there's a good chance he'll let you do some chores to pay back what you owe." He rested against the back of his chair. "But before I contact either one of them, I need to know what you've seen. I can't keep you safe if I don't know who's after you."

She shook her head, her blond hair swishing against her back.

"Then you leave me no choice. I'll have to contact Child Services and send you back to your last placement."

"No!" The sharp word flew from her lips, surprising him. The sheer terror in her wide eyes spoke volumes.

"You don't want to go back? Why not?"

"I can't say. But I don't want to put any of them in danger. If you send me back, others might get hurt because of me. He knows them."

"I see. Then we're at a crossroads." Wade drummed his fingers on the wooden surface, mulling over his options. He could take her back to her last placement, but he didn't want to put anyone in danger. Or he could call Child Services and tell them his theory. Or he could— A noise in the outer office caught his attention.

"Hey, Regan, can you buzz me in?" A familiar voice floated across the squad room.

A few seconds later, Bernadette appeared in his office doorway, breathless. "You are not going to believe this." She set her satchel in the empty chair, not even noticing Leanne. "But I took your advice and prayed about … well, you know what—and when I arrived at the office around ten, a realtor friend of mine called saying she'd won a gift certificate at a raffle two towns over for The Flying Pig Barbeque. They expire today and asked if I wanted them." She blinked and followed Wade's gaze. "Oh, you're not alone."

He grinned. "No, not quite."

"Hi. I'm Bernadette." She offered the teen her hand.

Leanne narrowed her eyes, not moving, then turned her attention to Wade. "Is this your girlfriend or something?"

"She's my realtor and a friend." Wade chose his words carefully. He didn't need half the office and the runaway teen knowing all his business. Besides, he didn't want to scare Bernadette away now that she seemed genuinely excited about their date.

"Do you often go out with your realtor?"

Glancing at Wade, Bernadette pulled to her full height and pointed with her thumb. "Who is this?"

"This is Leanne Hopkins." He rose from his leather chair and circled his desk until he stood in front of them.

Bernadette gave her the once-over. "Nice shoes." She pursed her lips. "I see I'm interrupting. I'll come back later. But I wanted you to know we're definitely on for dinner tonight." Then she beamed. "My treat." She grabbed her satchel and turned to leave, but Wade stopped her.

"Wait a minute, would you?" He faced Leanne. "Stay here." Shutting his office door, he placed his hand in the small of Bernadette's back and moved her toward the break room.

"What's this all about?" She took quick steps to keep up with his long strides. "I take it Leanne is our lockbox hacker."

"Yes, she is. Regan caught up with her this morning, thanks to the information you gave us, but I have a bit of a problem." Wade slid his fingers over the scar on his left cheek and down his jawbone.

"What's that? She seems a perfectly lovely girl."

Wade didn't miss the sarcasm in her tone. "I need a place for her to stay. When I mentioned sending her back to her last foster home, she panicked. Said the others there would be in danger."

Concern entered Bernadette's eyes. "I didn't know. Can you share what the issue is?"

"No, because I don't really know the whole story myself. But I do know she's afraid, and someone is looking for her."

"You don't think there's something funny going on in her last placement, do you?"

He shook his head. "She seemed genuinely concerned for their safety, more than being afraid of them. Truthfully, I think she knows something about the string of burglaries, but I can't be sure." Wade stroked his cheek again. "Didn't you say your parents are licensed by the state to foster children?"

Bernadette eyed him. "I did. But they are fully booked for the next two weeks at the bed and breakfast. They don't have the time or the energy it would take to keep up with a teen. Especially one that's prone to run off."

"I'm only asking as a temporary solution until I can convince the girl to cooperate." He pulled out one of the four chairs ringing the marred table.

Bernadette dropped her satchel onto the tabletop and took the seat across from him. "Can't Regan take her home with her? I'm sure Child Services would make an exception since she's a witness to a crime."

Wade laughed. "There's no way I'm sending Leanne home with Deputy Perez. They'd kill each other." He shook his head. "No, it needs to be someone else. Someone Leanne might open up to. Not a cop. Someone who knows about foster kids but doesn't have an agenda." His eyes locked on Bernadette. Tilting his head, he let the new idea he'd landed on churn in his brain. "You know—" He raised his eyebrows.

"Oh no, no, no. Not me." She waggled her finger at him, avoiding eye contact. "I'm not good with teens."

"Sure, you are. You did a great job working with the foster kids when you were younger."

"That's because I didn't know any better, and I wasn't fully responsible for them. My parents were." She rose and picked up her satchel. Shaking her head, she pushed her chair under the table. "Besides, I'm not licensed."

Wade rose and planted his fists on the tabletop, pulling him closer to her. "No, but like you said, Child Services might make an exception while we're sorting this out."

She shelved her hand on her hip, frowning. "What about you? Why can't she stay at the ranch? There's plenty of room, and it'd give Nikki and Dan some practice."

"For what? It's not like their giving birth to teens."

Bernadette scowled at the sarcastic remark. He didn't want to upset her and give her a reason to say no, so he softened his answer. "I think you'd have the better chance of gaining her confidence and persuading her to tell you what she's hiding. It's obvious she doesn't trust cops. You're the better choice."

Bernadette tightened her grip on the handle of her satchel and shifted her weight. Her lips flattened into a straight line. "Fine. I'll do it. But I can't promise you any results. She'll have to tell me in her own time. I won't hound her."

"That's great." Happy that she'd agreed to take the girl, Wade needed her to have a sense of urgency. "Just remember, someone out there is looking for her. And Reseda County isn't that big." As she moved toward the hallway, he remembered why she'd come to talk to him and followed her to the door of the break room. "So, I'll be seeing you tonight?" He called, watching her retreating frame.

She scoffed but didn't stop. "Oh yeah, right, if I can find a babysitter."

"I'm sure you'll have no trouble getting your mom to keep an eye on our witness." He grinned. "If you tell her you're going out with me."

She paused at the threshold of the squad room and glanced back down the hall. "You certainly are full of yourself, Sheriff."

"Not at all, Bernie. You've just given me a reason to hope." His heart raced. Somewhere along the way his high school infatuation had matured into something else.

A softness flooded her eyes as the corners of her mouth shifted into a gentle smile. She shook her head, meeting his gaze. "I'll see you tonight."

Chapter Ten

Frodo's repetitive barking from the kitchen alerted Bernadette to her mother's presence at the back door. She tucked the edge of the comforter under the pillows and scanned the room. Not quite a teen's dream, but it would do for now.

"It's just me, baby girl," Darlene called from the other room.

Bernadette scurried through the living room, glanced at Leanne, and breezed into the kitchen. "Thank goodness you're here. I have the guest room all made up, but I need to hustle." Still wearing her lime green robe with her hair in sponge rollers, she'd tried to make the most of her time by multi-tasking, but instead she'd wound up with everything half done. "Wade's picking me up at seven."

"You'd better get a move on then." Her mother stroked the thick white fur on Frodo's back. "How's my good boy?" Frodo snuggled next to her thigh enjoying the attention.

"Follow me, and I'll introduce you to Leanne."

Her mother paused, dropping her purse onto the counter next to the door. "How is she doing?"

Bernadette stopped mid-stride. "For everything

that's going on, pretty good." She lowered her voice. "She can be a little testy. I'm not sure if that's because of her situation or if it's the fact she's a teenager." She gave her mom a knowing look.

"I think I can handle it." Her mom patted her shoulder to reassure her.

What would she do without this woman? "Thanks again for agreeing to do this. I know the B&B is busting at the seams with people this weekend—it being the Fourth of July and all."

"Not a problem. Your dad is covering the front desk, and Tina agreed to stay until ten in case any of the guests needed something." She checked the microwave clock. "You'd better get a move on, or you'll be having dinner with Wade in your robe." The corners of her eyes crinkled.

"I'm never going to make it in time. That's what I get for multi-tasking." She threw her hands up. "I know better. If I try to do too many things at once, I don't get any of them done."

"Not to worry. I'll keep him occupied until you're ready."

"Bless you." Bernadette leaned in and planted a kiss of appreciation on her mother's cheek. "Now, let's go meet *your* dinner date for this evening."

Rounding the corner into the living room with her mother behind her, Bernadette found Leanne in the same position as earlier, plopped on the couch with her feet on the coffee table scrolling through one of her streaming services. The movie covers displayed on the screen grabbed her attention.

"Have you ever seen the *Boogeyman*?" Leanne asked.

The two women answered in tandem. "No."

Leanne shook her head, a sour expression puckering her brow. "A bunch of scaredy cats. I wish my sister were here. She'd watch it with me. Or Jay."

Bernadette added. "Well, this house is a G or PG-rated house. We don't do slasher movies or ones with too much violence. In fact, if it's a regular TV show, and it gets too heavy-handed with the blood, I turn it off."

Leanne looked over the back of the couch toward Bernadette's mom who stood in the entryway from the kitchen. "Who are you?"

"I'm your dinner date tonight, Darlene," she announced with an upbeat air.

"You mean my keeper." Leanne turned her attention back to the screen and continued to scroll. "I'm not hungry." She shifted in her seat and crossed her feet at the ankles on the coffee table.

Darlene strolled toward the chair adjacent to the couch. "Too bad you're not hungry." She lifted her shoulder then dropped into the chair. "I guess I'll have to eat the whole pizza myself."

Leanne cut her eyes toward Darlene.

Bernadette pressed her lips together to smother the giggle rising in her chest. Her mother, child expert. Now, she remembered why her mom and dad made such good foster parents. They understood what made teens tick.

"What kind of pizza?" Leanne asked, her attention ping-ponging between Darlene and the screen.

"Meat lovers all the way." Bernadette's mom licked her lips. "Oh yeah, and the sausage makes it smell so good."

Now, Leanne abandoned the screen all together. Darlene had her full attention. "Can we add mushrooms and pineapples?"

"Sure. I love a fully loaded pizza." Darlene's head bounced in agreement. "And while we eat, we can watch a movie."

Rolling her eyes, Leanne turned back to the screen. "You're tricky. Thinking you can bribe me with food."

"I'm not trying to bribe you." Bernadette's mother placed her hand on her chest as if she were offended by the accusation. "I'm merely being a good keeper." Her lips twitched.

Leanne smiled for the first time since Bernadette had met her. She had a nice smile too. One that radiated warmth and innocence.

"As your keeper for the night, I think we should watch something fun. How about *Cheaper by the Dozen* or maybe the new *Little Mermaid* movie? The one with real people."

Leanne popped up. "Ooh, the *Little Mermaid*. I heard it's awesome."

"Me, too." Darlene glanced toward Bernadette. "Don't you need to get ready?"

"Yikes." Bernadette gasped and raced down the hall to her bedroom with Frodo on her heels.

Half an hour later, her bedroom looked like a clothes bomb had exploded. She'd gone through several renditions of her favorite outfits, combining this top with those shorts or that skirt. But nothing screamed "second date with a guy I like but are afraid to get serious with, so tonight we're just friends, I think." Apparently, she didn't own that outfit.

Sighing, she picked up the first pair of white shorts

she'd tried on and the flowy red and blue shirt. A patriotic theme. Everybody and their brother would be wearing it this weekend, but it would have to do.

A knock sounded on the front door. Frodo jumped from her bed where he'd been watching her madness and bolted for her bedroom door, barking.

"Yes, I know, I know." Running a brush through her hair, she checked her reflection. The curlers had done their job and added some softness to her otherwise tangled mane. Tucking a strand behind her ear, she touched her earlobe. *Earrings.* She'd forget her head if wasn't attached. Bernadette poked through the pile in her jewelry bowl and found two white heart-shaped earrings and secured them into place.

Frodo had worked himself into a frenzy. Scratching on the door, he whined.

Grabbing her purse, she opened the door, freeing her protector. Frodo shot down the hallway to the living room.

She took one last look in the mirror. *Okay, Lord. I'm stepping out in faith here. I hope the gift certificates were the sign I believed them to be.* Oh, the gift certificates. They hung on the refrigerator under a magnet. Where was her head tonight?

She hurried into the living room on her way to the kitchen to retrieve the gift certificates and stopped dead when she rounded the corner. Handsome didn't begin to describe the man standing in front of her. The gray tee-shirt he wore hugged his body, reenforcing the fact he was in great shape and drew her attention to his strong broad shoulders, one of his best features. That and his smoky green eyes.

When he caught sight of her, his mouth wreathed

into a smile, making her heart hammer against her ribs. A warm light radiated from those dark eyes. She had to make herself breathe. How was she ever going to stay *just friends* with the man, when his very gaze sent tingles zipping straight to her heart?

~

They stood in front of the mural which covered the entire back wall of the restaurant. Wade tilted his head to the side. "Wow, that's—" Wade's eyebrows winged up, "something."

Bernadette giggled at his reaction. Most people reacted the same way at seeing the famous wall art. And since The Flying Pig didn't exist when Wade had lived here as a teen, she figured he'd be impressed. "Yes, it's quite the conversation piece."

The five pink pigs with wings spread wide did somersaults in the blue sky as lazy white clouds floated along. One piggy lay on his tummy on a fat cloud near the top left corner and looked down on his fellow acrobats as they swished in the heavens.

"I love it." Wade declared, taking a step back to get the full effect. "It has character. Makes the place unique."

She glanced over her shoulder and found those smoky green eyes resting on her. Heat rushed to her cheeks as a swarm of butterflies awakened in her stomach. Uncomfortable with the sensation, she searched the restaurant for an empty table. She hadn't considered the holiday weekend when she'd accepted her friend's offer of the gift certificates. The place was packed. "We'd better find a seat."

"You're right. Are you hungry?" He placed his hand in the small of her back and directed her toward an empty table for two in the corner. Private and cozy near the mural. Leaning closer to her, he whispered, "Thanks again. I owe you one."

She turned, her lips inches from his. His eyes moved to her lips then back to her eyes. "Yes, you do." She teased while her heart pounded in her chest. Friends, Bernadette, just friends, she recited in her head as she concentrated on making it to the table, weak knees and all.

When she went to pull out her chair, Wade stepped beside her and did the honors. "Thank you." She slid into the seat. Wade always treated her like a lady. Opening doors, helping her out of his truck when they went house hunting, and now pulling out her chair. She wasn't surprised by his good manners, but she was surprised she'd never given his kindness a second thought. How long had he been doing these things?

As Wade took the seat across from her, she unrolled her silverware from the paper napkin and placed the fork and spoon on the red checkered tablecloth. He did the same. Pulling the menus from the holder on the table, she handed one to him.

"Thanks. So, what do you usually order?" he perused the choices on the plastic-covered sheet in front of him.

"My favorite is the Little Piggy Goes to Market. It comes with a side of coleslaw and corn on the cob, buttered within an inch of its life." She peeked over her menu and waggled her eyebrows. "And it's not too spicy."

Wade pointed to the column with the spicier choices. "I think I'll take a chance and order the All the Way Home." His eyes peered at her from over the menu in his hand. "It says it's got a little kick, and it offers a sampler of three sides and cornbread." He laid his menu on the table. "It sounds almost like a religious experience." He laughed.

"Now I'm starving." She grabbed his menu with hers and put them back in the holder, brushing against his arm. "Oh, sorry." The momentary contact sent a jolt of electricity racing up her arms.

A playful grin emerged on his lips. "Don't be. I've been sitting here trying to figure out a way to hold your hand without it being awkward." He focused on her hand, then took a breath. "So, here goes."

A smile pulled at her lips at his honesty. He slid his hand under hers. The warmth of the touch made her heart skip a beat. And the intensity in his eyes when she lifted her gaze made those butterflies in her stomach do somersaults like the pigs in the mural behind her.

"Why don't we go ahead and give thanks?" Wade suggested. "While I've got your hand captured."

She nodded her agreement and bowed her head.

"Father, thank you for this time together, and thank you for Your provision." He squeezed her hand. His voice rumbled the words, "You have been so good to us. Please direct our steps in this new adventure. In Jesus' name, amen."

The words of his prayer swirled around her heart, causing a new cascade of emotions.

Before she could gather her thoughts, Frieda whisked to their table. "What can I get for you folks? Did you have time to look at the menu?" She eyed the plastic-covered sheets of paper standing in their holder.

"Yes, we know what we want." Bernadette withdrew her hand from Wade's. "I'm going to have

Went to Market."

"Good choice." Frieda winked at her before jotting down the order on her pad. "And you?" She pointed to Wade with her pen.

"Put me down for an All the Way Home."

She gave him the once-over. "That should fill you up, big guy."

"Wait." Bernadette pulled her purse onto her lap and fished out the gift certificates. "I have these."

Frieda inspected them. "You're cutting it close. These expire today."

"That's why I brought them. A friend won them in a raffle a few months ago and never got the chance to use them."

"Lucky for you then." Frieda handed back the slips of paper and pushed her pen behind her ear, freeing a strand of her salt-and-pepper hair from her bun. Hearing her name called from somewhere behind her, she yelled over her shoulder, "Hold your horses." Turning back to them, she said, "I'll put these orders in right away." Then she scurried off to help the other table.

Not sure if she should take his hand again, Bernadette dropped her hand to her lap, deciding to stick to familiar territory. "I finally got everything in shape to show you the ranch I told you about. It'll be perfect for you."

"That's wonderful. Are you available tomorrow?"

"That should work." She hesitated. "But I might need to bring Leanne with us. Mom and Dad are swamped at the B&B. She had to get Tina to stay overtime to sit with Leanne tonight."

"I'm sorry about all this. It's inconvenient, and you

didn't sign up for any of it. But I ran out of choices. At least I know she's safe with your family."

"It's all right." Bernadette shrugged. "There's nothing to be done. Leanne needs to be protected, and if she thinks she'll put her foster parents and the kids in danger by going back, then she's probably right. From what I've seen of her, she's a pretty smart cookie."

"Yeah, I picked up on that too. But she's determined to keep her guard up, especially with me. She doesn't trust men, and she doesn't trust law enforcement."

"Mom seemed to connect with her tonight. Before I left, she had her eating out of the palm of her hand. They'd planned to order a pizza and picked out a movie to watch."

"Wow, that is progress. Maybe Darlene can convince her to tell us what she knows. Meanwhile, I had Deputy Perez go talk with her foster parents, Mr. and Mrs. Pittman, this afternoon after y'all left to let them know she's safe. They had filed a missing person's report with us and Child Services. I figured they'd be worried." He pressed his crossed arms on the tabletop. "Seems they have no idea what caused her to run. They're at a loss like us, but they did say her behavior changed not long after school let out for the summer. Sometime in late May."

"That's odd. Usually, kids are less stressed during the summer. You know—looking forward to playing video games or going to the movies or camping."

"It had to be something that came about because of the change in her routine." Wade's brow furrowed, and he ran his fingers across the scar on his cheek. "I also had Perez find out what she could about her sister Mia."

Bernadette liked the scar. It made him look manly. "Yeah, she mentioned a sister tonight. I figured she must be older."

"No, apparently when her last foster parent, Nadine Nichols, became too ill to care for the children, the sisters were separated. Mia is only eleven. Now, I understand why Leanne acts tough and tries to take care of the other kids in her foster home. She's used to looking out for her sister."

"Being apart must be tough on her." Compassion for the young teen gripped Bernadette's heart. She'd try to be more patient and give her a little breathing room while she stayed with her. "I can't imagine what her life's been like. And now, with someone after her, she must be scared senseless."

Chapter Eleven

Wade realized he'd drifted into work mode, and that was the last thing he wanted to do tonight. He'd have time to examine the case after he dropped off Bernadette, but for now, he needed to give the beautiful woman in front of him his full attention. And that's exactly what he intended to do. It was time to move out of the friend zone because frankly, it wasn't working for him anymore.

As he reached to take her hand, Frieda arrived carrying their orders. "One Went to Market. And one All the Way Home." She eyed him. "Be sure to eat the rolls I brought with the meal. It'll break up the heat, and I'll bring you a tall glass of water, too." A glint of mischief gleamed in her eyes. "I wouldn't want to get in trouble with the law for 'frying the sheriff.'" She snorted a laugh and slapped the table. Shaking her head, she heaved a sigh to stop the chuckles in their tracks. "I'll grab that water for you."

Bernadette tucked a napkin in the collar of her shirt. "Frieda is a real character. She's as famous as the mural. Part of the experience, in a way."

"Yeah, I got that." Wade nodded toward the

napkin. "Should I follow suit?"

"Only if you want to leave stain-free. Otherwise, have at it."

With the plates, drinks, and extra sauce between them, Wade gave up hope of holding her hand and directed the conversation to what she loved. "So, tell me more about the ranch." He took a bite of his barbeque. The moment the meat hit his tongue his eyes watered. Swallowing, he snatched a roll from the basket in the center of the table, tore off a piece, and shoved it into his mouth. The bread did the trick.

Grinning like a kid at the circus, Bernadette leaned back in her chair, twirling a curl. "Hotter than you thought? I should've warned you. Sorry."

Frieda appeared with the promised glass of water. Wade grabbed the glass from her hand and downed it. Frieda perched her fist on her hip. "Ah, so you tried it. What did you think?"

"Good," Wade croaked over the rim of the glass. "But I might need more bread."

"Smart move." Frieda glanced at Bernadette. "You didn't warn him, did you?"

Bernadette shrugged and seemed to be enjoying herself.

"Shame on you." Frieda tsked before moving to greet the occupants of the table in the opposite corner.

Bernadette waved off Frieda's reproof and answered Wade's question about the ranch. She went into detail about the square footage and the acreage of the property. Then she described the wooded area with the stocked pond and the gazebo. She ticked off the number of stalls in the stable, how large the barn was, and a myriad of other facts about the property.

The way she described it made it sound like Heaven on earth. "Sounds perfect."

"I think it is for you. Can I ask you something?" Bernadette pushed her now-empty plate to one side still wearing the napkin tucked into her collar. "Why a ranch? I thought your brother Dan was the rancher, and that you didn't want any part of that lifestyle. Why not a condo, or for that matter, a whole apartment building?" Her pink lips lifted at the corners, and she rested her cheek on her fist.

A stray hair hugged her jawline, and his fingers itched to push it back into place. Instead, he fiddled with the fork sitting on his plate. "There's no elbow room in a condo. A man's gotta be able to breathe and move and have a place to hang his saddle." Wade shrugged. "You can't do that in an apartment or a condo."

She tilted her head. "Well, technically you could, but the horse that goes with the saddle might present a problem." The corners of her eyes crinkled, and the tenderness he found in them melted his resolve. He didn't care what she'd said about two friends going out. Looking at her there with her auburn hair, soft skin, and barbeque napkin tucked in her shirt, he knew his heart belonged to her. They'd talked about taking it slow, but his heart had a mind of its own. He hoped to convince her their friendship could grow into so much more. "Why did you move back to Orange Blossom after college? I mean, you could've gone anywhere. Why here?"

"Family. Plain and simple." She clasped her hands together under her chin. "I couldn't imagine being anywhere else. My mom and dad are here, and as you've seen, I apparently know half the population of our small town." A sigh floated out, soft and long. "Dorothy was right. 'There's no place like home.'" Meeting his gaze, she asked, "How about you? Why did you move back? Besides the elbow room."

"Same as you. Family. I swore I'd do better this time, since I missed the chance to get to know Dan's first wife, Lilly. And with Dan and Nikki expecting, there was no way I was missing out on the lives of my niece and nephew. I mean—" He drew closer to her and lowered his eyes in mock humility. "Could you imagine them growing up without their Uncle Wade's expert advice?"

"Not a chance," she teased. "But expert advice about what?"

"Well, everything, of course." Wade chuckled. "Seriously, I couldn't see any reason not to move back and every reason to do so." Pinning her gaze with his, he reached past the sauces and half-empty drink glasses and took her hand. "Now I'm very glad I did." He rubbed his thumb across the back of it. The feel of her soft skin against the callouses of his own made him want to protect her from the rough world he had known.

A look of apprehension appeared in her eyes. She squeezed his hand and let go, pulling her napkin from her collar. "Well, yeah. Being the new sheriff has its privileges."

Not wanting to let his disappointment show, he conjured up a smile. "Yes, and I couldn't ask for a better realtor, who springs for dinner."

~

The conversation flowed during the drive home. They chatted about the houses he'd viewed, discounting the ones without enough acreage or floor plans that didn't work for him. They talked about the heat index that had pumped up over the last few weeks, making this Fourth of July holiday a scorcher. They'd even discussed Leanne. But every time Wade glanced at Bernadette, his mind wandered to the goodnight kiss and how good she'd taste if things led that way.

He wrestled to push the idea out of his head and remembered he'd agreed to go slow. Tonight's date centered around friendship and getting to know one another, but he couldn't help imagining how wonderful she would feel in his arms.

Turning into her driveway, Wade cut the engine and rolled down his window with the hand crank. Bernadette followed suit. The heat of the night rushed into the cab of the old Chevy and mingled with the cool air from the ancient air conditioner, making the windshield fog up.

Bernadette rested her head against the seat and turned toward him. A slight smile pulled at her lips. The features of her face lit by the yellow glow of the streetlight.

The quiet of the evening settled between them with only the chirping of the cicadas ringing out around them. Wade turned toward her and took her hand. "I had a great time tonight."

"Me, too." The streetlight shone on her face. "I haven't been on a date in a while, but you made this one as painless as possible."

Wade's eyebrows winged up. "I had hoped for something a little more positive than simply painless."

She shrugged. "Okay, maybe it was a lot better than painless."

"Was it good enough to try for a third date?" Wade's heart drummed in his ears. It had taken him months to work up the courage to ask her out, and even then, she'd been the one to make the first move.

"I believe so." She squeezed his hand and lifted her head. "I'd better go. With the B&B completely full for the weekend, Mom's going to need a good night's sleep." But she didn't let go of his hand. She didn't make a move for the door handle.

Wade intertwined his fingers with hers. "I imagine there's a lot involved with hosting that many guests. How many people does the B&B hold?"

"The main house has five guest bedrooms upstairs. My parents have a bedroom downstairs by the kitchen with a small sitting room, and they have two bunkhouses. They use one bunkhouse for groups who come for the cowboy experience." She emphasized the last two words. "So, yeah, it's a lot, but Mom and Dad love it. The Belles and Beaus was their dream." She rested her head against the seat again as if she were settling in for a long stay. "When I was little, I loved the B&B. The people coming and going, and the foster kids made my family seem so much bigger than just the three of us."

"Do you think you'll ever take over for them? Run the place yourself one day?"

She furrowed her brow. "I don't know. Maybe? It would be a lot of work, and to do it right, I'd need to love the B&B like they do. I'm not sure I do." She sighed. "They have their hearts set on leaving me the place. There's not much I can do about it."

"Who knows? Maybe by then you'll want to do something like that. You'd be an excellent hostess of your own place."

"That's easy for you to say. You don't know the financial struggle it can be. I remember many years during the off-season—Mom and Dad picking up odd jobs around town to make ends meet. Unlike some of us in this truck, not everyone has money bursting out of their pockets."

"I don't have money bursting out of my pockets." Wade stroked her cheek with his finger as the light from the streetlamp draped her in a yellow hue. "Most days I'm broke. All my money is either invested in Pop's company or is put back into Silver Spur ranch."

"Don't tell me you're the classic poor little rich boy." She lifted her head and fixed him with her gaze. "I'm not buying it."

Wade couldn't keep the smile off his lips. "So, you're not going to cut me any slack?"

"Uh-uh, no way."

"Fine. Then I'll spring for dinner next time." His heart raced. "I'll be sure to have cash."

Her face lit up like one of the stars in the night sky. "You're crazy. You know that?"

He lifted a shoulder. "Maybe a little." He gravitated toward her like a magnet, but the flash of alarm that appeared in her eyes stopped him from pulling her to him and claiming a kiss.

Her shoulders stiffened. "I'd better go for real this time." She released his hand and picked up her purse from the floorboard.

"I'll walk you to the door."

"If you like." She hopped out.

He met her in front of the truck. Taking her hand, they walked in silence up the driveway to the front porch steps. The buzz of the cicadas around the porch light drifted on the night air.

Wade paused. "Do you hear that?"

"I don't hear anything," Bernadette said.

"That's the point. Shouldn't Frodo be barking?" Wade's hand went instinctively to his side. He'd left his gun in the glove compartment for the evening. "Wait here."

Hustling back to the truck, he opened the passenger side door, popped open the glove compartment, and pulled out his gun, removing it from the holster. With a quick glance, he checked the magazine and clicked it back into place. Motioning for Bernadette to follow him, he headed toward the back of the house. She fell into step with him as he rounded the back corner and strode to the kitchen door. "Keys." He extended his hand.

She slipped her fingers into the front pocket of her purse and produced a key ring.

The jangle of the keys hitting together set his already tense nerves on edge. He stiffened.

"Sorry." She cringed. Finding the right one, she passed it to him.

He mounted the steps and peeked through the window of the back door. The counters were littered with crushed soda cans, and two pizza boxes sat with their lids half open, but he didn't see anyone. Not even Frodo.

Wade slid the key into the lock and quietly opened the door. Bernadette followed close behind him, holding onto his shirt. He stole a glance at her over his shoulder. Her eyes were wide, and her lips pressed into a thin line. Fear and worry warred on her features.

A low murmur floated from the living room. He froze to listen.

"That sounds like the TV," Bernadette whispered.

Wade nodded. His hand grasped the gun tighter, and he slid off the safety. With caution, he rounded the entrance leading into the living space. He stopped.

Bernadette bumped into his back. "What—" Then she stepped around him and stood gaping at the sight.

Darlene lay on the couch with a throw over her legs and the remote dangling precariously from her hand. Her chest rose and fell in a peaceful rhythm. To the right of the couch, Leanne dozed, cuddled in a chair with her feet resting on the ottoman and her chin to her chest. Frodo, the fierce protector, lay across her lap, sound asleep.

"Well, I guess that explains that," Bernadette whispered.

Relieved, Wade pushed the safety into place, shoved the gun into his belt, and covered it with his shirttail. He tilted his head toward the kitchen where they could talk without waking anyone. Wade moved as quietly as he could, but the thud of his boots didn't make it easy.

At the back door, he waited. Bernadette joined him, standing close. The smell of her fresh scent wafted around him. "I guess I'd better go. At least it looks like Leanne cooperated. I have to give your mom kudos. She knows how to handle teens." He grinned at Bernadette. "She must've had plenty of practice."

"I'll have you know I was the picture of sweetness and grace as a teen." But the mischief in her eyes told him a different story.

"As I recall, you got into trouble on more than one

occasion."

"Faulty memory." She shook her head. "It happens to the best of us. A certain sign of age, I hear."

"I'm sure." He hesitated. "So, are you interested in going out again? I'll try to keep it as 'painless' as possible."

"With an offer like that, how can I refuse?" She shrugged, letting her right-hand fall onto his arm.

Her touch set off a cascade of delightful prickles zipping through him. If she only knew what she did to him. "Good. Maybe Thursday night? We could go watch the fireworks at the Senior Citizen Center. I hear Spike has a great show lined up." He covered her hand with his.

"Hm, sounds nice. He always puts on a great show for the community."

She stood close, drawing his full attention, but he tamped down the urge to wrap his arms around her and pull her to him. "Yeah, he's done a great job as the Community Events Director."

"Bernie, is that you?" Darlene called from the living room, her voice rough with sleep.

"You'd better go." Bernadette straightened and opened the door in one motion. She pushed against Wade's chest. "If she sees you, we'll have to answer a million questions. How was the food? Were there a lot of people? Did Frieda wait on you? Is her arthritis any better?"

A squeak sounded from the living room like a groaning couch spring. Bernadette looked over her shoulder. "Go, go. I'll call you tomorrow about touring the ranch." She gave Wade one last shove across the threshold then shut the door and closed the curtains on

the little window.
For Wade, tomorrow couldn't get here fast enough.

Chapter Twelve

"How was dinner?" Her mom asked as she entered the kitchen toting a plate with a half-eaten piece of pizza on it and a mound of crusts.

Bernadette dropped her purse on the counter by the back door, forcing herself not to look out the curtain for one last glance. She didn't miss the gleam in her mother's eyes. "Delicious as always." She figured her mother referred to the date, but she didn't want to talk about it. The evening had been everything she'd hoped for and more. She didn't want to spoil it by recounting it, one fluttering butterfly at a time.

"Did you introduce Wade to the Brownie Caramel Melt Delight?" Her mother waggled her eyebrows. "Just thinking about it makes me want a piece."

Bernadette ambled to the counter and peeked inside one of the pizza boxes. "No, and how could you possibly be hungry?" Lifting the other lid, she shook her head and pointed to the empty containers. "You've finished off two pizzas."

"Did we?" Darlene's eyes grew round, and she touched her lips. "I had no idea. I just kept sending Leanne back into the kitchen for two more slices." Moving her hand to her stomach, she wrinkled her nose. "Maybe that's why I feel so stuffed. I thought it was the carbonation from the soda."

"Mom, you should know better. I hope Leanne doesn't wind up with a stomachache the first night in my care."

"Don't worry. She'll be fine." Mom dismissed the thought with a wave. "It's harder to break kids than you think. Besides, she's been living on her own for a couple of weeks now. She just needed a good hot meal and some fun. A girl her age shouldn't have to carry this burden all alone," she tsked.

Bernadette pulled out one of the stools from under the island ledge and took a seat. "What burden? Did you convince her to tell you why she ran away?" Bernadette was all ears.

"Not exactly." Her mother opened the trash can and pitched the remains of the pizza. Placing the plate in the sink, she joined Bernadette at the kitchen island. "Leanne said she was worried about the safety of her foster family, and she didn't want to bring them any trouble. She seemed nervous and scared when she talked about them, so, I didn't linger too long on the subject."

"That was probably wise. We don't want her running again. Did she mention why she thought they'd be in danger?"

"She said she'd seen something. I tried to get her to say what, but she refused. When I pressed her a bit, she added that they knew where she lived."

"Who knew?"

"I don't know. She changed the subject, and I decided to let her have the evening. I figured Wade or one of the other officers would be questioning her again soon enough."

"Wow, what a big burden for a fourteen-year-old to carry, worrying about the safety of those who are supposed to be taking care of her." Bernadette reached down and petted Frodo who stretched his front paws along the tile, then let out a massive yawn. "I wonder what she saw. Wade thinks it had something to do with the burglary ring that's been hitting houses while the owners are out of town."

"But that doesn't tell us why she ran away, or why her foster family would be in danger." Mom rested her chin on her hand, her brow furrowed.

"No, it doesn't." Bernadette frowned. "Wade said he talked with her foster mom, and she told him Leanne started acting strange a few weeks after school let out. A day or two later, she left. They filed a missing person's report with the sheriff's office once forty-eight hours had passed." She crossed her arms and rested them on the counter of the island. "Did she say anything else?"

"We mostly watched the *Little Mermaid* movie and ate pizza. But she did tell me she and her little sister, Mia, have been in the foster system since Leanne was eight."

"That's six years." Bernadette whistled, unable to imagine being without her mother for six years at such a young age. She could barely go a day without talking to her mom as it was. "Where's Mia now? Is she with Leanne's foster family?"

"No. They were separated after their time at Nadine's. She's the lady who fostered her before she came to live with the Pittman's. Leanne's not sure where Mia is." Her mom shook her head. "She carries that burden, too. No wonder the poor girl thinks she's all alone."

"Well, it looks like you've made a friend. The way you guys were all comfy and cozy, sleeping in the living room when I came in."

"She needed food, a safe place to be, and some sleep." Mom raised one shoulder and let it drop. "The basics." She stood and pushed the stool back under the counter. "Tomorrow's when the real work starts. She'll be feeling better and be ready to go back to doing things her own way."

"Wade might have a few surprises for her. He's not going to give her the opportunity to slip away. Wades planning on contacting the gas station owner and Harry at the Hardware store to see if they'll let her work off her debt."

"I didn't know she'd been stealing." Her mom turned her gaze towards the living room where Leanne slept. "That breaks my heart to think she was so desperate."

Bernadette stood and wrapped her arm around her mother's shoulder. "That's why you and Dad made wonderful foster parents, even if the kids were only temporary placements. Your hearts were always with them."

Her mom leaned her head against Bernadette's shoulder and wrapped her arm around her waist for a hug. "I wonder if that's why you always root for the underdog."

"Maybe." Bernadette squeezed her mom a little tighter.

Mom straightened. "I can tell you one thing. That young woman in there, needs all the help she can get."

She released Bernadette and stepped toward the counter to stack the empty pizza boxes. Picking them up, she reached for her purse sitting near Bernadette's. "You're doing a good thing for her, baby girl. She won't forget it." Her mother met her gaze. "And neither will the Lord."

Bernadette watched from the small window as her mother deposited the empty pizza boxes into the large green trash can before slipping out of view around the corner of the house. Sighing, she grabbed her purse from the counter and headed toward her bedroom to change.

Rounding the doorjamb, Bernadette pulled up short when she found the chair where Leanne had been minutes earlier empty. Panic raced through her until she heard the water running in the bathroom.

Her pounding heart slowed, and she allowed herself to breathe. What had she been thinking, agreeing to take care of a teen who didn't want to be here? She wasn't cut out for this, worrying every second Leanne might run again, or worse, the people looking for her might find her. It hadn't even been twenty-four hours. Why had she agreed to help?

The calm answer rang in her heart. Because Leanne needed someone.

Looking heavenward, she hugged her purse to her chest and prayed, *Lord, show me how to do this because without you, it'll just be another one of my messes.* She opened her eyes and continued toward her bedroom, feeling a bit more settled.

As she neared the bathroom, her foot slipped without warning, and she caught herself against the wall. Glancing down, she discovered water spilling out from under the bathroom door. "No, no, no."

Pounding on the door, she called for Leanne. No answer. She jiggled the doorknob. Locked. She slid her purse strap over her head, freeing her hands. Just as she braced to put her shoulder to the door, the shower turned off.

"Leanne, open the door."

Nothing.

"Where did all this water come from?" Leanne asked.

"Hurry up," Bernadette snapped, all the calm from earlier evaporating.

"Okay, I'm coming. Give me a minute." Two seconds later, the door opened, and a whoosh of steam rushed out of the space. Leanne stood in the middle of the wet floor wearing an oversized tee shirt with a towel wrapped around her wet hair. The teen's eyes stared down at the inch of water covering the entire area then met Bernadette's frown. The look of trepidation on Leanne's face pushed Bernadette to control her temper.

"Grab some towels from the shelf," Bernadette ordered, fighting to keep her voice even. "What happened?"

"I don't know. I woke up and heard you talking with Darlene, so I decided to take a shower before I went to bed. It's been a while since I've had running water. I had no idea the floor was flooding." Leanne bit her bottom lip but did as Bernadette had asked and grabbed some towels. She tossed two to Bernadette and then spread two on the floor. Standing on top of them, Leanne moved the towels across the wet floor by twisting her hips.

Bernadette eyed the shower curtain. The girl had

forgotten to place the liner into the tub. Swallowing a groan, she flapped the towels open and spread them out on the tile and into the hallway. Glancing toward Leanne, Bernadette giggled. Leanne danced around on the towels like she was at a sixties' music festival. Knees bent. Arms pumping. Hips swaying. All they were missing were the Beachboys.

Bernadette shrugged. Why not. She stepped onto the towels and joined her, twisting her hips and pumping her arms to slog the towels over the area by the door. Her purse flopped in the air in one direction while her body twirled in the other.

Catching sight of their reflection in the partially fogged mirror, Bernadette laughed. What a pair they made, her purse flapping every time she wiggled, and Leanne trying to keep the towel on her head from falling into her face.

Leanne glanced over at Bernadette who pointed to the mirror and then twirled, and pumped, and wiggled.

Then one of the best sounds ever to hit Bernadette's eardrums floated her way as she exaggerated her antics. A giggle. One lone burst of laughter. Then another and then another.

Leanne doubled over, wiping her eyes, which made Bernadette put more energy into her show.

Before long, Leanne added her own antics to the fun, and Bernadette couldn't keep the tears from rolling down her face. She pointed at Leanne as she tried to moonwalk with the wet towels glued to her feet. Then Bernadette tried to do the Egyptian without knocking over the toilet-paper holder. She laughed so hard her sides hurt.

Later as she slipped into bed, Bernadette let her

mind wander over what had transpired that evening. Her date with Wade and all the possibilities their friendship held. And her time with Leanne—all the fun she'd had with her, even in the midst of Leanne's troubles. They'd laughed, and time had stopped for a minute.

She fluffed her pillow. Marilyn was right. God does work in weird ways.

~

Leanne sat on the top rung of the wooden fence of the corral near the barn. Her blond hair hung around her thin cheeks framing her face, her sapphire blue eyes remained trained on the pasture. Wade thought she looked almost serene, but that just might be wishful thinking. Frodo dragged a long stick as he trotted toward her. She lifted her hand to her brow, blocking the sun as she watched his progress.

Bernadette had allowed Leanne to bring Frodo on their tour of the Percy ranch, The Bar K, named after Kilroy Percy. It was good the girl had connected with someone, even if it was just the furry member of the group. Bernadette had told him Leanne and Darlene had bonded over pizza and the movie, *Little Mermaid*, if Wade remembered right.

Wade hooked his elbows on the wooden fence with his back braced against it. He crossed his right foot over his left, digging the toe of his boot into the dirt. Bernadette stood beside him gazing out over the pasture, the midday sun causing her to squint. "So, what do you think?"

"About the ranch?" The house and property were everything she'd promised. The floor plan suited him, and for a while he'd only use the downstairs rooms until he started a family.

Wade cut his eyes toward Bernadette. He'd found it hard to sleep last night after their date. Her scent had lingered in the cab of his truck, sending his mind spinning on the drive home. Today, his concentration wasn't much better.

Bernadette blushed under his scrutiny. He'd been staring. "It's perfect." He couldn't take his eyes off her.

Frodo dropped the stick on the ground in front of Leanne who jumped down from the fence with a thud. "Good boy." She rubbed the spot between his ears and picked up the stick. "I'm gonna go find a smaller one and see if I can get Frodo to fetch it."

"Good luck with that. I've never been able to get him to bring me any of his toys. If I throw one, he grabs it and hides it." Bernadette grinned. "I usually find it a few days later buried in my dirty clothes hamper or stuffed between the cushions of the couch."

Leanne shrugged. "Well, maybe he will for me."

"Go for it. You never know."

Leanne took off toward the line of trees at the edge of the pasture with Frodo following. "She seems to be doing all right. Much better than yesterday when Regan found her."

"Yeah, she's a pretty great kid. She's really taken to Frodo, and he's taken to her. He slept in her room last night. I felt a little betrayed." Bernadette lifted her chin. "But I'm glad Leanne's settled in. It makes me feel a little more confident she won't run away."

"I can see that. Plus, your idea of bringing her today was a good one. The more she's around us, the more she'll trust us. That's another reason you should go with me to the Fourth of July celebration." He hesitated. "For Leanne's sake. So, we can build some trust."

Bernadette's eyes narrowed. "Really? That's the only reason?"

"It's not the only reason." Wade glanced down at his boots before meeting her gaze. "I thought it might build a little trust with you too."

Her eyes flashed with mischief. "I trust you; It's me that I'm unsure of. But I'm glad you asked me. Taking Leanne is a wonderful idea. Thanks for inviting us."

"No problem. Besides, she'll love the fireworks at the Senior Citizens Center. They've got the gazebo decked out with patriotic bunting for the occasion." Wade straightened. "I appreciate what you're doing for her and me."

Bernadette bumped her shoulder against his. "What are friends for, right?"

Friends, he hated that word when it pertained to her. "Yeah, right. So, a hundred acres with a pond. A two-story house with five bedrooms, one on the main floor, and a back porch big enough to host a barbeque for the whole town."

"And don't forget a fireplace for all those cold southern Texas nights." She laughed. "Who puts a fireplace in a house in the south?"

"I guess Kilroy Percy does. Or at least one of his ancestors." Wade turned toward her and gave her a sheepish grin. "If I'm going to buy the joint, it'll need a new name. So, what do you think I should call it? Any suggestions?"

She spun toward him, her face beaming. "Heaven." She glanced up to meet his eyes, her hand over her brow to ward off the blinding midday light.

"I think that one's taken." He loved her quick wit. She'd always been like that, ready with just the right thing to say, a piece of encouragement or a funny reply.

"I guess you're right. Does that mean you're taking the place?" She tilted her head and pressed her lips together, anticipation lighting her eyes.

"I supposed it does."

Bernadette gave a whoop-whoop and pushed her hands into the air just as Wade lifted her. She wrapped her arms around his neck and squeezed as he spun her around in circles. "I knew you'd love it," she whispered close to his ear.

Just as quick, she loosened her grip. He took his cue from her and eased her back to the ground. The celebratory hug had only lasted a few seconds, but boy, she'd felt wonderful in his arms.

Regaining her composure, she tugged at the hem of her blouse to straighten it. "Sorry. Usually, I send a fruit basket." She grinned. "I'm sure you're making the right choice." Then spotting Leanne, she changed the subject. "So, what have you found out about our girl?"

Wade swallowed the words that threatened to spill out. Words about the future and wanting more than a friendship, but he stuffed them back in their box for another day. "I did some research into her background. Seems she and her sister Mia were taken from their mother six years ago because of neglect. Several neighbors lodged complaints against their mother over a period of about four months."

"Yeah, her sister Mia. She talked to my mom about her."

"She'd mentioned a sister when we first picked her

up yesterday." Wade pursed his lips and kept his attention focused on Leanne.

"So, where's the mom, now?" Bernadette rested her back against the fencepost.

"Willow Hopkins has been in and out of drug rehabs. Never stays to finish the programs. Can't keep a job. You know the story." A knot tightened in his stomach. He despised what addiction did to families. There were always other victims besides the addict, loved ones who became collateral damage. His heart broke for the kids. "She hasn't been able to regain custody."

Bernadette hung her head. "That's so sad. What about their father?"

"He ran off about a year before. That explains why Leanne doesn't trust men."

"Maybe that's also why her mother spun out of control." Bernadette turned back to watch Leanne with Frodo.

"Or maybe her addiction was the reason he left. Either way, seems to me it's Leanne and Mia who've been dealt the bad hand."

Leanne found a stick and threw it a few feet beyond Frodo. The white fluff ball bounded to the stick, picked it up, and toted it halfway to Leanne, then dropped it and flopped onto the ground beside it. Leanne shook her head and tried again. After several attempts, she took the stick and dragged it on the ground behind her, enticing Frodo to follow her as he tried to bite it. When she flung the stick several feet away, Frodo bounded after it, picked it up, and dropped it at her feet as pretty as you please.

Wade hollered, "Great job!"

Leanne bowed, then hustled over to them, dragging the stick behind her.

"I don't know how you got him to do that." Bernadette shook her head. "I've tried for two years to get him to fetch."

Shrugging, Leanne reached down and petted Frodo. "I've worked with Radar, the collie at Mrs. Pittman's."

"I didn't know they had a dog." Wade's brows pulled together.

"Sure do. Taking care of Radar was part of my daily chores besides homework. I had to feed him, check his water, and walk him once a day."

"If you did all that for Frodo, he'd drop me like a hot potato."

Leanne giggled and gave her a look of disbelief. "Frodo is a good dog, and so is Radar. It makes it easy when they're good."

"I find most dogs are good-natured." Bernadette petted Frodo who stood panting.

"I've been in some homes where the dogs were mean." Leanne squatted to Frodo's level. "It's usually because the owners were also mean."

Concern clouded Bernadette's face. "Have you been in many homes where the owners were that way?"

"A few, but not for long. Miss Nadine's was the best home I've been in. She really cared about what happened to us, but she didn't let us get away with much."

"Good for her. What about Mrs. Pittman?" Wade asked.

"She's fine. But she's got four of us, and that makes it harder on her. That's why she asked me to take charge of Radar. Besides, I like dogs." Standing, she asked, "Can I go wait in the car? My feet hurt, and I'm hungry."

"How about the back porch?" Wade checked his watch. "And we'll catch something to eat on our way back to Bernadette's."

Leanne smirked, displaying her crooked top teeth. "Don't trust me?"

"No, you're way too clever for your own good." Wade nailed her with a look then broke out into a grin.

"I have to be." Leanne turned, flipping her stringy blond hair behind her, and sauntered toward the back porch.

Bernadette clucked her tongue. "The more I learn about her, the more I want to roll her in bubble wrap. It just hurts my heart to know the load she's carried, on top of everything else in her life."

Wade engulfed her in his arms. "Leanne's going to be all right, Bernie. I'm going to solve these burglaries. She won't have to carry the fear and worry much longer."

She stepped back out of his embrace and grinned at him. "I know you will. If anybody can help her, it's you." Adopting her realtor's stance, she crossed her arms and cleared her throat. "So, you want the ranch. I'll get in touch with the seller and set a date for the inspection and then the closing."

"That'll be great." Wade cocked his head, amazed at how quickly she changed gears. If he didn't know any better, he'd swear her resolve had weakened. "Do you think I could get a key soon? I have some renovations I'd like to have done before I move in, and the sooner I get started, the sooner I can get out of Dan and Nikki's hair."

"I'll see what I can do." Bernadette's eyes drifted over to where Leanne sat on the porch steps. "That reminds me. I need to get a key for Leanne. It'll make her feel more welcome."

"That'd be good. At least until we can safely return her to Mrs. Pittman's care."

"Yeah, at least until then," she murmured.

Wade studied her. Something had shifted in Bernadette where the teen was concerned, but he wasn't sure what.

Chapter Thirteen

Monday came too soon. It was time to pay a visit to Leanne's foster parents to see if they could shed any further light on what had triggered her to run away. Wade knocked on the screen door and waited. The sound of movement came from inside the house. A dog barked in spurts. It must be the one Leanne mentioned the other day when they were at the Percy property.

Deputy Adams had secured footage from a doorbell camera of three culprits breaking into the house on Maple Lane. Even though the photos were grainy, Wade wanted to see if the Pittmans recognized any of the suspects. It hadn't helped that the camera's range was limited and that the suspects had entered the property from the side yard and not the driveway. The doorbell camera only caught flashes of the perps as they dashed by.

Wade knocked again. The thump of footsteps on the wooden floor grew louder. The door swung open, and a plump woman stood in the doorway. Her glasses sat on top of her head, and she sported a tee-shirt encouraging moms to 'keep the faith.' Carolyn Pittman blocked his view of the room behind her. "Can I help you?"

A black and white border collie poked his head around her leg and growled. "That's enough, Radar." Turning her back to Wade, she called, "Michael, come get the dog and take him for his walk, will you?"

"Sure, Mrs. P., I'll handle it." A boy in his early teens strolled into the living room. Squatting, he called the dog to him and grabbed his collar. "I'll go out the back."

"Thanks, Michael." She turned to Wade. "Now, how can I help you, Sheriff?" She pushed open the screen and peered over his shoulder at his vehicle. "Is Leanne with you?"

"No, she's still with my colleague." Well, that was mostly true. Bernadette was a colleague of sorts. "Until we figure out why she ran in the first place, I don't think it's safe for her here." Wade hooked his sunglasses on the top button of his uniform. "May I come in? I have a few photos I'd like to show you."

"Oh, sure." Mrs. Pittman stepped back into the living room holding the door open for him. "Excuse the mess. With three kids, a dog, and a husband, it's never truly picked up." She pointed to an empty spot on the couch. An overflowing laundry basket occupied one end while a black backpack similar to Leanne's sat on the middle cushion.

Wade dropped into the spot she indicated and placed his sheriff's hat on the seat beside him.

Carolyn moved a pile of folded laundry from the recliner to a basket on the floor and took a seat. "How is Leanne?" She scooted the basket out of her way with her foot before settling into the chair.

"She's doing well. But she won't tell us much. We're still in the dark about what scared her and why she ran."

"Stan and I have been wracking our brains trying to figure that one out. She seemed happy here. Her grades were good, and she'd even expressed interest in joining the karate club next year."

"I don't think it has anything to do with you or Mr. Pittman. In fact, she's afraid of putting you in danger if she returns."

Carolyn shook her head. "Sounds like her. She acts all tough, but she cares deeply. Once she likes you, she's loyal."

"Yeah, she's talked about a woman named Nadine. She seemed very fond of her."

"She loved Nadine. Nearly killed Leanne when she heard she'd died of cancer. She didn't know about the funeral until it was all over. Leanne asked me to take her to her gravesite this past spring to put flowers on the grave."

Wade pulled the photos from the doorbell camera out of his shirt pocket. "We believe Leanne witnessed something to do with all the break-ins that have been occurring over the last four months."

Carolyn nodded. "I've read about them in the paper. There was a break-in not far from here back in May, a house in the subdivision adjacent to our street. It's the big house at the back of the cul-de-sac. Kind of secluded. Way off the street. I was shocked when I saw the article. It's always a little disturbing when something like that happens close to home."

Frowning, Wade made a mental note about the break-in. He didn't recall seeing any information on it, but if it had been within the city limits, the city police would've been called. He'd have to have the information sent to his office. "Do you remember the name of the family who was robbed?"

"North…Nevell…Newson. It started with an N. I can't remember the exact name."

Wade wondered if it was the Norton family that Marilyn had mentioned when she came in to report the hacked lockboxes.

Carolyn chuckled. "I'm lucky to remember what I had for breakfast. But I do remember they were out of town. At the time, I thought it was fortunate they were gone. I can't imagine how frightening it'd be to experience a break-in. People in your house, taking your things while you're there."

Wade leaned his forearms on his knees, holding the photos in his hand. "The name's not important. I just thought if you knew what it was, I might swing by and speak with them while I was in the neighborhood. But it would be helpful if you could walk me through Leanne's last day here. Maybe something will stick out."

Carolyn raised her shoulder and let it drop. "Sure, I'd be glad to go through it with you, but I gave this information to the officer who came by after I filed the missing person's report in May."

"I understand, but I'd like to hear it again if you don't mind."

Tapping her chin, she squinted, her eyes focused on the far wall. "School had been out for less than two weeks, and the kids were already getting bored. The younger two had begged Leanne to play Go Fish with them, and they wound up playing several different board games that morning in the upstairs playroom." She met Wade's gaze. "Leanne is always such a help.

Great with the younger kids and the dog, too."

"How so?"

"She's the one who always took Radar for a walk in the evenings. In fact, she'd been walking Radar in the neighborhood next to ours when the burglary happened. Of course, I didn't realize it until I read the article in the paper the next evening. I asked her about it, but she didn't seem to be aware that anything had happened."

Wade furrowed his brow. So, Leanne had been out walking the dog during the time of the burglary. Another item to check out. "What happened the rest of that day?"

"That's the odd thing. Not a lot. Leanne came down from playing with the kids upstairs. She asked me what we were having for lunch, and I told her grilled cheese sandwiches with veggie soup."

"How did she seem?"

"Happy. Her usual self." Carolyn shifted her weight in the recliner. "Then someone was at the door, so I asked her to go see who it was because I was in the middle of preparing lunch. I could've sworn I heard her open the front door, but after a minute, I heard them knock again. After the third time, I went to see who it was."

"Who was it?" Wade rubbed his thumb across the smooth paper of the photos.

"It was the mailman. He had a package that needed a signature. An official document for one of the kids."

"And you'd asked Leanne to answer the door, but she didn't?"

Carolyn shrugged. "I don't know what to tell you. I could've sworn I heard the door open, but obviously, I was mistaken."

"Anything else out of the ordinary happen?"

"Not really, we ate lunch. She played with the other kids in the backyard. The four of them came in when Stan got home, and we had dinner. Same old, same old."

"Did she walk the dog that evening?"

Frowning, Carolyn tilted her head, and tapped her chin. "No. Now that I think about it, she asked Michael to do it. She said she wasn't feeling well and headed upstairs to her bedroom earlier than usual. Later, when I went to say goodnight, I found her asleep." Carolyn released a long sigh. "But when I went to wake the kids the next morning, she was gone. Stan and I have been worried sick. I can't tell you how relieved we were when Deputy Perez contacted us Friday."

"I can only imagine."

"You don't have kids of your own, do you?" A smile grew on her lips.

"No, ma'am. I do not."

"Well, when you do, you'll understand how terrifying it is when they pull a stunt like this. You're so mad you want to ground them for life, but you're so thankful for their safety, all you want to do is bundle them into your arms and hug them until they can't breathe."

"That sounds about right." He grinned and held out the photos to her. "I'd like for you to take a look at these and tell me if you recognize any of these men."

She took the pictures from his hand and studied them. "They are rather fuzzy."

He couldn't argue with her. The quality of the photos left a lot to be desired, but it's all he had to work with at this point. "Can you look again?"

She studied the photos in her hand. "This guy looks familiar, but I couldn't tell you where I've seen him. You know how you see people, but you don't really see them. It's like that. I probably bumped into him at the grocery store or Walmart." She handed back the photos. "Sorry."

"No, that's all right. But if you could keep your eyes open, maybe you'll run into him again." Wade rose and picked up his hat. "If you do, please let me know right away." He pulled a card with his name and number on it from a leather pouch on his utility belt.

Taking the card, Carolyn followed him to the door. "Please tell Leanne we miss her."

"I will." Wade pushed open the screen door. "By the way, what time does your mail usually come?"

"Around lunch. Maybe a little later. But always by two. Why do you ask?"

Wade slipped his hat into place. "I wanted to make sure Leanne didn't answer the door like you asked her. Just running down every lead, even the small ones. It's probably nothing."

"In that case I guess I should mention the mailman asked about her later that week. He knocked to give me the mail and said something about not seeing my oldest around lately. I told him she'd been busy. I didn't think it was any of his business what was going on."

"That's interesting." Wade tipped his sheriff's hat to her. "Thank you for your time." He hurried down the steps to his SUV. He'd have Hilda find out about the burglary in the nearby subdivision of Pinehurst and have the city police department send over a copy of the file. Plus, he'd ask Regan to talk to the postman. He didn't like the fact that the mail carrier had asked about Leanne. Maybe the guy had seen something or had information about what had upset her.

While Regan worked on that, he'd swing by and speak to Leanne. He'd show her the pictures and see what she had to say. Hopefully, it would be more than she had shared. He wasn't holding his breath.

~

Sliding behind the wheel of the SUV, Wade tapped the number for Bernadette's office before pulling out of Pittman's driveway.

"Bernadette Stewart speaking. How can I help you find your dream home today?"

The realtor jingle always caught him off guard. "I think you already did." He placed the phone on its stand and pushed the call through to his SUV's hands-free device.

"Well, hello there." The smile in her voice quickened his heartbeat.

"Do you have a minute?" he asked.

"Sure, what do you need?"

"I wondered if I could swing by your place and see Leanne. I need to ask her a few more questions. There's been some new information come to light." Wade decided not to tell Bernadette about the photos. Wade didn't want her to mention them to Leanne, giving the teen time to prepare her response. He needed to see her knee-jerk reaction to the pictures. Only then would he know if she recognized any of the men.

"Sorry, Mom picked her up earlier for a sleepover. Leanne wanted to go on the trail ride with the B&B guests this afternoon and participate in the campfire sing-along tonight. They do it twice a month. The guests love it. Makes them feel like they've been on a real cowboy adventure. Leanne will be back in the morning. She has to be at Harry's Hardware by nine to work off her debt to society." There was a long pause. When Wade didn't answer, Bernadette added, "If it's important, you could go see her at Mom's."

"No, it's not urgent. Besides, I'd hate to ruin her fun." Realizing he wouldn't be able to talk with Leanne, he flipped on his blinker and made a U-turn, heading back toward the Pittman's' neighborhood. "She's had so little of it in the last two months. I'm still amazed she made it on her own for as long as she did."

"She is a resourceful girl with wicked hacking skills, but she did borrow a few items from others. I think that counts as help," Bernadette said.

"I guess you're right." He recalled his first encounter with Leanne. In his report, he'd described her as surly and uncooperative. But after a few visits with Bernadette's mom, Leanne's attitude had thawed. She still didn't want to talk about the reason she'd done a runner, but overall, he'd caught glimpses of the sweet young lady that lay underneath her tough exterior.

"I'm just thankful you were able to talk Harry and the gas station owner into letting her do odd jobs to pay them back. She doesn't need a police record for shoplifting following her into adulthood."

"No, she doesn't. She's already got enough obstacles to overcome. Plus having her work off what she owes, will do more for her than having her locked up." A grin pulled at his lips. "Besides, it's hard to take advantage of people once you meet them."

Bernadette scoffed. "Tell that to my mechanic. I gave him a deal on his house and my fees, and he still charged me full price when I had my brake pads replaced."

Her indignation made him laugh. "You poor thing."

"Laugh all you like, but don't expect a break on your fees."

"Hey, now wait a minute," he protested. Turning right, he entered the Pinehurst subdivision and followed the main road around several curves. As it wound towards the north, he took one of the side roads leading to the cul-de-sac at the back of the subdivision. "Listen, I've arrived at my destination."

"You sound like the lady on my GPS."

"I take offense to that. My voice hasn't sounded like a lady's since I was thirteen and had hormones playing tricks on me." Wade pulled into the long driveway of the large two-story house.

"Plus, I thought we weren't supposed to drive and talk on the phone. Too distracting and all that."

If he didn't know any better, Wade would've thought she sounded worried. "It's okay, *Mom*. I made it safe." Wade joked then softened his tone. "Bernie, I used the hands-free function in the truck."

"Oh, well," she stammered, embarrassed. "I'm glad to know my Sheriff follows the law."

Deciding to let her off the hook, he redirected the conversation to the Fourth of July celebration. "Are we still on for Thursday night?"

"Definitely, Leanne was really excited when I told her. Plus, she doesn't have to work at either the gas station or Harry's that day."

"Great, then I'll pick you both up at six, since the festivities start at seven," Wade said.

"Can't wait." The lilt in Bernadette's voice made his heart skip a beat.

"Me, either." Pushing the button, he ended the call. He grabbed the radio attached to his utility belt. "Dispatch, I need information on a dwelling, 2031 Pinecrest Drive in Orange Blossom city limits. I believe the owners were involved in a burglary back in May. Can you get me their names? Try asking Hilda. She might know."

"On it, Boss."

"And see if you can get the police department to send over a copy of the report. It might help shed some light on what Leanne saw."

"Anything else?" Penny asked.

"Yeah, send Regan over to the Pittman's' house and tell her to talk to the mailman about the day Leanne went missing. I think he might know something. He's usually in the area around lunchtime."

Deciding to proceed, he rang the doorbell and waited. Wade noticed the doorbell was one of the new ones with a built-in security camera. Maybe the owners had caught some footage of the robbers. If so, the images had to be better than what he had with him.

The door inched open. "Can I help you?"

Two dark brown eyes and a fluff of salt-and-pepper hair were all Wade could see through the slit. Wade pulled his badge and ID card from his left shirt pocket and opened it. The woman read it. "I'm Sheriff Thibodeaux of Reseda County, and I wanted to speak with the owners of the house. Are you the owner?"

The woman stepped back and opened the door a little wider where Wade could see the logo on her tee-shirt. The dark green emblem read *Maid Perfect*. Her hand shook as she raised it to her throat. "No, they not here. But I give message if you want."

From her accent, Wade figured she was one of the many immigrants who sought a new life here in the States. "Maybe you could help me. Have you worked for the family long?" Wade shoved his ID back into his pocket.

"Si, almost two years. I work for the Nortons' and two other families in town. Everyone treats me nice. Especially my boss at Maid Perfect Cleaning Service. She's very good to me." The woman fidgeted from foot to foot, displaying clear signs of anxiety.

Wade needed to make her feel more at ease if he wanted to get any information from her. Apparently, she misunderstood the reason for his visit. "I'm sure you do a great job, and that they are lucky to have you. But that's not why I'm here. I wanted to speak to them about the break-in back in May. Were you here when the burglary took place?"

Her eyes widened even more. "Oh, no, Señor. I wasn't here. I did not take anything." Her hands flew to her cheeks, and her eyes flooded with worry.

"No, you misunderstood me. I know you didn't have anything to do with the burglary. We know the suspects are male." He hoped this information would ease her mind. "What is your name?"

"Anna Garcia."

"Anna, did you come to the house after it happened? Maybe on your regular day?"

The woman let out a nervous giggle. "I understand. No, I did not come that day because the owners were away. They ask me to come the day before they come back, so I can make everything nice for them."

"What did you find when you got here?"

"Everything messed up. Broken glass on the floor by the back doors. And the TVs and computers gone." She turned toward the interior of the house and waved her hands as she spoke. "I call my boss, and she tells me to leave it. That Mr. Norton would have to make a police report, so I no clean it up." She shrugged. "So, I left."

"How long were the Nortons gone?"

"Maybe a week? They go visit their new grandbaby."

"Do you remember the exact dates they were out of town?"

The maid pulled her phone from her back jean pocket and tapped the calendar app. She scrolled back to the month of May and brought up the daily display. "They left on May 15, a Wednesday and returned on Tuesday, May 21."

Wade fished out a small pad and pen from his pocket and jotted down the dates. "So, you came to the house on that Monday. Correct?"

"Si." She nodded.

"And you didn't call the police?"

"My boss say the Nortons would call when they return. That way they can tell the police what's missing." The maid slipped her phone back into her pocket. "So, I didn't call."

"Did *you* notice anything missing?"

She glanced off to her left. "I went into the office where sometimes Mr. Norton works. I know there is a safe. So, I checked it before I called them. It was empty. The pretty diamond necklace her mother give Mrs. Norton on her wedding day, gone."

"And you have no idea when the break-in actually happened?"

"*Clara que no*, do I know this."

Wade's Spanish was a little rusty, but he believed she'd said no way. He pointed to the doorbell. "I noticed the doorbell camera. Did the Nortons get any footage of the thieves?"

Anna frowned and shook her head. "No, they put it in after they got home from their trip."

Wade closed his pad and stuck it back in his pocket, clipping the pen to the edge of the fabric. "All right, I think I have everything."

The woman went to shut the door, but Wade caught it before it closed. "One last thing. What did the diamond necklace look like?"

"It hung to here." Anna pointed to her collarbone. "And it was one long string of pink and white diamonds. So beautiful. I saw it on Mrs. Norton once when she wore it to a party. Magnifico."

Wade pulled out of the Norton's driveway. He needed to see the report from the Orange Blossom Police Department about the break-in. If Anna's description of the diamond necklace was accurate, that piece alone would be worth thousands.

Chapter Fourteen

The red, white, and blue bunting on the gazebo danced in the hot July breeze as Bernadette stretched her legs out in front of her. She crossed her ankles and settled into one of the three folding chairs Wade had brought for them, ready to enjoy the evening. He'd also brought a blanket to spread on the ground, so they could have a better view of the fireworks later. She'd been looking forward to this evening since they'd gone out Friday night.

Leanne lay on the plaid blanket with her head resting on her backpack, playing a game on Bernadette's tablet. A red and white plastic cooler filled with soda and water bottles sat between her chair and Wade's. Bernadette had packed the cooler and a tote with snacks. She'd learned over the past week with Leanne, teenage girls could eat.

Glancing around, Bernadette made note of who was there. She spotted several members of the Cowboy Community Church. Pastor Connor and his wife were present along with their two grown daughters. A little farther away, Bernadette picked out Purdy and her daughter and granddaughter, Sarah, standing among a group of retirees. She'd half expected to see her parents but couldn't find them in the growing crowd on the lawn of the Senior Citizen's Center.

Wade picked up his soda from the top of the cooler and took a sip. "This brings back memories." He glanced at her with a winsome smile on his lips.

"I know. My parents and I come almost every year." Bernadette nudged Leanne's shoulder with her toe to get her attention. "What about you? Have you seen any of Spike's famous fireworks shows?"

Leanne rolled over onto her stomach. The gray of twilight hung in the sky, not yet dark enough for the fireworks but dark enough to paint everything in shadows. Bernadette couldn't make out the expression on the teen's face.

"I've seen one. Nadine took us the year before she got sick. Jay and my sister, Mia, and I loved it. Nadine even let us have bottle rockets when we got home."

Wade groaned. "Don't even mention bottle rockets." He held up his hand, palm out. "I still have nightmares about those things."

Straightening in her chair, Bernadette teased, "A big strong sheriff like you afraid of a little ole light? This I've got to hear." Leaning on the fabric arm of the chair, she planted her chin in her hand. "I'm all ears."

Leanne tapped the screen of the tablet and laid it aside. "Me, too."

"Well, if you must know—" Wade rubbed his hand across his chin and leaned forward settling his forearms on his knees. "When I was eight and Dan was about ten and Brent was six—"

"Who are Dan and Brent?" Leanne interrupted.

"My brothers," Wade answered. "Pops gave us some sparklers along with some bottle rockets to celebrate the Fourth of July since we couldn't come into town for the big show."

"Uh-oh, this isn't going to end well, is it?" Bernadette chuckled.

Leanne sat up and hugged her knees.

"Anyway, after Pops gave us some instructions about how to aim the bottle rockets away from the house and how to miss a stand of trees not too far away, he told us to stay on the concrete patio, but my brothers and I had the bright idea we'd have more room out by the barn. That way we definitely wouldn't hit the house."

"Safety first," Bernadette razzed.

"What happened?"

"Dan decided to set off a bottle rocket, but the bottle we were using for the base was aimed more sideways than upright. It took off, whizzing around and chasing me and Brent. We dove out of the way. I landed on the other side of the tractor, knocking the breath out of me, and Brent went headfirst into a pile of … well, let's just say he needed a bath when we were done. But the bottle rocket headed straight toward the barn and landed in a bale of hay not far from the barn door. Caught fire before we could say Holy Cow."

"Oh, man." Leanne giggled, rocking back and forth holding her knees.

"We both ran to the faucet near the watering trough for the horses. Dan yanked the hose to the hay that was ablaze while I manned the water spigot, attaching the nozzle and turning on the water. When the water hit the hay, smoke filled the air. We coughed and sputtered, and my eyes stung. About then, here comes Brent with Pops in tow." Wade ran his hand over the scar on his left cheek. "The look on Pops' face told us all we needed to know. Boy, were we in trouble, big trouble!" Chuckling, Wade scooted back in his chair. "That's still one of my favorite Fourths, being with my brothers here in Orange Blossom."

"Did you put the fire out before it reached the barn?" Leanne asked.

"Sure did. But Pops made us get up early every day for the rest of the summer to do chores." Picking up his soda, he shook his head. "I don't ever remember being as ready for school to start as I was that year." He took a sip. "What's your favorite memory?"

Bernadette shrugged, unable to pull a memory as interesting as his from her years of coming to the Reseda County Fireworks show. "Mine are kind of tame compared to yours."

"Nonsense," A familiar voice called from behind them. Bernadette twisted in her chair to see her mother approaching from the side closest to Wade. "Don't you remember the year you volunteered to help at the vet's office? You wound up with eleven dogs all going nuts because of the noise. Howling to beat the band."

"I do remember that. It was also the year I had to cut one of those hounds loose with my switchblade before he strangled himself with his leash." Bernadette laughed.

Wade narrowed his eyes. "Switchblade? What on earth were you doing with a switchblade?"

"Daddy gave it to me. It's harmless. Probably wouldn't cut through marshmallow cream." She grinned. "But I still carry it in my purse in case I need to open a package of chips or something." Giggling, she turned her attention to her mother. "So, where did you come from? I looked for you earlier and didn't see you."

"We got held up at the B&B, but we made it." Darlene sang out. She glanced at Leanne. "I promised a certain someone she could sit with us and have ice cream sandwiches. Do you mind?"

Leanne jumped up before Bernadette had a chance to answer. Grabbing the chair still in the bag and her backpack, she offered up the device. "Here's your tablet back. Thanks for letting me use it."

"Well, I guess that's a yes." Bernadette's brows winged up. "We'll find you after the fireworks."

"No, that's okay. We'll just drop her by your house on our way back to the inn. It'll probably be easier after it gets dark than trying to find you again." Mom handed her two ice cream sandwiches in their wrappers. "These are for you."

"Thanks." Turning to Leanne, Bernadette asked, "Hey, do you have your key?"

"Sure do." She patted the front pocket of her backpack.

"Great. Then we're all set." Her mother bent down and kissed Bernadette on the cheek. "And I'll be sure she locks the doors if we beat you there."

"Sounds good." Bernadette watched them as they drifted off into the crowd.

As they ate their treat, the gray sky gently turned to a thick inky black, and the stars popped out. The night air sizzled. They ate their ice cream quickly, racing to beat the heat. Even so, drops trailed down Bernadette's hand, making her fingers sticky.

The taste of the chocolate wafer and vanilla ice cream reminded her of other summer evenings spent in good company. She watched Wade close his eyes before he took a bite. He repeated the action with each mouthful. A smile crept onto her lips. The man certainly enjoyed the little things in life.

Taking his last bite, he reached over and took her wrapper out of her hand and tossed both into the open cooler. He pulled out a bottle of water. Opening it, he rinsed his hands and offered it to her. She took it, glad to wash off the sticky residue.

A quiet hush fell over the crowd as they waited for the fireworks with only a few murmured conversations sprouting up here and there. When the moon rose in the sky, Bernadette leaned toward him and whispered, "The show should be starting soon."

"Then we'd better get to our spots." Wade stood and pulled Bernadette to her feet.

After they'd settled on the blanket with the black sky spread out before them, Wade reached over and took her hand. "Now, it feels like a date."

Bernadette could hear the smile in his voice as he tucked his other arm under his head. "Leanne sure is smitten with your mother."

"She's great with teens. After hearing your story tonight, I have to admit I'm a bit envious. Being an only child has its drawbacks. You and your brothers seem so close."

"Yeah, we were while we were growing up, but we went our own ways when we got older. So, I made the conscious decision to put family first. My career in the FBI didn't leave a lot of leeway for relationships, romantic or otherwise." Wade shifted onto his side with his head in his hand, looking down at her. "It was a good decision though. I don't regret moving back here one bit."

"Really? You don't miss the adrenaline rush of bringing in some of the country's biggest threats? The thrill of the hunt, the excitement of the chase?"

"Nope." He rubbed his thumb across the back of her hand sending goosebumps shooting over her skin despite the warm night air. "The price was too high."

"I get it. Family is important."

"How about you? Do you want a big family?" Wade asked. "Your folks are going to make some wonderful grandparents if you do have kids."

Rising on her elbow, she faced him. "I don't know about big, but someday, I think I'd like to be a mom. Have my own or maybe adopt." She rolled onto her back and stared at the vast canopy of darkness with its pinholes of lights, twinkling brightly. "Or perhaps, both."

"Adopt? Hmm, I hadn't figured you for one to adopt, but I guess it makes sense with your parents participating in the foster care program."

Images of the kids that had passed through her home while growing up floated through her mind. Each with their own needs and set of circumstances. Diane from a broken home with a mom who was an addict. Simon, whose mom was in prison and had no idea who her father was. James, just a baby, left behind, waiting for the grandmother to gain custody. So many needed a safe place, a loving home.

"My parents had a way of making me feel important and loved. I had zero childhood trauma compared to others. Guess that's why I root for the underdog. My parents made me feel like nothing was impossible as long as I had them and God on my side."

Gratitude welled up in her, causing her chest to tighten. She was so blessed. Maybe someday she'd bless a child with that same unconditional love she'd received.

"Either way. You're going to make a great mom."

The warmth of his hand against hers with their fingers intertwined felt right. He'd been correct. Now, it felt like a date. She swallowed the lump in her throat and forced a chuckle. "If my dog ownership reflects any of my skills, I'll be lucky to remember to feed the poor kid. Besides, I need the whole husband thing before I consider becoming a mom. With my track record, it's not looking so good." Why had she said that to him? She tucked her head, thankful for the darkness to hide her embarrassment.

"That might not be as big of a problem as you think." He picked up her hand and held it to his lips. Gently, he kissed her knuckles then pulled her toward him.

She rose onto her elbow, and he leaned in to meet her lips, a natural act as if they'd been kissing under the dark sky all their lives. Soft at first, a mere whisper. Then with a rush of urgency.

Releasing her hand, he cupped her cheek and deepened the kiss, his hand on her face, his lips pressed against hers. Her breath caught. He tasted sweet like chocolate, summer evenings, and everything good in the world.

Giving in to the feeling, she ran her hand over the nape of his neck and sunk her fingers into his hair, returning his kiss. After a minute, he pulled back and rested his forehead against hers.

A quick, sharp whistle through the air and a loud pop signaled the beginning of the Reseda County

Fireworks Show.

Wade stroked her cheek, meeting her gaze. "That was nice."

Slowing her breath, she tried to steady her racing heart. "It certainly was and a little unexpected."

"Like whizzing bottle rockets." He chuckled.

"And billionaire sheriffs."

He planted one last kiss on her lips before he settled back on the blanket, tucking one hand under his head and taking hold of her hand with the other.

Sliding back onto the blanket, she tried to focus on the fanfare before her. Another round of explosions lit up the sky, sending waves of oohs and aahs rippling through the crowd. But Bernadette wasn't paying attention. She'd already experienced the most amazing fireworks of the evening.

Chapter Fifteen

"Good morning," Marilyn called over the obnoxious tune of the front door chime as she entered William Keys Realtors. "How's this Monday treating you?"

Glancing up from her computer, Bernadette found her friend standing in her doorway. "Don't you mean good afternoon?" She looked at the clock on her screen. "It's nearly lunchtime. I was just about to leave to pick up Leanne from Harry's Hardware store." Bernadette couldn't believe it'd been almost two weeks since the teen had become part of her life.

"What's she doing there?" Marilyn entered and chucked her satchel into one of the two chairs sitting in front of Bernadette's desk. "Did she get a part-time job for the summer or something?"

Not comfortable sharing about Leanne working off a debt, she skirted the question by changing the subject. "I have some good news. You'll be pleased to know Mr. Percy accepted Wade's offer."

"Really? He agreed to all the upgrades?"

"Yes." Bernadette squealed and rose from her chair. "I just made my biggest sale ever." Her eyes widened with excitement.

Marilyn held up her hand for a high-five, and Bernadette obliged then followed it up with a knuckle bump. "Way to go, girl. You got the guy and the sale. Pretty impressive." Marilyn sing-songed the last word.

Heat rushed up the back of Bernadette's neck and painted her cheeks. "You don't think he bought the house because we're …" Bernadette hesitated. She didn't know what to call it. They'd only gone out a handful of times, and then there was that kiss. But because of Leanne, they did see each other almost daily.

"Dating." Marilyn filled in the missing word. "You're dating. I know it's a foreign concept to you because the last time you went out with anyone, we had a different president, and flowy sleeves were trending, but surely you remember what a date looks like."

"Well, of course, I do. And I don't appreciate the snark." Great. Now, she had something else to worry about besides keeping up with Leanne. Had Wade bought the ranch simply to help her out? With his inheritance from his pops, he had the means to buy the ranch and twenty others with no problem.

"Uh-oh, I know that look." Marilyn dropped into the chair across from Bernadette. "What just happened? What's wrong?"

"You don't think he bought this house just so I could get this commission, do you? I mean, he pretty much bought the most expensive one on the market."

"Bernie, don't be silly. You've dragged him to every ranch within twenty miles of here for months, and he told you to keep looking, until now."

Bernadette pursed her lips, giving Marilyn's point some thought. "That's true."

"If he only wanted to help you out with a commission, he'd bought the first one you showed him. Besides, does it matter?"

Plopping into her chair, she crossed her arms. "Yes, it does. I don't want Mr. Big Bucks to think he has to help me out financially. I mean, I own my house. My car is paid off. I can take care of myself."

"Um, girl, there are days I don't understand you. You're dating one of the hottest bachelors in the county. He has money, manners, and he attends church. If he were any closer to perfection, we'd have to name the town after him." Shooting up in her chair, Marilyn pointed at her. "You're looking for a reason to sabotage this relationship."

"I am not." Bernadette protested, glaring at Marilyn. But if she were honest with herself, maybe she was. That kiss they'd shared the other night under the rocket's red glare had made bombs burst in her heart, to say the least. She'd been so distracted with him being next to her she missed most of the show, even though she'd been staring right at it.

Marilyn laughed and clapped her hands together. "That's it. You must really like this guy if you're looking for a reason to ditch the relationship."

"Relationship?" Bernadette's heart raced. Panic oozed through her as her fear of commitment kicked into high gear. "It's not a relationship. We've agreed to go slow. I told him I didn't have such a great track record with men."

A stern look swept across Marilyn's face. "Don't you dare let one little hiccup with Peter Finch discourage you from pursuing what could be a terrific relationship with Wade."

Bernadette sighed. Marilyn had a point. "I won't."

"Promise?"

"I'm not going to promise. You'll just have to take my word at face value." Bernadette raised her eyebrows. "I won't let my past relationship with Peter affect what I'm building with Wade." She placed her elbows on her desk and narrowed her gaze. "But I am going to let the Lord affect it, and if he says it's a no-go, then I'm not going to push to get my way."

A smile spread across Marilyn's lips. "So, your way is to keep dating Wade. I knew it." Marilyn popped out of her chair and snatched her satchel from the other seat.

"Grrr, you are so infuriating sometimes." Bernadette grabbed a piece of paper from her desk and wadded it up, throwing it at Marilyn as she darted for the door, missing her by inches.

"Yeah, but you love me anyway. And Wade." Marilyn shut Bernadette's heavy wooden door with a thud, causing the second wad of paper to bounce off it.

Glancing at the screen, Bernadette saw the time. She needed to leave if she didn't want to be late to pick up Leanne. Plus, she expected to see Wade there. He wanted to ask the teen a couple of questions, but he didn't mention what they were.

Twenty minutes later, Bernadette pulled into the gravel parking lot of Harry's Hardware Store which sat off Deadwood Drive. She scanned the small parking lot but didn't see Wade's black SUV with the Sheriff Department logo on it.

Bernadette carefully trekked across the white gravel in her navy-blue heels, hoping not to scratch the faux leather. She'd dressed nicely today because she had a meeting with a new client. At least that's what she'd told herself when she'd spent extra time on her hair and makeup. It certainly didn't have anything to do with seeing Wade.

Lifting her chin, she swung open the glass door and stepped inside expecting to be greeted by Harry or Leanne, but the place appeared to be empty. Sidling up to the counter, she rang the bell for help. The ding echoed through the space.

"Be right with you," Leanne called from somewhere near the back of the store. The place wasn't that big, but Harry did carry quite a variety of merchandise that caused the place to seem bigger than it was.

"No rush, just me."

Leanne's tennis shoes slapped against the tile floor. Moments later, she appeared at the end of one of the aisles with a feather duster in hand. "Can I finish dusting the top shelves on aisles ten and eleven? Harry had to pull out a ladder and everything, and I don't want him to have to get it back out tomorrow. It seemed like a struggle, and the ladder almost won."

"Sure, take your time. I'm in no rush. Besides, I talked to Wade earlier, and he's going to meet us here around one. We have time." Apparently, Wade's observation about it being hard to take advantage of people once one got to know them might prove true in Leanne's case. Bernadette couldn't stop the pang of pride that sprang in her heart at Leanne's concern for Harry.

Leanne's brows pulled tight together at the mention of Wade. "What does he want?"

"I'm not sure. He said he had a few more questions

for you.”

“He’s wasting his time. I’m not putting my foster family in danger. So, he can ask all the questions he wants, but I’m not talking.” Leanne’s lips grew pencil thin as she pressed them together. Jutting her chin out, she crossed her arms and let the duster dangle in her hand.

Stubborn as a mule, but she’d let Wade handle the attitude. “Fine but hear him out.”

Leanne shrugged one shoulder. “It’s a free country. I can’t stop him from talking, can I?” With that, she spun around and headed back down the aisle.

Harry appeared from the back room wiping sweat from his forehead with a handkerchief. “Sorry about that. I was outside helping Bill with the propane.” He checked his wristwatch. “Is it that time already? Where did the morning go?”

“It is. Bet you’re glad to have the first two weeks behind you with Leanne.”

“Not really. She’s been a big help. It’s made me think I might need to hire a teenager for the summer. I forget how flexible they are.” His shoulders shook as a belly laugh rumbled through him. “I can’t get up and down a ladder anymore.” He patted his midsection. “The ladies who work for me would rather not climb that high either.”

“No, I imagine not,” Bernadette said. With his white beard and rather chunky form, Harry often played Santa in the Orange Blossom Christmas parade. He fit the part perfectly.

“Truth is none of us are getting any younger.” He sealed his statement with a wink. “So, it’s nice to have someone around young enough to do some of the more athletic chores like dusting the items on the top shelves."

"I'm just glad—" Before she finished her thought, the front door whooshed open letting in some of the mid-July heat. The mailman walked in carrying a rather long, thin package and a stack of letters bound together with a rubber band.

"Oh, great. Sam's paddles are here. He'll be glad." Harry glanced at Bernadette. "He bought a canoe last summer and lost the paddles over the winter. Has no idea what he did with them. So, he's been waiting for these to come in to take his grandkids out on the lake."

"Here you go, Harry." The mailman lifted the package over the counter and handed it to the store owner. Harry stashed the package out of the way in one of the corners behind the counter.

"Okay, I think I'm done." Leanne rounded the end cap of aisle ten and stopped dead in her tracks. A look of terror washed over her face.

"Are you all right, Leanne?" Bernadette hurried toward the teen, not sure what had happened.

Leanne's eyes widened, and Bernadette followed her gaze. The mailman stood watching the two of them, his face drawn. For a moment, Bernadette could have sworn she saw a flash of panic in his eyes.

Harry turned. "You got anything else for me today?"

The mailman tore his eyes away from Leanne and slid the bundle of letters onto the counter. "Yeah, here's the rest of it." Nodding to Harry, he made a beeline for the front door.

"Thanks." Harry loosened the rubber band and sorted through the small pile.

Crossing her arms, Bernadette turned her attention to Leanne. "What was that all about?"

Leanne pressed her lips together, and the stubborn glare Bernadette had become familiar with over the past two weeks appeared in the girl's eyes. "Nothing. I just wanted to see if Wade was here yet. I'd heard the door, but I guess it was the mailman."

"Are you finished dusting?" Bernadette narrowed her eyes, not buying this explanation. She'd read fear on Leanne's face when she'd spotted the mailman, not simple curiosity. "It's past quitting time. I'm sure Harry won't mind if you pick up where you left off tomorrow."

"I just remembered there's one more thing I need to do. It'll only take a minute. Like I said, I don't want Harry to have to get the ladder out again." Her gaze darted toward the front door before meeting Bernadette's gaze. "Besides, don't we have to stay until Wade gets here with all his insane questions?"

Okay, this sounded more like the Leanne Bernadette knew. She studied the teen's face for a moment. "You're right. Go ahead."

"Thanks." Leanne took off down the aisle.

Fifteen minutes later, Wade strolled into the store wearing his sheriff's hat pushed back on his head with beads of sweat peppered across his forehead. "It's a hot one today." Wade pulled his hat from his head, fanned his face with it for a moment, then laid it on the glass counter near Bernadette. "So, how did today go?"

"Fine and dandy." Harry brushed off his overalls. "She's a hard worker. Makes me think I might need to hire someone young to help around here more often."

"Now, don't get any ideas about paying her, Harry.

Remember she's repaying you for the items she took." One corner of Wade's lips lifted in a half grin as he tapped the top of the display case. "Don't go soft on me now. This is for her own good."

"I know, I know." Harry grumbled.

"Speaking of Leanne, where is she?" Wade scanned the front section of the store.

"She's finishing up some dusting on the last two aisles. I'll go get her." Bernadette headed to aisle eleven, but when she reached the end cap and peered down the aisle, it was empty. A tall aluminum ladder leaned against the last section on the right with the feather duster tucked neatly between two of the steps. "Leanne?" Bernadette called. No answer. Turning, she caught Wade's attention. "She's not here."

"Where could she be?" Wade walked to the first aisle and checked down each consecutive one.

"Maybe, she's out back." Harry offered. "I'll go see." Moving from behind the counter, Harry hustled to the back room that led to the back lot.

Bernadette began with the last aisle and moved toward Wade, meeting him in the middle of the store. "She's not here." Panic rose in her. "She must've been spooked. I should've known she'd run." Bernadette worked hard to tamp down the fear that squeezed her heart.

"What do you mean she was spooked? What happened?" Concern and irritation mingled in Wade's words.

Chapter Sixteen

The back door slammed with a thud before Wade saw Harry emerge from the back room. "No sign of her, and her backpack is gone from the storeroom."

Bernadette groaned. "I should've known she was frightened."

"Bernie, tell me exactly what happened," Wade pressed.

Bernadette rehashed the situation. Worry etched in her features with each word. Finishing, she said, "she acted odd, but I couldn't be sure if it was because of the mail carrier or if something else had happened." Bernadette covered her eyes with her hands. Hanging her head, she let out a deep sigh. "What are we going to do? We have to find her."

Wade fought the urge to wrap her in his arms and tell her everything would be all right. He hated seeing her worried. Instead, he turned his attention to the owner of the store. "Harry, you said she acted fine all day."

"Right, until the mail carrier came in to drop off a package that wouldn't fit in the mailbox. A pair of paddles for Sam's canoe." Harry gestured toward the odd-shaped package leaning in the far corner. "She came around the end cap, chatting and froze when she spotted him. But then after Bernadette talked with her, she said she wanted to finish the dusting and seemed fine."

"How long between the mail carrier leaving and my arrival?" Wade's mind raced. What if the mail carrier had something to do with the burglaries and had abducted her?

"Maybe fifteen minutes," Bernadette answered before Harry could reply. "Why? What are you thinking?"

Fishing the photos out of his shirt pocket, he showed them to Bernadette. "Do any of these men look familiar?"

Bernadette flipped through the photos. Wrinkling her nose, she pointed to the last one. "I think this is the mail carrier, but it's so blurry it's hard to be sure." She locked eyes with him. "Are these the robbers?"

"We think they are. One of the homes had a doorbell camera, and the owners were able to supply us with these photos. Though they aren't the best quality."

"Oh man, what should we do?" As if she'd read his mind, Bernadette's eyes widened, and the blood drained from her face. "What if the mail carrier took her?" She touched her stomach as if she might be sick.

"Now, now, Bernadette, it's going to be all right." Harry patted her shoulder. "Remember mail carriers work for the federal government. I'm sure none of them would abduct a teenager and tie her up in the back of their mail truck." Harry gave a weak chuckle. "Talk about special delivery."

Wade pushed down the groan rolling inside him. Harry only wanted to quell Bernadette's fears, but

Wade had seen too much over the years. His experience had shown him when faced with exposure, criminals would do anything to stay under the radar.

Something had happened, and Leanne was missing. They needed to determine if she'd been taken by force or left of her own volition, but he didn't want to frighten Bernadette unnecessarily. "We don't know what's happened. She was probably just scared and ran off. It's what she does." He handed the pictures to Harry. "Do you recognize any of these men?"

"Not these two, but maybe this one. I think he was the guy who was here today." He pointed to the same man Bernadette had identified. "I really wasn't paying attention. When he handed me the paddles, all I thought about was contacting Sam to let him know they'd come in." He shrugged. "Sorry."

Wade scowled. "Don't you know your mail carrier? I thought everyone knew everyone in Orange Blossom."

"Not this one. My usual mailman is Terry. He's been delivering my mail for years." Harry stroked his short white beard and studied the photo. "But I'd heard from Winston, the postmaster, that Terry's wife had a stroke a few months back and isn't recovering well. This guy must have picked up his route."

Wade processed this new information. He needed to get his deputies moving. "Bernie, call your mom and see if she's heard from Leanne. I'm going to radio for backup and get everyone looking for her."

"What can I do?" Harry asked.

"If she shows up after we've gone, let me know. She might simply be hiding to avoid my questions."

"That's a good point." Wade heard the hope

ringing in Bernadette's words. "Maybe, she's hiding because she doesn't want to chance putting her foster family in danger. Maybe she's hiding from you. After all, she wasn't too keen on the idea of having to meet with you today."

"Maybe," but Wade doubted it. His gut told him this had everything to do with the mail carrier and nothing to do with him. "The important thing is that we find her and the sooner the better." He grabbed the radio from his utility belt slung around his hips. "Dispatch, we have a 10-65. A Leanne Hopkins. Be advised she may be in danger."

Penny Martin's voice rasped over the air waves, "What do you mean she's missing?"

"Penny, just get everyone looking for her. And send Donnie over to talk with the postmaster. I need to know who worked the route out on Deadwood Drive this afternoon."

"10-4."

Replacing his radio, he glanced toward Bernadette. "I'm going to head over to your house. See if she's there."

"I'm going with you. I'll call Mom on the way." Bernadette hurried to the door. "If she shows here, call me," she instructed Harry.

Leaving her car, Bernadette jumped into the passenger side of the Sheriff's Department black SUV.

"I'll bring you back once we've found her." Wade hoped he sounded more confident than he felt. Leanne had avoided law enforcement for over a month, the first time. Wade glanced at Bernadette who sat biting her fingernails. "It's going to be all right."

"What if it's not? What if she's in real trouble?"

"Call your mom. See if she's seen her before you start mutilating your manicure." Wade nodded toward her hand.

Shooting him a scowl, she dug her phone from her purse.

Pulling out onto Deadwood Drive, he headed toward Bernadette's house, Wade hoped with everything in him they'd find Leanne slouched in a chair watching her newest favorite movie, *Little Mermaid*, the one with real people in it.

Chapter Seventeen

Bernadette punched her mother's number into her cell phone and waited for the familiar buzz.

"Hey, sweetie. I was about to text you. Had the phone in my hand."

Bernadette cut her off. "Have you seen Leanne?" She worked hard to keep the panic out of her voice but failed miserably.

"She's with me. We just pulled into my driveway. No need to worry. That's why I was texting, to let you know where she was. I would've contacted you sooner, but you know how I detest texting and driving, and I haven't quite figured out how to use Bluetooth. Besides, with Leanne in the car, I figured safety first." Her mother's voice rose a notch.

"Leanne's with you?" Relief flooded through her. She let out the breath she'd been holding. Glancing at Wade, she mouthed, "Go to Belles and Beaus."

"Yeah, honey. She's right here. Hold on a sec."

Wade made a three-point turn in the middle of Hoover Road. Headed in the right direction, he mashed the gas pedal to the floor.

Bernadette clung to the grab handle above her seat and pressed the cell phone harder to her ear with her other hand. Muffled voices sounded on the other end and then a hard thud.

"I sent Leanne on into the house. You sound stressed," her mother said. "If I'd known you'd be this upset, I'd have called you before we left your house. Really, I didn't think you'd mind. Besides, she seemed like she could use some company."

"No, it's fine. It's just that we were worried."

"We?"

"Wade is with me. We were looking for Leanne because he had a few questions to ask her, that's all. And when we couldn't find her, I got worried she'd run off again."

"I don't believe that's all there is to this. Not after the way Leanne behaved when I opened the back door unannounced. She looked scared to death and stood there in the middle of the kitchen holding a broom above her head as if she was about to whack me senseless with the silly thing." Her mom said. "It's a good thing she recognized me before she started swinging."

"Mom, we were worried because she was missing, and with her track record, we weren't sure if she went back into hiding." Bernadette hoped her mother would be satisfied with this answer, but she doubted it.

Wade scowled. Glancing at her, he shook his head.

"Look, I need to go. We're headed in your direction, and we can talk when I get there." She needed a minute to get her story straight with Wade and find out how much information to share. "If you could keep Leanne with you, I'd appreciate it."

"So, Wade's with you. And you were worried Leanne had gone back into hiding?"

"Yes, that about sums it up."

"Uh huh, I see." Which meant her mother had a good idea there was more to the story than she was telling.

"I'll see you in a bit." Bernadette ended the call and tossed her phone back into her purse.

Picking up the mic on the police radio in the SUV, Wade contacted dispatch and had Penny call off the manhunt.

"Thank the Lord, you found her. I've been praying for that girl's safety since the minute you called it in."

"Has Donnie gotten back with the information about the mail carrier?" Wade asked.

"Not yet."

"Fine. Contact me the minute he does."

"10-4." Penny signed off.

Wade sped around the curves leading to Belles and Beaus Bed and Breakfast. "I swear that girl's going to be the death of me." He grumbled, replacing the mic on the radio.

"I thought you had experience dealing with the worst of the worst during your stint with the FBI. Don't tell me you can't handle a lanky fourteen-year-old and her drama." Bernadette teased, her own heart fluttering with relief that Leanne had been found.

Wade drove like a man on a mission. They arrived at Belles and Beaus in record time. Bernadette hurried through the spacious back porch, catching a glimpse of Leanne through the window in the kitchen before she entered. Wade followed close behind her. Leanne sat at the table in the breakfast nook where Bernadette's parents took their meals. The main dining room was reserved for their guests.

As they entered, Leanne slouched in one of the chairs, eyes wide with a mouthful of cookie crumbs. She jumped up, scooting the chair back with her legs, nearly spilling the glass of milk on the table.

"Don't even think about it." Wade spread his hands wide as if he were calming a scared pup. "It's going to be okay."

She froze and inched her way back into the seat.

Tossing her purse onto the island in the center of the kitchen, Bernadette moved toward the teen who kept her eyes glued on Wade. Anger coursed through her. She'd been so worried earlier she hadn't had time to be angry at the girl's actions. Crossing her arms, Bernadette scowled. "Do you have any idea how worried I was?"

"*We* were," Wade corrected.

Bernadette glanced at him over her shoulder, not happy with the interruption. "We were worried."

Her mother replaced the milk in the refrigerator. "Think I'll excuse myself and go upstairs. I have a few rooms I need to prepare for tomorrow's guests." As she passed behind Bernadette, she whispered, "Go easy on her. She's had a real scare."

Bernadette studied the girl for a moment then pulled out the chair next to her.

Wade joined them taking the seat across from her.

"Look, I'm sorry you didn't feel like you could trust me to keep you safe," Bernadette huffed. "But running away isn't an option anymore."

Wade laid his forearms on the tabletop and clasped his hands in front of him. "We know it has something to do with the mail carrier you saw today at Harry's Hardware. I need you to tell me what you know."

"No. I don't want to put anyone in danger." Leanne's hands shook. She crossed her arms, clamping them against her sides.

"The only person you're putting in danger is you." Bernadette touched her shoulder, wanting to comfort her.

Wade pulled the grainy photos from his pocket and laid them out single file in front of Leanne. "I need you to look at these. One of the homeowners caught the perpetrators on their doorbell camera. They're not great pictures, but if you can identify any of them, it would give us enough reason to pick up the guy and question him."

Leanne pressed her back against the chair, turning her head. "You don't understand. He saw me that night and then a few days later, he saw me at the Pittman's. He knows where I live. I had to run, or he'd hurt them."

"Why do you think that?" Bernadette asked.

"Because he told me he would when I answered the door to get the mail."

"Did he seem surprised to see you? Or do you think he knew you lived there?" Wade asked.

She shrugged. "What does it matter? He said he'd hurt them if I told anyone what I saw."

"Would you look at the pictures? Please," Wade asked.

Leanne shook her head. The line of her lips pulled pencil thin.

Scowling, Wade leaned his chin in his left hand and ran his finger across the scar on his cheek. "Look, Leanne, if you want to keep the Pittman family safe and Michael and the other kids, your best bet is to identify the thief. That way I can get him off the street and behind bars. The sooner I can do that, the safer they'll be."

Leanne lifted her chin but refused to make eye contact.

"What about your sister?" Wade asked.

Her head jerked toward him, and Bernadette read the concern in her eyes. "What about her? She doesn't know anything about this."

"No, but if he's desperate, he might go after her to keep you quiet. But if we get him, then you won't have anything to worry about. She'll be safe and sound."

"Just take a look." Bernadette kept her tone calm, in spite of the torrent of emotions bubbling over inside her. "It's the only way to keep everyone safe. Including you."

Leanne cut her eyes toward Bernadette then lowered her gaze to the pictures stretched out in front of her. Reluctantly, she pointed to the same man Bernadette and Harry had identified as the mail carrier who had delivered Harry's mail. "That's him. I'd know him anywhere. I saw him the night the Norton's were robbed while I was walking Radar. He was climbing into a white van with a utility logo on it, carrying a black bag. Not tools."

Bernadette ran her hand across Leanne's shoulders. "You did the right thing."

Standing, Wade strode to the back door and stepped out onto the porch.

Leanne pushed the pictures aside and laid her head in the crook of her arm as if all the fight had gone out of her. "If anyone gets hurt, it'll be his fault."

"No, Leanne. Wade's doing his job, and he's good at it. He'll get the guy and his partners. Everyone will be all right."

"That's what they said about Nadine. That she'd be all right but look what happened." A tear glistened on her cheek, and Bernadette fought the urge to wipe it away. "She's dead, and no one could stop it."

"This is different, honey. There's not much you can do when someone is dying of an illness, but this…this we can do something about. Trust me, Wade Thibodeaux has your back."

"But what if they get to Mia? What if he can't stop them?" Leanne's tears fell in earnest. She rose and caught Bernadette in her arms in a hug so tight Bernadette struggled to inhale.

Chapter Eighteen

"Did you get the guy's name who worked the route on Deadwood Drive this morning?" Wade spoke into his cell phone working hard to keep his voice low. He didn't want to upset Leanne any more than he already had. He'd hoped stepping outside onto the back porch would put him out of earshot of both Bernadette and Leanne.

"The carrier's name is Artie Burton. He's worked for the United States Postal Service for over twenty years. The postmaster, Winston Humphrey, said he's been an exemplary employee. Never late. Runs his route in a timely manner, and he's great with the customers, although Winston did say he's had maybe a handful of complaints over the years about Artie, usually to do with lost mail," Deputy Donnie Adams rattled off the information in an all-business tone.

"So, nothing personal? Like a threat or being aggressive toward a customer?"

"No, nothing along those lines. But this was interesting. The postmaster did say Artie should've returned while I was there. Since he's given him one of the morning routes, Artie's been arriving back at the post office before two. I waited around for a few minutes, but he never showed."

"Did you get a copy of his route?" Wade asked.

"Sure did, Boss." Deputy Adams drew out the word.

Wade hated it when Donnie called him boss. Granted, he was his boss, and pretty much everyone else called him that as well. But ever since they'd both campaigned for the job, when the word came from Donnie's lips, it felt more like a jab than a show of respect. Ignoring his irritation, Wade proceeded with the next logical steps. "Good. Have one of the patrol cars ride his route. Let's see what's happened to Artie."

"Do you think he's in trouble? Or just ran off?"

"I'm not sure. Either way, we need to find him. He's key to cracking this burglary ring. And get Deputy Henderson to secure a warrant for his arrest. I don't want any loose ends once we find him. Tell the judge we have an eyewitness who's identified Artie Burton as one of the robbers."

"So, Leanne finally spilled the beans." Deputy Adams chuckled. "It's about time."

"Yeah, she saw him today delivering mail at Harry's Hardware. It really shook her up." Wade's eyes darted toward the window. Leanne was hugging Bernadette. He let out a long sigh. "She told us she happened to be out walking the dog and came upon a burglary in progress. That's when she saw Artie's face. Later, he found her at the Pittman's house and threatened her, so she ran."

"That's rough." Wade could hear the sincerity in Deputy Adams' voice.

"She's scared, and I want to make sure there isn't any reason for her to be scared. So, let's make this happen."

"On it. I'll let Henderson know, and I'll get one of the other deputies to drive the route."

"Keep me in the loop. And do me a favor. Check on Leanne's sister, Mia Hopkins. Let's make sure she's in a safe place." Wade had hated to use the question of Mia's safety to coerce Leanne to talk, but he had to make sure nothing happened to either of them.

"Do you think the thieves know about her?"

"No, I doubt it, but I don't want to be the one to tell Leanne that we could've protected her sister and didn't."

"Copy that."

"If you need me, I'm headed over to the post office to see the postmaster myself. I think I know what's been going on, but I'd like to confirm a few facts." Wade stepped back inside the kitchen to let Bernadette know he was leaving.

"Did you find out anything new?"

Glancing toward Leanne who was helping Darlene unload the dishwasher, Wade walked over to Bernadette and kept his voice low. "Yeah, we got the guy's name, and now we're looking for him. Seems he hasn't come back to the post office."

Nodding toward Leanne, Bernadette moved even closer to him. "You should've seen her once you left the room. She melted into a puddle." Meeting his gaze, she added, "She's terrified. This guy did a number on her. Telling a kid who's lost so many people in her life he'd take more from her." Bernadette's face flushed with anger. "I'd like to get my hands on him. Threatening a girl like that. I'd like to see how he does next to someone his own size."

Wade's heart warmed at the sight of the ferocious love she had for this teen whom she'd only known for a short period of time. "You're going to make a good mom."

She scowled. "What on earth are you talking about?"

"Nothing." Without thinking, he leaned over and placed a kiss on her cheek. Glancing toward the sink, he found two sets of eyes watching them. "See ya later." He strode to the door but stopped, looking over his shoulder. "Darlene?"

"Yes?" She answered without looking up as she wiped the inside of a bowl with the dishtowel.

"Would you mind taking Bernadette to get her car? I need to follow up on a lead, and I don't know when I can get back."

"No problem. Don't give it a second thought. I'll make sure she gets to her truck." Darlene slid the bowl on top of the stack in the open cabinet.

"I'll see you later, Leanne." Wade nodded.

"Fine." She shrugged, but when she met his gaze, he spotted the fear in her eyes. He needed to get to Artie Burton soon, or Leanne would run, and this time who knew where she'd end up.

~

Winston Humphrey looked much younger than Wade had expected. Early forties at best. Yet it didn't take Wade long to recognize how efficient the man was at his job. He kept his small office neat and tidy, nothing out of place. Even his desk, which sat facing the wall, lacked the usual piles of papers, which for Wade was the bane of his existence. He'd never figured there'd be so much paperwork attached to being a sheriff.

After explaining his interest in Artie Burton, Wade had a couple of questions for the postmaster. He had a theory about the robberies, and it all hinged on the fact Artie worked for the post office.

"Okay, if a person wants to put his mail on hold—let's say for a week or two while he's on vacation—how would that work?" Wade sat in the chair next to the postmaster, both men facing the computer on the desk.

Winston tapped the computer keys and pulled up a form. "There are two ways for a person to do that. You can go online and fill out this form with all the information, then the form is routed to us here. Then, I print it out and give it to the carrier." Winston opened a side drawer in the wooden desk and pulled out a yellow card, handing it to Wade. "Or the customer can fill out one of these yellow forms and turn it in to the clerk who will then give it to the carrier."

"So, each carrier is responsible for holding the mail for the people on their route. Is that right?" Wade scowled and studied the yellow card.

"Yes. Each carrier has a station called a mail case where they sort the mail for their route, and each address has a cubby."

"Can I see them?" Wade asked.

Winston shrugged. "Sure, follow me." He led the way further back into the post office. Across the side wall stood several U-shaped stations, each one labeled with a route number and a mail carrier's name. Wade stepped into one of the cramped stations.

"This is what is called a mail case. As you can see, there is one for each route. The carrier sorts his mail here before going out on the streets." Winston pointed to a yellow stick lying in one of the cubbies. "That yellow stick indicates the mail is on hold for that address. We have several different colored sticks. Each one means something different. Like red is for a vacant address." He picked up a blue stick. "Or blue which means to forward the mail." He laid the stick back on the metal desk.

Stepping back out, Wade surveyed the layout of the mail cases. He noticed a yellow card taped to the side of a blue tub on the floor of one of the units. "What's that?"

"Most carriers, when they have a hold, will assign that address a tub. If the occupants are gone any longer than a few days, it starts to pile up and won't fit in the cubby."

"I see." Wade shook his head and frowned. "So basically, anyone who works here could find out who had their mail on hold anywhere in Reseda County." Wade grumped. "Isn't there a better way to do this? Something a little more secure?"

"I hadn't really given it much thought. This is just how it's done." Winston crossed his arms. Tilting his head, he studied the different U-shaped areas. "I suppose if you had the mind to break into a house or two, this would be one way of finding out who wasn't at home."

Wade nodded toward the tub with the yellow form attached. "What happens to the yellow cards after the mail carriers are done with them?" With security so slack, he wouldn't be surprised if they just threw the cards in the trash with all that personal information on them.

"Once they're no longer needed, they're supposed to be shredded. We have a machine located outside of my office."

The radio on Wade's utility belt squawked to life. "Excuse me, I need to take this." He pulled the radio from his belt and pressed the button on the side as he took a few steps out of the postmaster's hearing.

"This is Thibodeaux. Go ahead." He released the button and waited.

Winston caught his attention and pointed toward his office.

Wade nodded.

"Sheriff, we've found an abandoned mail truck just north of Harry's Hardware. We're having it towed to the impound yard," Penny said.

"Excellent. Send a car over to Artie Burton's house and sit on it. If he shows, I want him taken into custody."

"Roger that."

"And tell Donnie and Deputy Perez to meet me at the office in thirty minutes. I think I know how the robbers are getting their information. If I'm right, then we may be able to blow this whole thing wide-open today."

"I'll tell Donnie, but Regan is off duty."

"Well, call her in, and anyone else who's out of pocket. Now that we know about Artie, the others in the ring will be scurrying into their rat holes. We'll need to find them before they can leave town."

Chapter Nineteen

Bernadette glanced over at the teen sitting in the passenger seat of her red Ford truck. She could only imagine how frightened Leanne must be, knowing the man who threatened her and her foster family was on the loose and had found her. What a shock to have seen him chatting with Harry in the store.

Leanne sighed and hugged her middle even with the seatbelt snuggly snapped in place.

Biting her lip, Bernadette searched for something to say to comfort her. It had broken her heart the way Leanne had clung to her mom, Darlene, when she'd dropped them off at Bernadette's vehicle outside the store. At that moment, Leanne resembled a frightened little girl more than the ferocious teen she'd first met in the sheriff's office two weeks ago.

Bernadette batted away all the questions and concerns flooding her mind and concentrated on Leanne. *What would be a safe topic of conversation? Something that would feel normal.*

"So, what do you think about having tacos tonight for dinner? I can stop by the store and pick up some ground beef. I have guacamole."

Leanne shrugged and kept her gaze pinned to the

landscape outside the passenger side window.

"Or we could order pizza. With pineapple and Canadian bacon. What do you think?" Bernadette worked at keeping her tone upbeat.

"I don't care." Leanne's voice sounded flat, as if all the fight had gone out of her.

Bernadette focused on the winding road in front of her. They neared the bridge that crossed a section of the Sine River which led back to downtown Orange Blossom.

Glancing in her rearview mirror, she noticed a blue pickup gaining on her. The truck was the only other vehicle on the road. She tapped her brakes. *Surely, the idiot would slow down.* But he didn't. Instead, he hugged her bumper.

"I can't believe this jerk," she murmured and pressed harder on the gas pedal, hoping to make it across the bridge, so she could slow down and let the guy pass. Her speedometer registered higher than she realized. Bernadette glanced at Leanne to double-check that she had indeed put on her seatbelt. Panic lurched through her. The guy in the pickup matched her speed.

Leanne turned in her seat as the truck behind them moved even closer. "They've got to be doing eighty." She glanced toward Bernadette. "Do you think we should slow down and let them pass?"

"They have plenty of room to pass. I'm just going to zip across the bridge and then pull over. He can have the road if he wants it that bad." Bernadette gripped the steering wheel under white knuckles. "And you can bet this month's rent I'm going to file a complaint with my local sheriff."

Leanne whipped around to face the windshield and

gripped the grab handle above her seat as the truck crossed onto the bridge with a loud clunk. "I don't think they're going to slow down."

Bernadette glanced in the left-side mirror. The truck veered into the other lane to pass. She lifted her foot from the accelerator but kept her eyes on the blue truck.

Then without warning, the guy in the blue truck gunned it.

"They're going to hit us," Leanne screamed, still holding tight to the grab handle.

"Not if I can help it." Bernadette accelerated.

The blue pickup rammed into the left side of her truck, pushing her Ford into the railing, and flinging them both forward. Bernadette wrestled to keep the steering wheel steady, while the metal of her side fender screeched against the barrier, sending goosebumps down her arms. The other vehicle jerked back into the other lane.

Yanking the steering wheel to the left, Bernadette pulled away from the railing. But before she caught her breath, the blue truck accelerated, ramming into them. The crunch of metal on metal screeched in Bernadette's ears. She stomped the brakes willing the railing of the bridge to hold.

They fell, engine first. Bernadette braced for the impact. "Hold on."

The last thing Bernadette saw before the airbags deployed was the terror on Leanne's face. Then came the splash of water as the truck hammered the surface of the river and the cracking of glass. Water rushed into the cab.

She beat back the deflated airbag to check on

Leanne. The girl's body lay still with her shoulders slumped forward and her face planted in the white bag, the passenger side door pinned her in place. Bernadette pulled the teen's head back making sure the girl could breathe before she tried to release her own seatbelt.

The shifting of the weight of the truck jostled her as she fought to release the belt. Cold water rushed in around her legs as the vehicle dropped lower into the river.

She had to get out. She had to save Leanne.

Ignoring her racing heart, she pushed the button on the seatbelt, and this time the clasp gave way. Fumbling over the console between the two seats, Bernadette shook Leanne. "Come on, sweetie. We need to move." No response.

The river rose in the cab around them. Bernadette didn't have much time. She dug by Leanne's hip and found the buckle. The water had risen to Leanne's waist, making it hard for Bernadette to see what she was doing. She felt for the big button on the latch and pressed, but nothing happened. She yanked on the belt as she pushed, but again nothing. The damage to the door had been too severe. Leanne's seatbelt tied her in place.

With Bernadette's movement, the truck tilted. And though Leanne's side rose a bit, Bernadette's sank deeper. Cold water swirled into the cab. Her heart thundered. *What to do? What to ...?*

She remembered her knife. The one her dad had given her on her sixteenth birthday. The one he'd won at the rodeo. Searching below the water line, she lifted her purse that dangled from the door handle. She dragged her hand across the bottom of the bag and stopped the moment her fingers touched the hard metal.

Two slashes and Leanne was free but still unconscious. Now, Bernadette had to fight to keep Leanne's head above water and find a way out of the vehicle.

The truck groaned as it dropped another foot in the water. *Lord, if ever I needed a miracle, it'd be now.*

Chapter Twenty

When he arrived at the office, Perez and Adams were waiting for him in the conference room. Wade dropped into one of the leather chairs that ringed the dark mahogany table. Deputy Donnie Adams and Deputy Regan Perez sat in two of the other chairs, facing him. He'd finished with the postmaster and let him know before he left, they had found Artie Burton's mail truck abandoned not far from Harry's Hardware Store. He caught the deputies up on what he'd learned from his trip to see Winston Humphrey.

"Basically, anyone who works at the post office knows who is on vacation." Regan shook her head. "You'd think there'd be more security or something." She curled her lips.

"Yeah, with them being part of the federal government and all." Donnie smirked and folded his hands across his middle. "Now, we know how Artie got the addresses for the burglaries."

"Why would someone who'd logged more than twenty years with the post office just suddenly decide to start robbing people? There has to be a reason." Regan placed her forearms on the dark wood table and drummed her fingers against the hard surface.

"That's why I want you to investigate his finances. He's doing this for some reason." Wade scowled.

Regan's fingers stilled. "It's usually gambling or some kind of debt. Maybe he got in with the wrong people, and this is his way of paying them off."

"Let's hope it's something like that for his sake. Maybe the judge would go a little easier on him if he'd been coerced into breaking the law, since his record is clean otherwise," Deputy Adams said.

"What else do we know about him?"

Donnie straightened in his chair and reached for the file folder on the table. "Burton's sixty-two. Started working at the post office in his thirties as a career change. He had been working in construction up until then. Was married for about eight years but divorced. His only living relatives are a daughter and granddaughter who live in Georgia."

"So, no connections here." Wade frowned. "That means he could be halfway to Timbuktu."

"I've been thinking about that, Boss. I don't think he's going to leave the area before they liquidate all the stolen goods. We've been keeping our ears open, and since the first few robberies, we haven't heard of them trying to pawn any of the items."

"Not since we almost caught them when Johnson from the Stop and Swap gave us a heads-up he'd been contacted." Regan said.

"Right. And I haven't heard anything since. Not from legit shops or from the more questionable sources. It's been quiet." Donnie rubbed the back of his neck.

"They've got to have the stuff stashed somewhere. We didn't find anything in Artie's residence when we searched it this afternoon." Regan frowned, shaking her head.

"Where are we on finding him?"

"Deputy Sanchez is watching his house, and we've stationed unmarked cars at each end of his block. If he goes back there, we'll nab him. Plus, I've notified the other agencies in the area and sent over his picture from the Department of Motor Vehicles."

Wade stroked his cheek. "He's not going back to his house, and if the goods aren't there, then the perps probably have a storage unit somewhere to stash them until they can find a buyer."

"I'll start compiling a list of storage units in Reseda County." Regan stood pushing the chair out of her way.

"Good. And ask Hilda to order some Chinese takeout for us before she heads home for the evening. It's going to be a long night." Wade ran his hand down his face. "Donnie, I want you take a hard look at Artie Burton's finances for me. Let me know what you find."

"Sure thing, Boss." Donnie slapped the file folder closed and pushed his chair back.

The door to the conference room flew open and Penny Martin, the afternoon dispatcher, stepped into the doorway. "Charlie Giles just called." Her voice was breathy, as if she'd been running.

Wade turned in his seat to face her. "So, what's he complaining about now? Did Bernadette fly by his house again?"

"Yes," the dispatcher panted, fighting to catch her breath. "But this time she was being chased in the direction of Milton Bridge." Her eyes grew wide. "By a blue truck. Charlie says they were going close to eighty-five miles an hour when they passed his place."

"And how would he know that?" Donnie asked.

"He has a radar gun." Penny pressed her lips together.

"Why that nosy old fart." Wade stood, tamping down the anger threatening to flare. Charlie Giles would have to wait. Grabbing his sheriff's hat off the table, he marched past Penny. "Do we have anybody close to Milton Bridge?"

She followed, doing double time to keep up with his long strides. "I think Deputy Henderson is the closest one. Everybody's spread all over, looking for Artie Burton."

"Get Henderson out there now. Tell him if they're following Bernadette, they might be linked to the burglaries. Approach with caution."

~

Seven minutes later, Wade pulled onto Milton Bridge, making record time, arriving before Henderson. He slowed when he spotted the railing along the right side of the bridge. Pulling to the side, he parked and walked to the edge. The railing wore scratches and dents. He touched the marks trying to remember if there had been a recent accident out this way.

As he neared the middle of the bridge, he spotted a gaping hole in the metal barrier. Running to it, he saw the end of a red Ford pickup sticking out of the water. The tag read H-O-M-E-4-U.

His heart plummeted to his stomach. No, this can't be happening. His mind spun. Throwing off his shoes, he grabbed his flashlight from his utility belt before unbuckling it and letting it slide to the ground as he made his way to the edge of the opening. Without hesitation, he plunged into the water, praying with every fiber of his being he wasn't too late.

Pulling hard with each stroke, he neared the truck. Gulping in air, he dove down several feet to the windshield. Cracked. Maybe this could work in his favor.

He turned on his flashlight and peered into the cab of the truck. Through the murky water, he made out two figures. *Oh no, Leanne was with her*. Bernadette held Leanne's head above the water line in a pocket of air that had formed as the truck had submerged. She turned toward him when she saw the light and hit the windshield with her free hand. Panic-stricken. The water touched her shoulders, and the room between the roof of the truck and the water line was shrinking. Wade didn't have much time.

Pushing to the surface, he drew in a breath and dove back into the frigid water. The instant he broke the windshield, the water would rush in, stealing their last remaining air.

Reaching the truck, he beat the heel of the flashlight against the cracked glass of the windshield. Once, twice, he swung the heavy flashlight, but the density of the water slowed the motion, making the impact minimal. Finally, instead of pulling his arm all the way back, he made a quick, sharp blow. The windshield gave way.

Just as he predicted, the water rushed in, filling the cab to the ceiling.

Bernadette pushed through the opening, fighting to bring Leanne with her, but she couldn't pull her loose. Grabbing Bernadette, Wade pushed her toward the surface.

Holding onto the edge of the truck, Wade propelled himself into the cab. He shined the flashlight in

Leanne's direction. *Trapped.*

Using her shoulders, he moved her toward him, twisting her body and loosening her hip that had been pinned. Free at last, he wrapped his arms around Leanne and pulled her through the windshield. Pushing off the hood of the truck, he rocketed upward, sending the truck sinking deeper into the river's water.

Breaking the surface, Wade placed Leanne's head on his shoulder and prayed the girl was still alive. Over his shoulder, he caught sight of Bernadette struggling to make it to the closest shore. She slapped at the water and then went under. His heart raced as he saw her appear, grab a breath, and then disappear again. He didn't want to have to choose, but he couldn't save both.

In the distance, a sweet sound met his ears. The blaring wail of a siren preceded the sight of the squad car making its way down a trail running parallel to the riverbank. Pulling with all his might, he reached the shore as Deputy Henderson reached the water's edge. Running into the water, Henderson took Leanne from him.

Without a second thought, Wade whirled around and headed for the last spot he'd seen Bernadette.

The water moved in front of him as her body popped above the surface. He raced to her with each stroke. Wrapping his arms around her middle and turning her onto her back, he rested her head against his shoulder. "Stay with me, Bernie. Just stay with me."

His arms ached as he pulled with his right arm and kept his grip tight around Bernadette's waist. The shore seemed miles away, though it lay only a few feet in the distance. Fighting the water and the fear gripping his heart, he inched his way to the sandy ground that surrounded the Sine River.

Dragging Bernadette from the water, he laid her on the sand. With one quick movement, he used her shoulders to turn her to her side to the recovery position, letting gravity pull the water from her mouth and throat.

Once the airway was clear, he laid her flat again. Tilting her head back and lifting her chin, he pinched her nose and sent a quick puff into her lungs. "One Mississippi, two Mississippi, three Mississippi," Wade counted off the five seconds between puffs before he blew into her lungs again, making sure her chest rose with his breath.

Then he touched her neck to feel for a pulse before starting compressions. A faint thump met his inquiring hand. *Thank you, Lord.*

Moving her head back again, he pushed more air into her lungs, counting off the seconds and repeating the process. Then he rolled her to her side. More water tumbled from her mouth.

Glancing over, Wade discovered Leanne was awake. Henderson knelt beside her, talking to her as she lay groaning on the soft sand with her arms across her middle. Gratitude flooded him as he directed his focus back to Bernadette. The teen would be okay.

"I've radioed for an ambulance." Henderson stood from his kneeling position next to Leanne. "I'm going to the squad car to get the emergency kit. She's got a head injury. Probably from where the airbag deployed." He left without waiting for Wade's answer.

Wade leaned over Bernadette, pinched her nose, and administered another round of quick puffs, counting off the time in between the life-giving breaths. "Come on, Bernie." Wade gritted his teeth. *Lord, I can't lose her now.* He'd waited his whole life for her.

Leaning his ear toward her mouth and nose, he listened and felt for a breath. Then he touched her neck again to confirm there was still a heartbeat. Yes, faint but present.

This time when Wade pushed air into her lungs, Bernadette gasped, her lungs taking over. Inhaling, she coughed and rolled to her side as more water spewed from her lungs.

Coughing, she sat up. "Wade, I ... I ..." Tears rolled down her cheeks as a sob choked off her words.

He grabbed her shoulders and pulled her into his arms as they settled on the soft sand. Daylight had rolled into twilight, and soon the darkness of the July night would descend on this corner of Reseda County. Wade didn't care. He'd sit right here in this spot and hold Bernadette for as long as she let him. "Bernie, you gave me such a scare. There for a minute, I thought I'd lost you. Shoot, woman, I just found you." He nestled his chin on the top of her head, letting her lean her weight against him.

"I've never been so terrified in my whole life."

"Not even when your horse ran away with you at Silver Spur ranch?"

Lifting her head, she looked deep into his eyes, peering through him, touching his soul. "You've saved me again."

"I'll save you every time, Bernie. If you give me the chance." Wade caressed her cheek with his knuckles, then tucked a matted strand of her damp auburn hair behind her ear.

Without warning, Leanne raced up behind them and crumpled beside them in the sand as she snaked her arms around Bernadette's neck. Wade rose, making room for the teen. Henderson had bandaged the cut on her head with gauze and tape from the emergency kit. She looked a bit like a wounded kitten.

"Leanne, are you all right?" Bernadette hugged the girl in a death grip, then held her at arm's distance to inspect her.

The sound of sirens in the distance announced the arrival of the other officers and the ambulance. "You need to let them check you out. Both of you." Wade held out his hand to Leanne. As she took it, her hands trembled. The poor kid had to be scared senseless.

Turning to Bernadette, he reached for her. She grabbed his hand and braced the other on his forearm to balance herself. Once she was on her feet, he held her by her shoulders to steady her. "They'll probably want you to go to the hospital since you weren't breathing there for a while."

The reality of his words tore through him. His thoughts filled with all the ways this could have gone wrong as he studied the woman standing before him. A need to touch her possessed him. Lifting her chin with the crook of his finger, he placed a soft, gentle kiss on her lips. They were warm while her cheeks felt cool against his skin. His chest shuddered. He wrapped his arms around her. She felt good, like she belonged right here.

Bernadette ran her arms around his waist and rested her head against his chest. Sighing, she tightened her grip before releasing him. "We'd better go to the ambulance. I don't want Leanne to be up there alone.

Will you keep her with you while I'm being checked out?"

"Of course." Wade let go of her and took a step back.

But before Bernadette moved, she rose onto her tiptoes and lifted her lips to his. Touching his cheek with her cold hand, she answered his kiss with one of her own. A kiss, that to him, tasted of hope and of a future.

Chapter Twenty-one

While the EMTs poked and prodded Bernadette and Leanne, Wade walked back to the bridge in his sock feet to retrieve his utility belt, boots, and vehicle.

A van from one of the local news stations drove past him and headed down the trail toward the other deputies. A second cameraman stood near his truck, taking footage from the bridge where Bernadette's Ford had gone through the railing. Wade had hoped to keep the event out of the press, but if Charlie Giles knew about it, then so would the rest of the county.

Wade needed to tuck Leanne and Bernadette away somewhere safe. They couldn't stay at Bernadette's house. Artie Burton and his accomplices would be looking for her to get to Leanne. He had to keep them where he could protect them. He grabbed his utility belt and flung it into the back of the SUV. Fishing his phone from the console, he dialed Dan's number.

Dan answered on the second ring. "Hey, bro, you're all over the news. They say you and Henderson are the heroes of the hour."

"Yeah, that's what I'm calling about. It's not safe for Bernadette and Leanne to go back to Bernadette's house." Wade glanced in their direction. Bernadette stood trying to escape the ambulance. "One of the robbers knows Leanne can identify him, and he saw her with Bernadette earlier today."

"That does complicate matters. Do you think the guy would be able to find her?"

"In a heartbeat. Bernadette's face is plastered all over town as an agent for Key Williams Realty."

"Oh yeah, they do believe in advertising." Dan cleared his throat. "Well, you could invite her to stay here."

"You don't think Nikki would mind? I mean with her pregnancy and all. Isn't she close to her due date? I don't want to put any undue stress on her."

"The babies aren't due for another five weeks." Dan chuckled. "Though she's ready to be done with this part."

"Then if it's okay with you, that's what I'd like to do. I need them somewhere I know they're safe until we have Artie and his two accomplices in custody." Wade furrowed his brow. "I know this is putting you guys out, but it's the best option."

"I'll let Nikki know. She'll be thrilled to have the company right now. There's no way she'd turn away one of the Bible Babes. They're thicker than the proverbial thieves."

Wade tossed the cell phone back onto the console and put the truck into gear. Maneuvering around the news vehicles that had appeared while he was on the phone, he parked as close to the ambulance as possible.

Slipping out, he propped against the truck door, hugging his middle to ward off the cool night air. His damp clothes from his plunge into the river only worked to intensify the chill prickling over him.

Goosebumps cascaded down his arms. He needed to change clothes at Silver Spur Ranch when he deposited Bernadette and Leanne safely in his sister-in-law's care.

The EMTs released Leanne with a word of caution about a concussion, but it took longer for them to give Bernadette the okay to head out. "You'll need to make sure she rests and is under observation for the next twenty-four hours." The female EMT nodded toward Leanne who leaned against one of the ambulance doors. "Neither one of them should be left on their own for a while. Do you have someone who—"

Before the EMT finished, both Bernadette and Wade answered, "Yes."

Bernadette scowled and glanced in Wade's direction. "I can go to my mom's. She'll be glad to take care of us."

Leanne perked up when she heard Bernadette mention her mother. "Yeah, Miss Darlene will know what to do."

"I don't think that will be the safest place." Wade hung his head, prepared for the argument to come. "Too many people around. The inn's too public."

Bernadette moved to the back of the ambulance, and Wade extended his hand to help her down. She took it, stepping onto the bumper and then the ground. Then released his hand. "We'll be fine," Bernadette protested, crossing her arms. "Mom can nurse us back to health."

Wade pointed in the direction of the water. "Might I remind you your truck is at the bottom of the river? And that your name and face are plastered all over Reseda County because of your profession? It would be too easy for the men looking for you to figure out where you were. Owning a B&B doesn't exactly make your parents invisible."

She shrugged. "I guess you have a point."

"I've called Dan. He's agreed for the two of you to stay with him and Nikki while I hunt for the maniac who did this to you."

"Well, it seems you've worked out all the details." Bernadette cocked her head to one side. "Except one. What about Frodo?"

Wade had forgotten about Bernadette's dog. Surely, Dan and Nikki wouldn't mind one more, hairy animal hanging about the place. After all, Niki loved all sorts of creatures. She'd even adopted a family of baby squirrels one summer, until they grew big enough to make it out in the wild, or in their case, the park. "I'm sure he'd be welcome. After all, Snowball and Blue were his parents. It'll be a nice, furry family reunion."

"Great. Another new place." Leanne huffed and kicked the dirt with the toe of her soggy, bedazzled shoe.

"Look, we don't mean to rush you," the male EMT said. "But whatever you're going to do, you need to get moving. Being out here in the night air in damp clothes isn't going to help. Plus, bantering back and forth over where to go is counterproductive to resting." He scowled. "I can put you both in the back of this ambulance and haul you to the hospital for the night." His partner swallowed a giggle.

"Fine, fine. We're going." Bernadette moved toward Wade's SUV. Wade followed her and Leanne.

Once settled in the vehicle, Wade cranked the engine and flipped on the heat. "We'll go to your house first and let you guys grab some clothes. While you do that, I'll get Frodo ready to travel."

"We could just shower and change there."

"No," Wade's voice rose, his tone stern. "It's too dangerous. We can't stay that long. You'll need to gather what you'll need for a couple of days, that's all. And then we'll have to go." He peered in the rearview mirror as they traveled across the bridge, and he met Leanne's gaze. "You'll need to stay close to the ranch house. I'll get Dan to put all the ranch hands on alert. If anyone tries to get to you, they'll spot 'em before they get anywhere near the house."

Leanne sniffled and nodded, but the muffled whimpers continued in the darkened backseat.

Bernadette glanced his way then turned to face the teen girl whose hands covered her face. "We're almost done. Hang in there. Wade will catch these guys. You've been so brave."

"My bag," Leanne blurted out.

Wade scowled, confused. "Bag. What bag?"

"My backpack with all my stuff in it. It's at the bottom of the river." The tears flowed, rolling down her thin cheeks. "My pictures of me and Mia. Everything important to me was in that bag. Now it's gone."

~

Once Bernadette and Leanne were settled at the Silver Spur ranch, Wade headed to the office to check on the progress of his deputies.

"Hilda, are you still here? I thought you'd have left for the evening hours ago." Wade walked toward her desk.

"And miss all the action." She leaned back in her chair. "Besides, I've got some calls in about Mia Hopkins. Deputy Perez went to her location to check on her.”

“Sounds good. Where is Deputy Adams?”

“In the interview room with Artie Burton.” Hilda stood and handed him a file folder. “And there’s Chinese takeout in the break room.”

“Thanks.” Wade took the folder and headed to the back part of the building where the interview rooms were located. Deputy Adams stood in the hallway. “Where did you find him?”

“Exactly where you thought he’d be. At a storage unit. Hilda made some calls for us to see if anyone remembered a man fitting Artie’s description. We had a few maybes, so Deputy Perez and I hit those first. Perez grabbed a better photo of Artie from the DMV database.” Deputy Adams smirked. “Sure enough, we found him at One Stop Storage, up to his eyeballs in stolen goods.”

“Great work. What about his partners?”

“They weren’t there, and the lady working behind the desk said no one else had been there this afternoon. I showed her the pictures from the doorbell camera, but she didn’t recognize either of the other two men.”

“Interesting.” Wade scowled. “Have you run those photos through the state database to see if we can get a hit on them?”

“Perez is doing that now.” Deputy Adams frowned. “But I don’t hold out much hope. Those photos are blurry, and the angles don’t help.”

“True.” Wade hooked his thumb on his utility belt. “Have you questioned him?”

“I was just about to give it another shot. So far, he’s been resistant. Claims the items in the storage unit are his. Oh, and he’s going to sue the department for wrongful arrest. I've got a few of the other deputies running down the serial numbers."

"Good. The sooner we have him dead to rights, the sooner we can convince him to tell us about the others involved in the ring." Specifically, the two who were responsible for hurting Leanne and Bernadette. Wade's anger stirred. But there would be time for that. Wade nodded toward the door. "You mind if I join you?"

"Be my guest." Deputy Adams placed his hand on the doorknob.

"Wait a minute." Wade flipped open the file and scanned the information. "I see he has a daughter and a granddaughter."

"That's right." The deputy nodded.

"Good. That might come in handy. If you don't mind, can you follow my lead?" Wade grinned, closing the file. "Let's see if we can't make him sweat a little."

Deputy Adams shot him a lopsided grin, then opened the door and let Wade enter first.

Artie Burton sat with his back to the wall, facing a two-way mirror. As Wade pulled out one of the two chairs on the opposite side of the table, the metal feet screeched across the black and white tile.

Deputy Adams cut his eyes toward Wade but didn't comment. Instead, he slipped into the seat closest to the door.

Settling in, Wade studied Artie who wiped his hand across his forehead. His eyes darted from the deputy to the sheriff. The sixty-something, gray-haired gentleman looked more like the grampa he was than a professional thief.

Wade tossed the file folder onto the table, smiled at the culprit seated in front of him, and waited, never taking his eyes off him.

Deputy Adams did the same, keeping his eyes fixed on the suspect.

Artie scooted back in his seat. He squirmed and shifted his shoulders.

Wade opened the file and flipped a few pages. Studying the contents, he glanced up at Artie and nodded.

Crossing his arms, Artie huffed and cocked his head to the right.

Good, he's trying to figure out his next lie. Wade's FBI training in interrogation taught him people tend to look to the right when they're engaging their imagination. *This ought to be fun.*

After a few more seconds of silence, Artie leaned forward and clasped his hands together on the table. "What are you going to do, bore a confession out of me? It's like I told your deputy here. You've got the wrong man."

"What do you want to confess? That you're a thief, or that you tried to kill two people today?"

Artie straightened. The color drained from his complexion. "Wait a minute. I didn't try to kill anyone." He shook his head. "I'm not a killer. No way."

"Well, someone ran Leanne Hopkins and Bernadette Stewart off the Milton Bridge this afternoon. They nearly drowned." Wade moved forward, his chest hovering over the table, his jaw tight. "And I aim to find out who rammed them through the barrier. So, if you don't want to find out how good cop, bad cop works—" Wade slammed his fist against the tabletop. "You'll give me the names of your partners."

"I can't. If … if he finds out I said anything, I'll be

the one swimming at the bottom of the river."

"Who? Who has you so afraid?" Deputy Adams stood, his fists planted in front of him on the table, his face inches from Artie's.

"Let me guess. Salvador Cervantes," Wade offered.

Artie flinched at the sound of the name as if it were a loud banging in his ears.

"I should've known." Deputy Adams groaned, straightening. "Anything more than a stolen bike and Sal Cervantes has his hands all over it."

"Who are the other two?" Wade pressed. "I have to know who they are."

"I can't say. He'll kill me. You know I'm telling you the truth." Artie ran his hand down his face. Fear flickered in his eyes.

"Did they share the storage unit with you? Or was that your take of the stolen goods?" Wade's voice rose. "Tell me. Was that all of it, or was that your share?"

Artie hung his head. "It was my share."

Deputy Adams smirked and glanced toward Wade.

"Deputy, let the record reflect Artie Burton has confessed to being in possession of stolen goods, and that the storage unit was in fact rented by him."

"My pleasure, Sheriff Thibodeaux." His words rang with respect.

"Now, if you give me those names, I'll speak to the DA and see if we can get your sentence reduced. But if you don't tell me who you're working with, I'm going to make sure you are charged not only with breaking and entering, possession of stolen goods, and destruction of private property, but also, with two counts of attempted murder."

Artie pressed his lips together and ran his hand

across the back of his neck. "I didn't sign up for this. I was only supposed to supply the information about who was out of town. To pay off a gambling debt to my bookie. But then, once I gave them the information, they blackmailed me. Threatened to get me fired or worse." He wrung his hands.

Wade could see the internal struggle on Artie's face. So, he played the only ace he held. He picked up the manila folder sitting in front of him. "If you go down for attempted murder, you won't get out. You'll spend your last years in some cinder-block cell and then you'll die in prison." Hesitating, Wade let his words sink in. "But, if you cooperate, I'll talk to the DA and press for a plea deal. Who knows? You might make parole before your granddaughter graduates from college."

Closing his eyes, Artie mumbled the names. "Lenny Greer and Carlos Diaz."

"What?" Deputy Adams bent closer to Artie. "Say their names again."

"Lenny Greer and Carlos Diaz." Artie's voice rang out, firm and clear. "That's who you're looking for. Carlos is one of Sal's men. He's more than likely the one who tried to hurt the girl and that woman. Lenny, he's another sap like me. Someone trapped by his own bad luck."

"No, Artie. You could've walked away. Told the authorities." Deputy Adams stood over him.

Artie plopped back in his chair and met the deputy's gaze, with a sullen frown. "You think so? Then you don't know these men. When they threaten your family, you do what they say." Turning to Wade, Artie face softened. "The only thing I ask is that you make sure my daughter and her family are safe. They're all I have."

"We'll put them somewhere out of reach, until I can notify the FBI. I know they'll be very interested in hearing what you have to say about Sal Cervantes." Wade stood. "If you cooperate, it might be your ticket out of this mess."

Chapter Twenty-two

Bernadette rolled her shoulders, trying to work out some of the soreness in her muscles from the accident. Though her accommodations at Silver Spur Ranch were comfortable, it wasn't home. They'd only been sequestered for two days, but she was ready to be back in her own space, living her own life. She rubbed her biceps, dreaming of a long, hot soak in her big tub.

"How are those cookies coming?" Nikki peered into the half-empty bowl of dough. "Did you eat some of that?" Glancing at the cookie sheet with the globs of dough, she scowled. "I'd better make another batch. You know everyone will want at least three cookies apiece tomorrow night."

Bernadette dipped her spoon in the cookie dough and shifted her weight. Everything on her body ached. "Yes," she agreed. "We do like our sweets."

"'Good food and the Good Book.' That's my motto." Nikki grabbed a second glass bowl and pulled out the flour, sugar, and salt. "So, you and Wade—" She bobbed her head as she stirred the dough. Setting the spoon on the pan, she poured in half the bag of chocolate chips.

Bernadette shrugged. "Me and Wade, what?"

"You know. Are dating." She hustled over to the oven to turn off the timer. Pulling the baking sheet from the oven, she deposited it onto the hotplates lining the counter near the stove.

Rolling her eyes, Bernadette leaned against the counter. She didn't want to discuss Wade right now. Her emotions couldn't be trusted. Her body felt too tired and her mind too overwhelmed. Sure, he'd saved her life as well as Leanne's, but the strong pull she felt for him had started long before the break-ins or Leanne's appearance in her life. Her feelings for him went back to their weekly chats about the speed limit and were rooted in those summer days as a teen when they'd worked together.

Nikki glanced her way. "Look, I don't mean to tease you."

"Yes, you do." Bernadette couldn't smother the grin tugging at the corners of her mouth.

"Okay, I do. But I'm also very happy for the two of you. Wade is a great guy. And you, well, you held out for someone special." Nikki removed the oven mitts and flopped them onto the counter. "You waited until the right one came along." Picking up the spoon, she stirred the chocolate chips into the dough.

"Nikki, it's not like we're serious or anything. It's all still new. Because of circumstances, we've been thrown together. First, the hacking of the lockboxes and now, Leanne and her welfare." The memory of waking up by the river to Wade hovering over her raced through her mind. She recalled the relief in his eyes, and the way he'd scooped her into his arms. She'd clung to him. Heat rose to her cheeks, and she hoped Nikki wouldn't notice.

"True, it hasn't been the usual sort of relationship, but then, maybe it's the kind of relationship you needed. One with excitement and adventure." Nikki placed her hand on her stomach. "Not everyone is cut out for the humdrum life of a rancher. Look at Wade. Mr. FBI for six years and now county sheriff."

"Yeah, he's not a man to stand still, is he?" Bernadette scowled. "He does keep things interesting."

"Oh, so you admit you do like him." Nikki waggled her eyebrows. Lifting the spoon, she offered Bernadette a taste of the dough.

Bernadette ran her finger along the curve of the spoon. The sweet dough melted on her tongue and invited her to lick her lips. "Umm, that's good."

"Thank you." Nikki spooned globs of dough onto a second baking sheet. "Would you put the others on the cooling rack?"

"Sure." Bernadette grabbed a spatula from the crock holding the utensils and lifted the golden-brown cookies off the pan onto the cooling rack. Should she confide her wayward emotions to her friend? "If I were totally honest, I'd tell you I do like Wade. Maybe a bit too much. But he's not the problem."

"So, what is?" Nikki looked up from the cookie sheet, meeting her gaze.

Not wanting to say, Bernadette scrunched her face and shrugged. *Why had she even brought it up?*

"Oh, Bernie, you've got to let that go," Nikki tsked. "Peter Finch, I know for a fact is happily married."

"How do you know that?"

"Facebook." Nikki met her gaze with a sheepish grin.

"Facebook?" Bernadette frowned. "You mean you friended Peter Finch on social media? How could you?"

Nikki held her hands up, palms out. "He sent me a friend request around Thanksgiving last year, and I accepted. His wife is a second-grade teacher at a private school, and he's working for some bank as an assistant manager."

"Great. So, he's got his life all together. Perfect." Bernadette huffed and turned back to the cookies, not sure why this news upset her.

"That's not the point." Nikki pinned her two fists against her broad hips.

"Then what is the point?"

"That he has moved on—" Nikki raised an eyebrow. "And so should you. Quit carrying around guilt, as if you ruined the man's life or something. You didn't."

"Yes, I did." Bernadette sighed. "Well, not completely. But for a while, I wrecked it."

"But that part is over. He's happy. You don't have to blame yourself for all the failed relationships in your past." Nikki lifted the empty bowl and placed it into the sink, turning on the tap to fill it with water.

Bernadette grabbed the cookie sheet and pushed it into the oven before setting the timer. Nikki was right. She didn't have to blame herself, but who else should she blame?

"All I'm saying is you need to forgive yourself." Nikki maneuvered her body to lean against the counter, facing Bernadette. "We all make mistakes along the way. Some of us in our dating lives, others of us with our parents or siblings. But any way you slice it, relationships are messy. You need to forgive yourself."

Her eyes softened. "I know God has."

"You think so?"

"According to His Word, if you've asked for forgiveness, then you're forgiven." Nikki moved forward and placed a hand on Bernadette's shoulder. "You've been praying for God's will all along. Maybe, backing out of the wedding with Peter was God's will. Have you ever considered that?"

"The thought has crossed my mind."

"Good." Nikki pulled Bernadette in for a bear hug but only managed a tight squeeze around her shoulders, Nikki's protruding belly getting in the way. Pushing herself back, she looked down at the bulge. "I will be so glad when these two arrive. Between the swollen ankles, the backache, and the false labor pains, I feel more like a baby factory than a person."

Looking down at Nikki's ankles, Bernadette nodded toward the table. "Maybe we should rest a minute. You sit down, and I'll pour us a glass of iced tea."

"Okay, but don't let me burn this last batch of cookies."

"No worries, I set the timer." Bernadette walked to the refrigerator and pulled out the pitcher of tea as Nikki slid into one of the chairs at the breakfast table, letting out a long sigh. "So, let's say that I am interested in Wade. And let's say maybe we shared a humdinger of a kiss or two at the fireworks display." Bernadette reached above her and pulled down two glasses from the cabinet.

"You what?" Nikki's voice rose. "You've been holding out on me, keeping a secret like that for a whole week?"

Bernadette glanced over her shoulder as she put the tea back into the refrigerator. Nikki sat with wide eyes watching her. "Not holding out. Just not sure what to do with all these emotions floating around willy-nilly." She handed one of the glasses to Nikki and sat in the seat across from her, hugging her glass between her hands.

"Well, what do you want to do with them? Do you care for him?"

"Honestly, I could see us together, but we've been such good friends for so long—I don't want to mess anything up." A flood of indecision washed over her. Her heart wanted to race full tilt into a relationship with Wade, but her head kept setting up roadblocks.

"It sounds to me like you've already moved past friendship into something more. Maybe being friends first will help the relationship thrive." Nikki sipped her tea. "Have you considered that?"

"It's possible being friends first might be the glue that my other relationships were missing, but that's a big risk to take. Once you start dating someone, it's hard to go back to being only friends if it doesn't work out."

"True, but according to Wade, you're already dating." Nikki shifted in her seat and slipped off her shoes, resting her feet in the chair near her.

"What do you mean?"

"The birthday party, the Flying Pig, the Fourth of July fireworks." Nikki ticked them off one by one on her fingers. "Not to mention all the house hunting the two of you have been doing. You're practically joined at the hip."

"Point taken. We've been dating." Bernadette

scowled not sure she liked this new discovery. Seemed everyone knew they were an item except her.

"So, tell me," Nikki's eyes sparkled, and a slight grin formed on her lips. "Was he a good kisser?"

Bernadette tucked her chin and let the memory of that evening fill her heart.

"Oh, I see," Nikki said.

Grinning, she couldn't resist the need to share. "Let's put it this way, Spike's fireworks weren't the only thing that night that took my breath away."

The two women broke out into a fit of giggles. "Good for you."

Bernadette's heart felt lighter than it had in days. Nikki was right. She'd already made her decision about Wade. Her heart just hadn't explained it to her brain.

"What's going on in here?" Dan stepped across the threshold and held the door open, waiting for Leanne to enter with Frodo behind her.

"Bernadette, you should've seen the baby goats. There's one, Dan feeds with a bottle because its mom won't have anything to do with it." Leanne's eyes widened, and her words tumbled out. "So, he let me feed her supper."

After shutting the door, Dan flopped into one of the empty chairs around the table. "She's a natural. Took to the animals like a duck to water."

Leanne made a face. "Don't say that. Not after what happened."

"Sorry." Dan glanced at his wife. "Are we interrupting anything?"

Nikki snuck a peek at Bernadette. "No, just girl talk."

"That leaves me out." Dan removed his hat and

fanned his face with it. "I forget how hot July can get in south Texas, even this late in the day."

Leaning forward, Nikki grimaced.

Dan straightened, dropped his hat on the table, and reached for Nikki. "Are you all right?"

"Braxton Hicks. They've been going on all day. It'll pass." Nikki focused her gaze on the glass in front of her and slowed her breathing. After a moment, her face relaxed. "There, see? All better."

"I don't like this. How far apart are they?" Bernadette asked.

"Several minutes, but it's been happening on and off like this for about a week, and they dissipate." Nikki patted Dan's hand on her shoulder. "Don't fret. I'm fine."

Bernadette touched her friend's arm. "Why don't you go up to bed and stretch out. Leanne and I can finish up the snacks for tomorrow night's meeting, and we'll clean up the kitchen." Glancing at Leanne, Bernadette caught her biting into a cookie. "Hey, those are for the Bible Babes."

"Sorry," Leanne mumbled around a mouthful of cookie. She stuffed the last bite into her mouth and licked her fingers.

"I think I will go up to bed." Nikki rose from her chair, and Dan stood to help her.

"Come on, hon. I'll tuck you in." He took her elbow, and Nikki sagged against him. Stopping at the end of the counter, he turned to Bernadette. "Would you leave the lamp on in the living room for Wade, and be sure to lock the doors? Both back and front before you turn in." Dan took another step. "And let Blue and Snowball out of the mudroom before you go upstairs.

We usually leave them in there, but tonight it'd be wiser to let them patrol the lower floor. Our built-in security guards—Never know what they might scare away."

Bernadette understood the implications of Dan's request, even though he'd tried to make light of it. All the precautions and extra security on the ranch revolved around her and Leanne. Artie's accomplices were still at large.

"Sure, I can do that." The timer on the oven buzzed, startling her. She'd forgotten all about the second batch of cookies. Popping up, she rushed to the oven. "Oven mitts, oven mitts," she mumbled.

Leanne grabbed the mitts off the counter and tossed them to Bernadette.

"Thanks." Bernadette donned the mitts and pulled the cookie sheet from the oven, placing it on the hot pads by the stove.

"No problem." Leanne snagged another cookie from the platter, then moved to the sink. "I'll start on the dishes."

"Oh, that'll be a big help." Bernadette placed the cookies on the cooling rack, wondering about the time. She half expected Wade to be home before now. He'd been working around the clock since the bridge incident. Eventually, he'd have to rest. The clock on the microwave read ten-thirty. "After you're done with those, head on up and get ready for bed."

"Okay. I'm tired anyway. Nearly drowning takes a while to get over. My legs are still sore." Leanne chuckled, but Bernadette wasn't ready to joke about what had happened. Nearly losing Leanne had highlighted for her the importance of each life. She'd grown fond of the teen in the short time they'd been together. With the threat still out there, she wasn't about to lower her guard.

"Hey, Bernadette, can Frodo sleep with me tonight? Do you think Dan and Nikki would mind?"

She pondered the request for a moment. "Go ahead, I don't think they'll mind, and it might be for the best."

After putting the cooled cookies into a plastic container, Bernadette checked both the front and back doors. Locked.

Bernadette moved to the mudroom to release Blue and Snowball but stopped. Though her body was tight and stiff and longed for a good night's sleep, her mind roared with thoughts of Wade, babies, and thieves in the night. No way she'd fall asleep this hyped-up.

Instead, she grabbed a cookie from the container and headed to the couch. Plopping into the seat with the ottoman in front of it, she nestled into the soft cushions. She closed her eyes and let the quiet of the house soothe her raw nerves. Inhaling, she breathed in the blessed aroma of chocolate. Without opening her eyes, she took a bite. The sweet flavors of sugar and chocolate mixed, coating her tongue.

Laying the cookie on a coaster, she spotted a cozy mystery on the end table. Intrigued by the cover, Bernadette opened the book to the first page.

The scream echoed throughout the house. Dianne Blancher heard the footsteps on the stairs. Where do you hide when death is chasing you?

Hooked, Bernadette stretched out her legs, pulled the blanket from the back of the couch, and settled in to find out who had screamed and how Dianne Blancher fit into the story. Sure, Wade would be home any minute.

Chapter Twenty-three

Wade pulled his old truck into the driveway at Silver Spur ranch. He'd left his SUV for one of the deputies to use. They needed everyone on duty out looking for Lenny Greer and Carlos Diaz. A twinge of guilt plagued him for leaving in the middle of the search, but he'd be no good to anyone if he pushed on, running on caffeine and adrenaline. After the events of the last two days, his body ached in places he'd forgotten he had. He'd catch a few hours of shut eye and be back to work by four the next morning.

Besides, he'd left word if they came across anything, they were to contact him, even if it seemed insignificant. Walking to the door, he checked the time on his cell phone. Midnight. That explained why the lower levels of the house were dark. He grinned when he spotted the lone glow of a lamp shining through the living room window. Nikki's doing. She always left a light on for him when he worked late. He'd miss those hints of family when he moved out.

Shutting the front door, he relocked the knob and threw the bolt back into place before stepping into the living room to turn off the lamp. A low moan drifted from the couch as his fingers grasped the switch at the base. Turning, he discovered Bernadette asleep with a book on her chest.

Not wanting to wake her, he debated about leaving her to stir on her own. But then a picture of her lying on the shore of the river flashed into his mind. He needed her upstairs, behind another set of locks. Not down here alone.

He touched her shoulder. "Bernie, it's time to wake up. You need to head upstairs. Okay?"

"Umm, five more minutes, Mom." She turned away from him, but the book in her arms caught on the back cushion.

A grin tugged at his lips. "Bernie, it's me, Wade. You need to get up, sweetheart. We need to move you to your room upstairs."

Her eyes fluttered open, but she struggled to keep them that way. "Wade. What are you doing here?" Her lashes drifted back to her cheeks, and she rested her hands on the book she'd been reading. "Come back tomorrow."

"You're at the Silver Spur, remember?" He placed his hand on the side of her face and ran his thumb along her delicate cheekbone. *Man, she looked good.* His chest tightened when she placed her hand on his.

"So tired," she mumbled.

He fought the urge to pick her up in his arms and carry her upstairs, so he could feel her next to him. *How long had he loved her?* He didn't know. It'd grown slowly over time and quickly near the end, like a flower blooming. Nothing but green leaves for months and then bam, a blossom appeared.

"Come on, Bernie. Up you go." Wade took her shoulders and pulled her to a sitting position.

"Nooo," she protested as the book dropped into her lap. "I'm comfortable here."

Wade removed the book and tossed it onto the end table. "I know but think how much nicer the bed's going to be. And you'll have a soft pillow instead of the armrest for your head."

Her eyes opened, and she gave him a wry grin. "You could sell feathers to a bird, you know that?" She straightened and stretched her arms over her head. "Okay, I'm up. What time is it?"

"A little after midnight. How long have you been asleep on the couch?"

"Not sure, I was still keyed up when Leanne and I finished cleaning the kitchen. I came in here to read for a while. Must've dozed off." She rubbed her eyes, then blinked. "I was really out, wasn't I?"

"In a big way." Wade slipped onto the cushion next to her, pushing the corner of the blanket to the side. "I hated to wake you, but it's safer if you're upstairs with people around you in case you need something. And a second set of locks can't hurt either. The next few days are all about safety for you and Leanne." Wade met her gaze. "Understand?" It wasn't a question.

"Trust me, we've got the message loud and clear."

Wade nodded and relaxed. "Are you settling in, okay?"

"You know Nikki. She's never met a stranger. She took right to Leanne. And because of Bible Babes, this feels like my second home." Bernadette rested her head against the back of the couch, tucked her feet under her, and pulled the blanket up to her shoulders. "Dan took Leanne out to the stables after dinner. She's in love with the baby goat Dan is bottle-feeding."

"She liked it, huh?" Wade's hand twitched, wanting to drape his arm around her shoulders. But then, he'd never want to leave and go to bed.

"She came inside floating on a cloud. I think she's got it bad." Bernadette pursed her lips. A tell-tale sign she had something on her mind. "So, how long do you think we'll need to stay? I do have other clients."

"Hopefully, we'll have the other two perps in custody soon. I can't imagine more than a couple of days. No more than a week." Wade met her gaze. "Why? In a rush?"

"More like in the way."

"What do you mean? You just said this felt like your second home. Trust me, Nikki and Dan like having family around. Why do you think it's been so hard for me to leave? Every time I mention moving, Nikki starts with those sad puppy dog eyes of hers and says something about family needing each other."

Bernadette laughed. "I've seen those eyes. She does make it hard to say no."

"Besides, Nikki thinks of you as family." Wade took her hand in his, giving into the need to touch her. "And Dan does too. Shoot, we all think of you as part of our clan."

"Is that what I am? Part of the Thibodeaux clan like Rod, your ranch manager or Mack, your lead hand? I'm Bernie, your realtor."

Wade rubbed his thumb across the back of her hand and swallowed the lump growing in his throat. "You must know how I feel about you."

"Maybe you'd better tell me. After this week, it's better not to leave things unsaid. You're not guaranteed you'll have a second chance to say them." Lifting her head, she rested her hand on his cheek. The warmth of her touch ran through him. "So, tell me, Wade Everette Thibodeaux, how do you feel about me?"

He put his hand over hers and drew her palm to his lips, placing a gentle kiss there before resting their hands intertwined on his knee. "Since I met you that summer in high school, I've had a crush on you. And whenever I'd come to Orange Blossom to visit Pops, I'd look for you in town, hoping to run into you. And now, all these years later, with getting to know you and spending time with you, it's only made my feelings stronger."

"It has?" Bernadette's eyes softened, and she snuggled up closer to him, laying her head on his shoulder. "You've had feelings for me that long?"

His voice came out low and rough. "Yes, I have."

"Why didn't you ever ask me out? You've been here for over a year, first campaigning and then taking the office of sheriff. Why'd you wait so long to ask me on a date?"

"Technically, you asked me out, remember?"

She straightened and met his gaze. "Yeah, that's right. I did. Were you ever going to ask me out?" Her eyebrows knitted together as her lips dipped into a frown.

"Eventually, yes. I just didn't want to start something I couldn't finish. My old job at the bureau made it hard to have any kind of lasting relationship, and I wasn't sure what kind of demands this job would hold. But now, six months into it, I think having a steady girlfriend could work." Wade loved the sassy look that spread across her face.

"Oh, you do now?" A spark of mischief flashed in

her eyes. "What about said girlfriend? Have you asked her how she feels about all this?"

"I'm asking now." Releasing her hand, he ran his finger down her jawline and captured her chin between his thumb and finger. His heart hammered in his chest. "I love you, Bernadette. I have for a long time."

"Oh, Wade." Her eyes softened, leaning forward she met him halfway. Her scent wafted around him dispelling all thoughts of the day. He only saw her, felt her lips on his, the taste of her, food for his hungry heart.

Someone cleared their throat. "Sorry to interrupt, but I wanted to let you know Leanne and Frodo are all tucked in upstairs."

Wade broke the connection and sat back against the couch. Pulling his attention from Bernie, he focused on his brother Dan who stood in the doorway. "Thanks for the update."

"No problem." Dan grinned like a cat who'd caught the mouse out of his hole.

Bernadette twisted in her seat to face Dan. "How's Nikki?"

"She's sleeping. Seems the Braxton Hicks have subsided for now. But I'll rest easier once she's seen the doctor. Now that we're five weeks out, the doc wants to see her weekly." Dan poked his hands into his pockets and looked down at his socked feet. "I'm starting to wonder if I'm ready for all this. I mean, what kind of father will I be, and having two at one time." He blew out his breath. "It's a lot."

Bernie rose from her place beside Wade, letting the blanket fall to the couch and went to Dan. Wade immediately felt her absence as the cooler air from the air conditioner swirled around him, sending a chill up his empty arms.

"You are going to be a great dad. That's what kind of dad you're going to be. No one is a perfect parent, but you and Nikki are ready for this. And the two of you will do a beautiful job." She laid her hand on his shoulder. "You've got this."

"Thanks. No wonder Nikki thinks highly of you. She said you have the gift of encouragement."

"I'm only telling you the truth." She gave him a warm smile.

"Thanks for helping tonight, finishing up the snacks for tomorrow night's meeting. Nikki won't let me help, especially in the kitchen. The minute she got into bed she deflated. She'd worn herself out."

Bernadette let her hand drop. "Leanne and I were glad to step in and do our part." She turned toward Wade. "Speaking of worn out, I think I'll head to bed."

"I'll see you tomorrow." Wade didn't miss the sparkle in her eye or the faint color of pink tinting her cheeks.

"Tomorrow." She stepped into the foyer and placed her hand on the banister of the staircase, then paused. "Dan, can you let Snowball and Blue out of the mudroom? I sat to read and didn't do it."

"Sure thing." Dan walked across the living room and plopped into the chair adjacent to the couch as Bernadette headed up the stairs. "So, are there any new developments?"

"No." Wade rubbed his hand across the back of his neck and shook his head. "We've notified all the storage companies in the area to be on the lookout for them. That is, if they even have a unit. Just because

Artie did doesn't mean the other two do. And he's not talking until his lawyer cuts a deal with the FBI. But the storage units are a place to start.

"And we've spoken with anyone close to them, family, coworkers. Plus, we've got men watching their residents." Wade put his feet up on the ottoman and rested his back against the couch. "What I don't get is why they're still hanging around. Why go after Leanne? Why not run? For some reason, they're after her."

"Well, she's a witness."

"Yes, but she only saw Artie, and he's in custody. So, why go after Leanne and Bernadette?"

"That's a good question, but until you figure it out, you're doing what you can. Keeping them safe." Dan put his feet on the ottoman and relaxed in his chair. "But for now, let's go over the instructions you want me to give to the ranch hands on how to handle any intruders. I'll update Rod tomorrow on what's happening. We need the men to stay alert until you and your team capture those scoundrels."

~

Were the dogs barking? Wade lifted his head to listen then rolled over onto his side and pulled the covers to his shoulders. He must've dreamed it.

He'd set his alarm for four, and it had been close to one when he'd finally slipped into his bed, with muscles aching and his heart reeling over what he'd said to Bernadette. But sleep had overtaken him the minute his head hit the pillow.

He moved to his back again and placed his arm beneath his head. Quick deep barks rang from somewhere downstairs. Wade pushed up onto his elbow and listened. Another round of barking, then a door closing. *That's not good.*

Throwing back the covers, he reached for a pair of jeans on the floor. He glanced at his alarm clock as he dragged the pants over his legs. Three o'clock. Taking every precaution, he left his light off and moved toward his walk-in closet.

Shutting the door behind him, he flipped on the switch. No time to lose. His heart raced pumping adrenaline through him. Fully awake, he grabbed a tee shirt and pulled it over his head before shoving his feet into his boots. Reaching up to the top shelf where he stashed his weapon, he pulled his gun from its holster and checked the magazine to make sure it was full. He tucked the gun behind his back into the waistband of his jeans. Before opening the door, he grabbed the flashlight from his utility belt and turned off the light.

With measured movements, he inched towards Leanne's bedroom to check on her. A board creaked beneath his weight as he pushed open the door. He stilled, not wanting to alert any potential intruders to his presence. Peeking into the room, he pointed the flashlight at the floor and ran it up the side of the bed to the top. Empty.

Panic gripped him, twisting his insides. How did someone get into the house without waking him? He moved to the landing to go search downstairs.

"Is everything all right?" Bernadette rubbed her eyes with the back of her hand. Her lime green robe tied snuggly around her waist made her look small and vulnerable.

"Leanne's missing. She's not in her bed." Wade kept his voice low and tried not to sound panicked.

"What?" Bernadette asked in a whisper.

"Shhh ... we don't want to let any potential intruder know we're awake. We need the element of surprise."

The dogs barked again. Both Bernadette and Wade stilled.

Wade strained to hear any other sounds. The ticking of the clock in the foyer echoed up the stairs but nothing else.

Dan poked his head out of his bedroom door. "Are the dogs barking?"

Bernadette and Wade swung his direction. "Leanne's missing," Bernadette answered. Her words filled with worry.

"Give me a minute, and I'll come with you."

"No, you stay here. There's no sense in both of us trekking around the house in the dark. Besides, Leanne's probably downstairs hunting for a snack. If I'm not back in ten minutes, then come find me."

"Us," Bernadette corrected.

"No, you're staying here. If there is someone else down there, I don't need to be worried about keeping you safe." Wade pinned her with a glare, but it didn't seem to have any effect on her.

Bernadette's shoulders stiffened, and her lips pressed into a thin line. "I'm going with you."

Aware he didn't have time to argue the point, he nodded his consent. "But you stay behind me, and if I tell you to do something, do it."

"Ten minutes," Dan said. "If you don't report back, I'll come looking for the two of you." He closed his door, leaving Wade alone with the one person he'd wish would listen to him.

Wade crept down the stairs with Bernadette holding tight to the back of his tee shirt. He stayed close to the wall as he took each stair. At the bottom, he peeked into the living room. All clear. No intruder, no Leanne.

Bernadette glanced around him. "It's empty," she whispered close to his ear. Her breath tickled and for a moment distracted him from his purpose.

Meeting her gaze, he lifted his finger to his lips to remind her to be quiet. He needed to be fully focused on the task at hand, not worried about her doing something to put herself or him in danger. Wade moved quickly and quietly from room to room, entering each one, sweeping his flashlight low across the floor, then checking behind the door.

Near the end of the search, Snowball and Blue bounded from the direction of the kitchen to greet them in the downstairs hall outside of Dan's office. Their toenails clicked on the wooden floor. With tails wagging, the two dogs whined to be petted the minute they spotted them. Bernadette squatted and scratched each dog's head.

Wade hoped the attention would quiet them, but Blue stretched and yawned, the noise rattling through the house.

Bernadette hugged the dog to her to muffle the sound.

Wade motioned for her to be still. Tilting his head, he waited. The house stood dark and silent. Then Bernadette gasped, her hand flying to her mouth as she stood.

"What is it?"

Her eyes grew round like saucers. "Frodo. He slept in Leanne's room tonight. Did you see him?"

"No, he wasn't there. He must be with Leanne,"

Wade reasoned.

"Then Leanne's not in the house, or Frodo would've followed these two."

Wade murmured under his breath. Grabbing her hand, he headed toward the kitchen and out the back door without slowing down, keenly aware the back door had been unlocked. Wade's long legs ate up the distance to the stable. Bernadette trotted alongside him.

The glow of a light streamed from the stable doors—one stood wide open and the other partially closed.

"Maybe she's checking on the baby goat," Bernadette suggested. He didn't want to squelch her hope, but his gut told him Leanne was in trouble. "If she is, I swear I'll have her hide for making us worry."

A growl, then three rapid yaps rang through the night air, coming from the stable. That's when Wade noticed the other noise, the low clatter of horse hooves. Something had them stirred up.

"It's Frodo. I'd know that bark anywhere." Bernadette tore off ahead of Wade, her feet pounding the hard dirt in her slippers, the tie of her lime robe bouncing behind her as she ran.

His mind reeled. "Wait." He needed to catch her. She was headed straight for the open stable door and whatever trouble waited for them on the other side.

Chapter Twenty-four

With each stride, her anger fueled her. How dare Leanne put her through another horrific episode after what happened Monday. Didn't she know she had people who cared about her? Hadn't Wade been specific in his instructions to stay in the house? But no, she'd snuck out in the middle of the night to feed a … a … a goat.

Bernadette burst into the barn at full steam. "What on earth are you—" Her words died on her lips as her gaze connected with Leanne's. The terror in the girl's eyes melted Bernadette's anger.

A man stood with his arm slung across Leanne's collarbone, holding her tight against him with a knife pressed to her throat. Bernadette froze. An unaided prayer floated heavenward. *Lord, help us.*

Several yips pierced the air, coming from inside one of the back stalls.

"Frodo." Before she had the chance to assess the situation, Wade rushed in and stepped in front of her with his gun drawn.

"Let her go, Lenny," Wade demanded. "Or you'll need a stretcher to take you out of here."

"I don't think so. You won't shoot. You've got too

much to lose if you miss." Lenny snickered. "Besides, I'm not alone."

A second man stepped from one of the stalls with a gun aimed at Wade. Using the other hand, he closed the latch to the pen. Several of the horses whinnied, and Sampson, the horse from Bernadette's youth, stomped the floor with his hoof. Barking persisted from behind the wooden slats.

"Carlos," Wade said.

Bernadette's heart stammered as fear knotted her stomach. What could she do?

Wade swung his gun in Carlos's direction and pushed Bernadette toward the open door. She shuffled to the side a bit, but if Wade thought she'd leave him to handle these two clowns on his own, he thought wrong.

Carlos shook his head. "Don't make me use this. The realtor stays until we conclude our business with this young lady. Besides, Sheriff, we'll be gone soon enough. We just wanted the girl. She's got something that belongs to us."

"No, it doesn't. You were stealing it." Leanne struggled against her abductor, but Lenny pressed the knife against her throat making a small cut. She winced as blood trickled down her neck, dripping onto the collar of her pajamas.

Bernadette gasped. "Leave her alone. She's just a kid." Suppressing the urge to run to her and snatch her from the man's arms, she willed her feet to stay put.

"A kid who caused me a lot of trouble. She snatched something from our van the night she spotted Artie. The girl's too curious for her own good." Carlos backed up without turning around, keeping his gun trained on Wade and Bernadette. He stopped when he reached the spot next to his partner. "Now, if you'll step away from the door, we'll be going."

Bernadette ignored the thug's directions. Keeping her voice calm, she focused on Leanne. "Honey, what's he talking about?"

Tears rolled down the teen's slim cheeks. "I'm sorry. I just needed proof. That's all. I didn't think anyone would believe me."

"It's okay. You did what you thought was right." Bernadette tried to ease the teen's mind to keep her coolheaded.

Wade took a few steps closer to where the men stood, putting distance between himself and her. "What did she take, Carlos?"

Carlos followed his movements with the gun then swung it from Wade to Leanne. "Stop right there." He warned, holding the pistol inches from her head.

Leanne whimpered and struggled in Lenny's arms. He tightened his grip across her shoulders, pinning her in place.

Wade stopped dead in his tracks but kept his gun trained on Carlos.

Without turning his gaze from Wade, Carlos asked Leanne, "Where's your bag?"

"It's not here." Bernadette lifted her chin and stepped sideways, planting herself in the middle of the open doorway. No way was she telling them the bag sat at the bottom of the Sine River. "So, there's no point in tormenting her any longer." Her stomach quivered as she stared down the man with the gun. She'd made up her mind. They weren't going anywhere with Leanne.

Lenny's eyes darted to Carlos. "I knew getting mixed up with Artie was bad news. This whole thing has gone south."

"But you were just following orders, right, Lenny? Sal's orders." Wade pressed, taking a few more steps closer to the men as he spoke.

"You don't know what you're talking about. We've never heard of the guy." Carlos sneered.

But Lenny's eyes widened at the mention of Sal's name. A droplet of sweat dribbled down Lenny's jawline. Using his shoulder, he swiped it away without letting go of Leanne. "Yeah, we've never heard of him. If you want princess here to see her next birthday, you need to get that bag."

Leanne met Bernadette's gaze. Her eyes filled with tears. "I'm sorry. I didn't mean for this to happen. The only reason I took it was so people would believe me about the robbery."

"Shut up." Lenny jerked Leanne, causing her to yelp.

"I can bring the bag here," Wade bluffed. "One phone call and it's yours."

"Do I look stupid?" Carlos groused. "You're not going anywhere or calling anyone." He turned to Leanne, his finger on the trigger. "Now, I'm done playing, Princess. What'd you do with the diamond necklace?" He pressed the gun to Leanne's head. She closed her eyes and turned away.

Bernadette's stomach lurched. *O Lord, don't let them hurt her. Give us strength.* She rushed to Wade's side. "Do something."

Wade pushed Bernadette behind him.

"The necklace isn't in the bag. It's somewhere safe," Leanne offered.

Bernadette studied her face. She told the truth.

"Where is it, Leanne? Tell them."

"I hid it in the flashlight, but the flashlight's not in my bag." Leanne turned toward Carlos. "But I won't tell you where it is unless you let Sheriff Wade and Bernadette go." Jutting out her chin, she glared at the man who held her at gunpoint. "That's the deal."

"We're not going anywhere without you," Bernadette protested, anger rushing through her. Had the girl lost her mind?

Wade widened his stance, set the butt of the gun in his left hand, and looked straight down the barrel of his Glock 22. "Looks like we're at a standoff. You want the diamonds, and we want Leanne."

A faint rustling came from the stable door to her left. Bernadette glanced in that direction. Dan was pressed against the building holding a rifle, peeking around the doorjamb. He lifted his finger to his lips and nodded, then he disappeared from her sight.

A moment later, the click of a rifle being cocked sounded from the direction of Sampson's stall.

Carlos yanked Leanne from Lenny with the gun still pointed at her head and pulled her close to him. "Go see what that was." Glaring at Wade, he cautioned, "Don't get any funny ideas."

"I'm not going unarmed." Lenny thrust the knife toward Carlos. "What good will this do?"

Turning the gun on his partner, Carlos commanded, "Go, or I'll kill you myself."

Scowling, Lenny jogged to the stall and lifted the latch, letting the door swing wide.

From her angle, Bernadette could see inside. Sampson stomped the ground and swung his head.

"Whoa, boy. It's okay," Lenny spoke softly to the

horse as he made his way around the huge black beast to the small window with bars.

Bernadette held her breath, hoping Dan wouldn't get caught.

"I don't see nothing," Lenny shouted.

"Fine, then get back out here." Carlos pinned her and Wade with a steely glare. Wade held his stance, not flinching.

Lenny took a single step before the butt of a rifle came down on the back of his head from between the bars of the window. He reeled, knocking against Sampson who reared and burst through the open door.

The frightened horse headed straight toward Carlos who dove behind one of the feeding troughs, shoving Leanne forward. The stunned teen jumped out of the way of the horse and landed on her backside in a pile of hay.

Wade dropped to his knee and took aim. "Move, Leanne."

Without hesitation, the girl pushed to her feet, and with all the power of her bedazzled shoes, she raced towards Bernadette's open arms. Bernadette pulled her into her embrace and held her tight. The poor teen clung to her, tears glistening on her cheeks.

"Oh Leanne," Bernadette murmured against the teen's blond hair. Holding her by the shoulders, she straightened her arms to look at her, making sure she was indeed all right. "You scared me to death." Then she pulled Leanne back to her, not done with the hug.

"Come on out, Carlos. It's over." Wade waited.

The man rose with his hands raised and stepped out from behind the trough. But instead of surrendering, he jumped for the gun lying on the ground near him.

Bernadette pulled Leanne to the side and ducked behind an old rusty barrel.

Carlos rolled on his belly and aimed the weapon at Wade.

But before he could get set, Wade got off two shots—Bam, bam. The noise rang through the space, sending the animals into a frenzy. Sampson trotted to the far back corner, nickering.

Carlos dropped the gun, groaning and holding his right shoulder.

"Nice shootin', brother." Dan waltzed into the stable with three of his ranch hands, all carrying rifles. "I figured you might need some help when you didn't come back." He grinned. "Though Nikki thought you might be enjoying the moonlight with Bernadette."

"I think I would've enjoyed that a lot more." Bernadette groaned from her position crouched behind the barrel.

"Bernie." Wade slipped his gun behind him into his belt as he hustled over to help her up. "Are you two, okay?" He offered Bernadette his hand. She slid her hand into his, grateful for the help. "Thanks to you. You and Dan saved us. Again." A warm heat crept up Bernadette's neck, and she felt the blush blossom on her cheeks, but she didn't care. She met his gaze and got lost in the love she found there.

Leanne got up and dusted off the knees of her pajama bottoms. "I'm fine, thanks for asking."

Wade grabbed the sassy teen and pulled her into a hug. She tightened her grip around his middle for an instant, then let go. "I'm going to check on Frodo."

"Wait a minute. I have a couple of questions. How did these guys get their hands on you? Did they get into the house?"

"Frodo needed to make a trip out and before I knew it, they had me and dragged me into here."

"Umm, that explains why they were able to do it without anyone hearing anything. Thank goodness the other dogs barked and made a fuss about being left inside."

Leanne laughed. "Remind me to give them a treat. Can I go get Frodo, now? He's got to be scared."

"Sure," Wade said.

Dan patted Leanne's shoulder as she passed him on her way to the far stall. "By the way, I called the sheriff's office before I came out here. The deputies are on their way." Dan nodded toward Carlos. "I'm glad you told me to only wait ten minutes before coming to look for you. Fifteen, and this might have been a different scene."

"Agreed." Wade pulled two reins from the hook on the wall nearest him. "Here, go tie up the guy in Sampson's stall and bring him out here." He grinned at his brother. "And try to make sure he's conscious before my men get here. We'll need to question him."

"Will do." Dan took the reins and trotted over to the stall to take care of Lenny. Glancing at Carlos, he asked, "Should we call for an ambulance?"

"Probably." Wade picked up Carlos's gun, took out the magazine, and laid both on top of the stack of small hay bales. Rolling the guy over, he tied his hands behind his back and propped him up in a sitting position against the hay.

One of the ranch hands moved toward Sampson with a lead rope. A few minutes later, the two criminals sat side by side next to the stack of hay bales, and

Sampson was back in his stall, happily eating oats. Frodo, the fearless ball of fluff, sat with Leanne receiving his due reward, belly scratches.

Deputy Adams and Deputy Henderson entered the stable and escorted the two robbers to the waiting patrol cars. Dan followed them outside.

"Now—" Wade turned his attention to Leanne. "Where is the diamond necklace?"

Leanne scratched Frodo's belly once more, then rose. Glancing down at her sparkling shoes, she kicked the dirt with her toe. "It's at Harry's Hardware Store. When I saw the mail guy there, I slipped it into my flashlight and then hid it with the other flashlights on the shelf where I dusted." She shrugged. "It seemed like a good hiding place."

"Hiding it in plain sight." Bernie squeezed her shoulders. "Smart."

"Boy, is Harry in for a surprise!" Wade's eyes twinkled.

"Yeah, a rather pricey one." Bernadette laughed. Glancing at Leanne, she asked, "Why did you take the necklace in the first place?"

"For proof, like I said. I didn't think anyone would believe me about the robbery. They'd think I was some foster kid making up stories for attention. Then when I opened the door that day at the Pittman's house and found the same guy standing on the porch, I decided I had to leave."

"Did he threaten you?" Bernadette studied the girl's face.

"Sort of. He said now he knew where I lived, and he'd be back to take what was his." Leanne's eyes grew round as she told the story. "So, I slammed the door and ran upstairs. I got Michael to walk Radar that night. Once everyone went to sleep, I took off."

"Weren't you afraid you'd be blamed? I mean, you do have some pretty hard-core hacking skills."

Leanne's smile spread across her face. "Not after seeing what they took. The van was loaded with electronics and jewelry and even an old record player. No way anyone would think I had taken them. I can't even drive." Bernie and Wade laughed at her wisdom.

"Well, with your testimony and a positive ID on the diamond necklace from the Nortons, those two and Artie Burton should be going away for a long time."

Bernadette pulled Leanne in for one more hug. "Not long enough for my liking." Releasing the teen, she sighed. "Are you all right?"

"I'm better now, thanks to you and Sheriff Wade."

Dan stepped back into the stable. "The EMTs examined Carlos's arm. He's on his way to the hospital with a police officer and the other criminal is on his way to county lockup. I'm going on in and check on Nikki. She'll be worried."

Leanne sagged against Bernadette as Wade led them to the doorway and said, "You two gals go with Dan, and I'll turn everything off out here. Then tomorrow, we'll go see Harry about a certain flashlight."

"Come, Frodo," Leanne called. "You've earned yourself some vanilla wafers."

Chapter Twenty-five

Bernadette stumbled into the kitchen, barely conscious. She'd slept hard, once she'd gotten to sleep after all the craziness in the wee hours of the morning.

The smell of bacon tickled her nose as she slid into the empty chair across from Rod Carson, the ranch manager. Nikki stood by the stove refilling a bowl with scrambled eggs. "Look who it is—Sleeping Beauty herself."

Bernadette leaned her cheek on her hand and propped herself upright with her elbow. "How long have you guys been up?" She glanced at the faces that greeted her through half-closed eyes. Dan and Wade sat to her left, and Leanne occupied the chair to her right. Rod grinned at her from his spot at the head of the table.

"Long enough for me to meet Harry at his store," Wade admitted, leaning back in his chair with his coffee cup hugged between his hands.

"Is that coffee?" She eyed his mug and lifted her eyebrows, giving him her most pathetic look.

Wade chuckled and rose. "I'll get you some."

"Thank you," she murmured.

Leanne patted her hand resting on the table. "And long enough for me to help with the horses." She beamed.

Bernadette smiled at the blond-haired teenager who looked no worse for the wear from her midnight escapades. "How did you sleep?"

"Great." Leanne reached for the platter of biscuits sitting next to the butter and strawberry jam. Taking a biscuit, she placed the platter near Bernadette. "Want some?"

Wade returned with her coffee and set it beside the plate in front of her. She took a biscuit before asking for the jam.

Nikki carried the bowl of scrambled eggs to her husband. "More eggs?"

"No, I'm stuffed." Dan slid his arm around her back and kissed her belly. "Rod and I had better get started on today's list." Rod nodded his agreement, stabbing his last bite of sausage.

"Finish your coffee. The chores will be there when you're done." Nikki placed the bowl on the table, and Leanne snatched it up.

"All the excitement last night made me hungry." She scooped a large helping onto her plate.

"Adrenaline will do that to you." Wade moved closer to her as if he had a secret to share. "That's why I'm always so hungry. Catching bad guys can work up an appetite."

Nikki gasped and grabbed the back of Dan's chair with one hand, while hugging her stomach with the other.

"Are you all right?" Dan set down his mug and stood.

"Just another Braxton Hicks." She took a deep breath. "There, all better. Now, sit and finish."

"I will if you sit too." Dan escorted his wife to the empty chair next to Leanne then retook his seat.

When both were settled, Rod glanced at Wade. "I hate that I wasn't here to help capture those varmints." He picked up the platter with the sausage and bacon on it. Dishing out a second helping, he placed the platter between him and Dan. "But Dolly and I both sleep rather soundly. I didn't realize anything was going on until I heard the sheriff cars and ambulance coming down the driveway with their sirens blaring."

"That's okay. I called one of the men in the bunkhouse and got him to bring reinforcements." Dan sipped on his coffee but kept his eyes fixed on Nikki. "Besides, it'd taken you longer to get here from your house, and we needed help pronto."

"Boy, I'm glad you showed up when you did," Wade said. "There for a minute, I wasn't sure how we'd get out of that situation. I wasn't going to take any chances with Leanne in the crosshairs."

Nikki groaned and leaned forward in her seat, her face stricken with pain.

"You are not all right," Bernadette scolded, knowing her friend tended to soldier on even when in agony.

Dan moved to Nikki and laid his hand on her shoulder. Squatting, he waited for the contraction to pass. "It seems these are coming closer together." His brows puckered.

Nikki relaxed and lowered back in the chair. "They're lasting longer. I'm glad my doctor's appointment is today."

"And I'll be driving you." Bernadette pinned her friend with a glare. She didn't want any arguments. Her friend needed help, and that's what the Bible Babes did—they helped each other.

Nikki snickered. "Bossy, a little?" Then she smiled. "Dan's going to take me. We'd discussed it last night before bed, and we both agreed it wouldn't be safe for me to drive."

Satisfied her friend would use some wisdom, Bernadette suggested, "Then at least go sit down in the living room and rest. I'll bring you a plate instead of you serving us."

"What about the kitchen?" Nikki protested like the true southern woman she was.

Bernadette scowled and gave her the stink eye. "I'm more than capable of cleaning this kitchen. In fact, you should've awakened me and let me help with breakfast. What kind of friend am I to let an eight-month pregnant woman wait on me hand and foot?" She clucked her tongue and pushed up from her seat. "Come on. Let's go."

"Are you sure?" Nikki glanced around the table then at Dan who still squatted next to her.

"Honey, she's right. You should've been resting more before this." Dan stood. "With two on the way, I should've insisted."

Nikki rose. Clutching her stomach, she doubled over. "Oh…my goodness." She clinched her belly with both arms. Then, she grew stock-still. Her eyes widened as she glanced down at the puddle on the floor. "I think it's time to go to the hospital."

Bernadette followed her gaze.

For a split second, no one moved.

Then Rod jumped up from his chair, knocking it sideways. "I'll go get the SUV and bring it around front." He nailed Dan with a hard stare. "And I'm driving. She'll need you with her in the back seat."

"Thanks, Rod." Dan swung his arm around Nikki and nodded for Wade to help.

"I'll get your bag." Bernadette rushed toward the entrance of the living room but stopped short. Pivoting, she asked, "Where is your bag?"

"Top shelf of the closet, and grab the two teddy bears next to it, please."

A smile lit Bernadette's face when she saw Dan and Wade on either side of Nikki, helping her walk. Leanne followed behind her with her hands positioned, ready to catch Nikki if she stumbled.

Bernadette dashed up the stairs, mumbling, "Two teddy bears." When she returned, the front door stood wide open, and everyone had gathered on the front porch, waiting for Rod to park the SUV. "Here's your bag and the bears." Bernadette held out the items.

Dan took the bag and stuck one bear under his arm and held the other in his free hand.

Rod opened the screen door and motioned for Dan and Nikki to follow him. Dan acted bumfuzzled with his hands full, not knowing how to help Nikki.

"Here, I'll take those." Wade grabbed the bag and bears from Dan's hands and hustled out to the SUV. He tossed them into the front seat then took the porch steps, two at a time, sliding out of the way of the couple, while holding the screen door for them.

Rod stood by the driver's side door waiting.

Nikki faced Bernadette. "Thank you so much." She slipped her arms around Bernadette's shoulders and hugged her.

Bernadette let the warmth of her friend's embrace soak into her heart. Things would be different now. Nikki would be busy with two little ones to care for, but Bernadette couldn't be happier for her. Nikki would have the family she always wanted. "Don't worry about anything. Leanne and I will clean the kitchen. And I'll make sure to straighten our rooms before we leave."

"And I'll feed the baby goat and look after the dogs," Leanne offered.

Nikki pushed back still holding onto Bernadette's forearms and met her gaze. "What about the Bible Babes meeting tonight?"

"I'm sure they'll understand that you're busy having *babies*." Bernadette shook her head and gave her friend one last hug. "Now, go make Wade an uncle."

Nikki sputtered, "But … but …" Nikki cringed and breathed through her mouth.

"We'd better go before we have these kids right here on the front porch with me as your doctor."

Nikki glanced at Dan wide eyed. "Good point. Let's go."

Bernadette shut the door, and Wade let out a long sigh. "What a way to start the day." He chuckled.

"I could think of worse ways." Bernadette picked up the throw from the couch and folded it.

"Yeah, I guess so." Wade bumped her arm, and she swatted at him.

Leanne moved toward the stairs. "I'm going to go change into some work clothes, then let the dogs out of the mudroom. They're probably ready to go outside and run."

"I imagine so." Bernadette watched Leanne as she ascended the stairs until she disappeared from her sight.

"I think Dan may have a new ranch hand." Wade followed Bernadette into the kitchen.

"Yeah, she's pretty great." Bernadette couldn't help but admire Leanne. She'd been brave, level-headed, and even self-sacrificing in the face of danger. Her heart swelled at the memory of how Leanne had demanded she and Wade be released.

"Brave and smart. She'll go far in this world." Wade picked up the platters and carried them to the counter. Grabbing a fork, he raked the crumbs into the garbage.

Bernadette gathered the plates and glasses and took them to the double-sided sink. "She outsmarted those thugs." She grinned at Wade. "Hiding it where no one would think to look."

"I wish you could've seen Harry's face when we pulled that diamond necklace from one of his flashlights in the bin. It left him speechless."

"Nah, Harry speechless?" Bernadette let the joy bubble up inside her. "I can't imagine that."

Wade grabbed the few remaining utensils and serving bowls from the table and placed them on the counter beside the sink.

Bernadette turned on the tap, rolling up the sleeves of her robe, and let the water run over her hands. Once the temperature felt right, she rinsed one of the plates. Wade sidled up next to her, their shoulders only inches apart. Her heart fluttered. The smell of his musk drifted her way as he bent to open the dishwasher.

Straightening, he took the plate from her hand and placed it in the rack. Piece by piece, they worked together. She'd rinse and he'd place the item in the dishwasher. They fell into a harmonious rhythm.

So, this is what it'd be like, marital bliss. She allowed her thoughts to explore the idea of her and Wade. She couldn't help it, not after what he'd said to her last night. *I love you* entailed so much. Today, tomorrow, a future full of living together, routine moments like this one. She stole a glance at him, standing beside her, working together. It seemed so natural, so right.

As if he'd read her mind, he asked, "So, have you thought anymore about what I said to you?" He glanced at her from the corner of his eye.

Bernadette feigned ignorance. "What you said?" As if she'd forget those three little words from the man she loved.

"Last night before Dan interrupted."

"Oh, that." She forced herself to focus on the glass in her hand, hoping to hide the heat coloring her cheeks. "There hasn't been time."

His fingers brushed against hers as she handed him the glass. Taking it in one hand, he captured her hand with his other. His gaze met hers. She swallowed and willed the gymnast in her stomach to stop doing backflips.

"Bernie, you don't have to be afraid. Our relationship is stronger because we are friends. I just want more."

Leanne strolled into the kitchen wearing a pair of yellow shorts, a tee shirt with a cat decal on it, and a pair of mucking boots. She'd pulled her hair up into a ponytail.

Grinning, Wade gave her a thumbs-up. "You look

like a real cowgirl.”

“Do I?” A smile spread across Leanne’s lips and made its way into her eyes. They sparkled with pleasure at the compliment.

“Definitely. Mucking boots are a sign of a true professional.”

Bernadette liked the way his eyes crinkled at the corners when he smiled. He had such an easy manner with people and especially with Leanne.

Sticking out her right foot, Leanne modeled the black polka-dotted, green mucking boots by shifting her foot from heel to toe and back to her heel. Then taking a few steps, while exaggerating the sway of her hips and shoulders, she turned and stuck out her left foot, repeating the pattern.

Bernadette giggled. “Pretty snazzy, if you ask me.”

“Nikki loaned them to me yesterday. She said around here I’d need them. And boy, was she right. That goat pen is not bedazzled-friendly.”

Wade let out a soft cough to smother a laugh, and Bernadette pressed her lips together. “Ranch life does call for a special type of footwear.”

Studying the mucking boots, Leanne pursed her lips. “I wonder if my gem machine would work on these?”

“Why don’t we wait until you get your own pair to find out?” Bernadette suggested.

Leanne shrugged and grabbed the back doorknob, but before she left, Bernadette called out, “Be careful and stay close to the house.”

“The trouble’s over.” With those words, Leanne’s face fell. Her eyes filled with concern. Glancing at Bernadette, she bit her lip. “I guess that means I’ll be going back to Mrs. Pittman's now."

Wade cleared his throat. "Actually, I had Deputy Perez find out about your sister, Mia."

"You did?" Leanne's eyes widened. The sparkle returned and dispelled the worry that had filled them moments earlier.

"You did?" Bernadette echoed the teen's words, her surprise evident in her tone. *Would the man never cease to amaze her?*

"She discovered your sister has been placed with a nice couple who has petitioned the court for adoption."

Leanne dropped her hand from the doorknob and plopped into the nearest chair. "Mia has found her forever home?" Her voice rang with awe and a bit of trepidation.

"Seems that way. But I wanted you to know, so you wouldn't worry about her." Wade leaned his hip against the counter.

"Do they live nearby?" The look on Leanne's face told Bernadette of the inner conflict she battled. She had to be both happy for her sister and sad they wouldn't be together.

Bernadette's heart squeezed tight within her chest. It had to be rough, knowing your sister had found a home, but you were still without roots.

Wade nodded. "They do, in Orange Blossom. Deputy Perez told them about you, too." He grinned. "And they want to meet you. What do you think about that?"

Leanne squealed and threw her hands into the air. "They do? They want to meet me?"

Bernadette turned off the water. Drying her hands, she moved to the table and sat in the chair next to

Leanne. "Did you hear that? They want to meet you. And why wouldn't they want to meet a smart, brave, awesome fourteen-year-old like yourself?" Excitement ran through her. Wouldn't it be wonderful if Mia and Leanne could be together?

But she had to admit her heart ached just a little. She'd grown fond of Leanne. It would be hard to give her up, even to a nice couple who could love and care for both Leanne and her sister.

"Now, don't get your hopes up, but I do have a good feeling about this," Wade said.

Leanne jumped to her feet and grabbed Bernadette's hands and swung her around in a circle. Then connecting elbows with Bernadette, Leanne stomped and thumped in her mucking boots, making them squeak and squawk something awful. Bernadette laughed, and together the two did a jig worthy of any Irish dancer.

Stopping mid-twirl, Leanne turned to Wade out of breath. "When do I meet them?"

"Next week. They've made an appointment with your caseworker, and then we'll see."

Bernadette sobered. "Where will she be until then?" She braced herself for his answer. Though Mrs. Pittman seemed to be a nice woman, she hated having to say good-bye already.

"With you. If you'll have her." Wade gave her a lopsided grin that spoke of roguish mischief.

Wrapping Leanne in a big bear-hug, Bernadette squeezed with all her might. "You'd better believe I'll have her. She can stay as long as needed."

"I can't breathe," came a muffled plea from Leanne.

Wade joined them in the middle of the kitchen. Wrapping one arm around both, he pressed a kiss on the crown of Bernadette's head as she released the teen. Bernadette ran her arms around his neck. Her hero, in more ways than one.

"Ooh, gross. I'm out of here." Leanne marched to the back door, but before she opened it, she turned to Wade. "Thank you for …" She shrugged. "You know." Then heading out the door, she let it slam with a whoosh.

Bernadette grinned at the man standing in front of her. "You have a fan," she teased.

"Um, so do you." He wrapped his arms around her tighter. "Now, about that conversation which got rudely interrupted twice." His eyes lit with an intensity she'd not seen before. "I love you, Bernadette Stewart. What do you have to say about that?"

Her mind whirled, and that gymnast in her stomach did a triple somersault. Why was she waiting? Why couldn't she forget all her past mistakes and forgive herself—like Nikki had suggested. Like God had done.

She did love him, so what was the problem? Bernadette tensed. She did love him. Had for a long time. She'd just been too stubborn to let herself face the fact they were already more than friends. "What can I say but the truth." She let her gaze drift from his eyes, breaking the connection. Her heart pounded, roaring in her ears. "You've been such a good friend."

Wade loosened his grip but didn't let go of her. "I see."

"You've rescued me more times than I can count. I feel like a cat with nine lives." She glanced up at him, hoping to read his face. "You've stood by me and made me feel safe when I shouldn't have. You've been nothing but wonderful."

"But? I'm sure there's one in there somewhere." He stepped away, releasing her. "You just want to be friends, afraid anything more might mess things up. I understand." He shoved his hands into his pockets, his eyes trained on the tile floor in front of him.

"No, I don't think you do." Urgency filled her. She stepped toward him and placed the palm of her hand on his cheek. He raised his eyes to hers. "I can't help but love you, Wade. I don't think I could be just friends with you now, even if I tried. Somewhere along the way, between traffic stops and birthday parties, I fell in love with you—crazy, stupid love. The kind that can scare a person."

"Bernie, that's the only kind there is. Love is scary. And crazy—" He pulled her to him. His scent surrounded her as she nuzzled beneath his chin. "And stupid. But I'd rather take the risk with you than be without you." He ran his finger down her cheek, then lifted her chin with the crook of his finger.

Her eyes met his, and the fire she saw in them took her breath away. "Wade, what are you thinking?"

That roguish grin reappeared on his lips. "That I'm going to kiss you—good and proper."

"You mean you've been goofing around up until now?" Her voice cracked a little.

"Uh huh," He leaned closer and pressed his full lips to hers, pulling her tighter.

The warmth of his body against hers shot through her. The kiss, gentle at first, tasted sweet like strawberry jam. Running her arms around his neck, she dug her fingers into his hair.

He deepened the kiss, making her dizzy. Out of breath, she pulled back. He rested his forehead against hers.

"My goodness. You have been holding out on me."

"Yes." He rubbed her cheek with his thumb. "And for both our sakes, I'd better keep holding out. Too many kisses like this, and we'll have to elope."

Elope? They'd only declared their feelings. Bernadette braced herself, waiting for the usual panic to raise its ugly head, but it didn't. Nothing but peace filled her heart. She had her hero; there'd be nothing to fear. God had brought her the man of her dreams, and she would trust He had everything well in hand.

"What's that smile about?"

"You." She rose on tiptoe and placed a kiss on Wade's cheek. "And that God does work in weird ways."

Chapter Twenty-six

The two movers lifted the ramp into the truck before one of them pushed the door closed and slipped the metal arm of the latch back into place. Bernadette stood on the front porch of Wade's new ranch house, watching him sign the last of the paperwork for the moving company who'd brought his things from storage.

She leaned against the post nearest her, crossing her arms. Though the weather stayed warm for most of the year, today the November air held a little chill as the sun dipped lower in the sky. It had been three months since Wade and his deputies brought down the burglary ring that had plagued Orange Blossom, causing everyone so much trouble, especially Leanne.

Her lips rose into a smile at the image that popped into her head, of the now fifteen-year-old. She'd settled in beautifully with the Yates, the couple who had adopted Mia. And now she waited for her own news about their adoption of her. A forever home with her sister. Leanne's greatest desire.

Bernadette hugged her middle and sent up a silent prayer of thanks.

Wade rapped on the back of the moving truck,

sending it rambling down the drive. Pivoting, he jogged in her direction, taking the four porch steps, two at a time. "All this moving has given me a powerful thirst." He grinned. "Can I interest you in a glass of sweet tea?"

"Yes, do you know which box has the glasses?" Bernadette straightened, prepared to go hunt for the items in question. He'd only been in the house for a week and still used paper cups and plastic forks.

"I do, indeed." He moved forward and kissed her cheek. "At least, I think so. Why don't you have a seat on the swing and save me a spot."

"Sounds good." She bumped his shoulder with hers as he moved toward the screen door. Sighing, she ambled to the swing. Her heart filled with what? Contentment? Yes, that was it. He made her happy, her hero.

She nestled into the seat and pushed her foot against the wooden planks, setting the swing in motion. The chains groaned with the use. How had she fallen so fast? And so completely? Now, she couldn't wait to marry this man and start a family.

An image of Danielle with a pink bow clipped to her single strand of hair, and David dressed in the smallest cowboy boots she'd ever seen, flashed into her mind. The Thibodeaux twins had to be the cutest babies in the county.

The front screen door slammed, pulling her from her thoughts. "What's got you smiling?" Wade offered her one of the glasses he carried.

"Just thinking about the babies. They're so cute." She sipped on the cool liquid, the sweetness quenching her thirst.

He slid onto the swing next to her. "Well, I am

biased, but I think they're pretty perfect."

"Yes, Uncle Wade, you'll have them spoiled before they can walk," She teased, placing her tea glass in the cup holder on the armrest of the swing.

"Walk? I plan on carrying them everywhere." He ran his arm along the back of the swing.

Bernadette laughed and snuggled closer to him, laying her head on his shoulder. "So, you're all moved in now that your storage has arrived."

"Thanks to you and Dan and Nikki. It's not every realtor who helps with the actual move. They usually take the money and run. You're lucky if they send you a fruit basket."

She shrugged. "Not everybody dates their realtor, but I'm still taking the money." She pushed her foot against the boards, keeping the soft sway of the swing going.

"You should. You earned it. I wasn't an easy client, but once we found this place, I knew I'd found my home." He rubbed his hand along her arm, sending a different kind of chill running through her. "It just fits."

"Yes, it does fit you." She let her gaze drift across the front yard to a stand of trees as she nestled against him. The place held such beauty. A hundred acres of pasture, woods, and trails for Wade to explore gave him plenty of elbow room. It's what he'd wanted.

"I was thinking," Wade stopped the motion of the swing and turned toward her. "This place, it fits you too."

"What do you mean?" Her heart thrummed hard in her chest.

"I'm saying I want this ranch to be *our* home, not

just mine."

Bernadette met his gaze. "What? Like move in together?" She scowled, disappointed by the suggestion. She didn't think she'd ever done anything to make him think that was an option.

Wade raised his eyebrows. His lips pulled pencil thin. "You know me better than that, Bernie." His features softened as he touched her cheek. "More like marry me."

"What?" Her mouth went dry, and she wasn't sure she'd heard him right. "Even with my messy past? And the possibility I might ruin all this?" She waved her hand between them.

"I'm sure, Bernie. You fit. When I'm with you, I'm home." His eyes lit up. "Marry me and make this your home, too."

Bernadette placed her hands on either side of his face and pulled his lips to hers. She let out a soft sigh as the warmth of his kiss mixed with the joy in her heart. There was that feeling again. She'd have to get used to being this content.

"So, is that a yes?"

Bernadette nodded. "Yes, I'll marry you."

Wade captured her lips with his, sealing the deal.

She settled back into his arms and rested her head on his shoulder, never wanting this moment to end. Wade pushed the swing into motion. A sharp rush of happiness washed over her as the sun sank below the stand of trees at the edge of the long driveway.

"You know you'll have to give this place a name." She considered some options for a moment. "But I guess most of the good ones are already taken, like Painted Rock or Three Arrows."

"Or Silver Spurs." Wade chuckled. "Don't worry, I've been mulling it over."

"It'll have to be something unique." A few ideas popped into her brain, but nothing stood out.

"I agree, but I don't think anyone has the one I've picked out."

Bernadette lifted her chin. "So, you have something in mind. What is it?"

Wade peered down into her eyes. "I figured since your beloved truck is at the bottom of the Sine River, we'd use your tag here for the ranch."

"Home-4-U? Isn't that a little too unique?" She asked.

Wade shrugged and nestled his chin against the crown of her head. "Not really. I was thinking more along the lines of Home-4-Us. And put it on a sign above a picture of all the foster kids we're going to have hanging around here."

Bernadette's heart soared. She wrapped her arms around Wade's middle, pulling her feet up onto the swing. "It's perfect." Planting a kiss on his cheek, she snuggled her head against his chest, right above his heart, the spot of her forever home.

The End

Dear Reader,

I hope you enjoyed meeting Sheriff Wade Thibodeaux and his realtor, the feisty red head, Bernadette Stewart on this return trip to Orange Blossom, Texas. Coming back to these characters brought a smile to my face. I loved meeting the Bible Babes of Cowboy Community Church and Bernadette's mom, Darlene, is a real hoot and a half, as they say in the south.

Writing happily-ever-after endings is one of my favorite things to do, but with a sheriff involved a mystery was necessary, so I threw in a teen lockbox hacker and a string of robberies just to keep it interesting for you.

As with any project, there are several people I'd like to thank. First, my hubby who always shows grace when I'm behind with dishes, or dinner is late again because I was busy pounding out the scene rattling around in my head.

I'd also like to thank all those who pray for me and my stories, the Jesus girls at my church and my prayer partners who listens to all my concerns.

And my Beta readers who read early copies for me and point out any plot holes or odd wording. Thank you all! The stories are stronger because of what you've added. I'd also like to thank Sherri Stewart, my editor, and Cynthia Hickey, my publisher. You two have made my dream of writing a reality.

Then there is you, the reader. Thank you for your time. I

know there are millions of books out there and the fact you picked mine to read thrills my heart. I hope it met all your expectations and left you encouraged in your own relationship with God, the Father.

May God lead you down the path He has for you,

Bonita Y. McCoy

Bonita Y. McCoy - Author

Bonita Y. McCoy hails from the Great State of Alabama where she lives on a five-acre farm with two dogs, two cows, and one husband who she's had since circa 1989.

She is a mother to three grown sons and a beautiful daughter-in-law, who joined the family from Japan.

Her background includes a degree in Journalism from Mississippi State University as well as ten years teaching high school literature and writing classes to some of the best students, ever.

Her publishing adventure started at the ripe old age of thirteen when she worked for two years as a staff reporter for her school newspaper, The Bearcat Chatter.

More recent adventures include publishing her Amy Kate Cozy Mystery series through Winged Publications and being a finalist in both the Selah awards and Silver Falchion Awards with that series. She also won an Angel Book Award for her contemporary romance.

The devotional books her Word Weavers group publishes has given her an avenue to encourage other Christians along the way. Their Coffee and Cookies with God won a Christian Indie Award and was a finalist in the Selah Awards, which helps to spread His Word even further.

She loves God, and she loves to write. Her blog posts, devotions, and novels are all an expression of both these passions.

On any given day, you can find her reading a good book, playing with her German shepherds, Heidi and Kaiser, or drinking coffee with her hubby on the front porch swing. Of course, that's when she's not writing her next cozy mystery or sweet romance.

She is an active member of both American Christian Fiction Writers and Word Weavers International.

Sign up for her newsletter at www.bonitaymccoy.com and become part of her newsletter family where she shares giveaways, book recommendations, recipes, and more.

 Scan here to see Bonita's Books!

Other Books by Bonita Y. McCoy

Amy Kate Mystery series

Twisted Plots

Family Twist

Twisted Vows

Sawyer Sweet Romance series

No Room in His Heart

Truth Be Told

Seeds of Love

Billionaire Brothers of Silver Spur Ranch series

Billionaire Cowboy Next Door

Billionaire Sheriff on the Move

Stand Alone:

Merry Christmas Mix-up

Only for the Summer

Contributed:

Coffee with God

Coffee and Cookies with God   at Christmas

Coffee with God to Bless Your Heart

Coffee with God On the Road

Chicken Soup for the Soul: Thanks Dad edition

Christmas Spirit

Handy Tips for Homeschooling Parents: When You're
Feeling Overwhelmed

275